Growland

Lelia Moskowitz

HUMBOLDT STATE
UNIVERSITY PRESS

Humboldt State University Press
Humboldt State University Library
1 Harpst Street
Arcata, California 95521-8299
hsupress@humboldt.edu
digitalcommons.humboldt.edu/hsu_press

Cover and interior photography by Louie Moskowitz
Cover design and layout by Tia Moskowitz
Interior design and layout by Maximilian Heirich

ISBN: 978-1-947112-34-6
LCCN: 2020933951

For Stewart Moskowitz, my favorite fantasy character

overnight

Celeste drove away from the sprawl of Los Angeles, heading north as the sky turned a garish pink-orange. She intended to go straight through the night—soaring through darkness—closing in on her destination, where no one could find her. But as evening descended her daughters began to bicker. They needed sleep in a proper bed. She squinted at fluorescent signs lining the highway, settling on the last crusty motel before the lights ended.

In a room at last, the girls nodded off. Celeste listened to their soft duet of breathing. With her need to be in motion thwarted, the minutes crawled like slow, delicate spiders over her skin. As she stared at the popcorn ceiling, her thoughts spun tighter and tighter while each word of the phone conversation that had begun her day replayed. Less than twelve hours had passed since Victor's phone call; somehow it seemed decades ago. Her world was so changed. She had been standing in the triangle of light that streamed into her kitchen in the mornings, every nanosecond of listening to his voice stretched and warped. Rage galvanized her. Finally a tiny muscle under her left eye twitched and she clicked off the phone. She was furious and queasy, yet her mind, cleared of its usual chaos, was singularly lucid; her heart drummed: *escape, run.*

Charging through the house, she bundled together belongings, filling the girls' suitcases as they watched from the corners of their rooms. Sophie gripped her stuffed dolly, asking why they had to go on a road trip. Alexa kept repeating: "Mom, I don't want to go. The sleepover's tonight."

"We're going."

Celeste loaded duffel bags and backpacks with a sense of weightlessness and superhuman strength. She flew to her bedroom and threw her suitcase on the bed, cramming it with clothes. Alexa followed behind her, and Sophie trailed her big sister, sniffling. When the suitcase wouldn't close, Celeste yanked some clothing out. Everything was expendable. She no longer cared about treasured belongings. *Leave it all behind*, a monument to what once was, to the lie she'd lived. The next day Victor would return home early from touring with the band. Her last glance inside her home, before she closed the front door, she saw through his eyes—without the girls, without her, the house was a hollow shell.

A clean break was needed to protect her daughters from gossip and humiliation. It would be Victor's job, his responsibility, to tell them. That could wait until later. She would keep them emotionally safe, swaddled in her love, even as she decimated their world. As unwilling as they were to leave home, Celeste exercised her terrible power as a mother and forced them to leap with her. Only time would prove her right. Or wrong.

Had she dreamed this outcome to her marriage? She had felt rumblings for months, maybe years. Something was approaching, the squeal of unforgiving metal against metal, a train on its tracks, getting closer and closer. One night she'd woken to find Victor whispering into his phone; once she'd extracted a stray, alien earring from his suitcase. Her own guilt she determined to keep secret, especially now, locking it away even from herself. Maybe if she hadn't held on for so long they could have avoided this indignity. She'd hoped her sacrifice—putting her children first— would ensure her whole family's happiness.

※ ※ ※

The next morning, back on the road, whatever it was the girls had argued about was forgotten in the new day. Celeste wanted to break up the long car ride so they stopped at the Golden Gate Park Aquarium in San Francisco. She tried to pretend it was just another outing, an entertaining experience on a last-minute summer road trip. Years before, she'd visited the aquarium with Victor. Watching Sophie push her nose against the glass, absorbed by the swooshing underwater scene, Celeste remembered when Victor had done the same, horsing around. They'd been bound together then, in a shared sphere. His antics, his smoldering gaze, his long, heavy, black hair had completely absorbed her; she'd lost almost a decade and a half to worshipful infatuation.

Yet she had her children, her prize. She would not crack, not in front of them. Even sleep deprived, with the crushing details looping in her head, worried they wouldn't reach Tom's before nightfall, she skillfully escaped the gridlocked Bay Area. But Celeste had erroneously regarded San Francisco as Northern California; she now realized it was barely half-way up the state. She gripped the wheel so tightly her knuckles turned white. That westernmost bump she'd located on the map: Humboldt County, a knob of land protruding out into the Pacific, was easily four more hours north. Had they been in Europe they'd be crossing borders, traveling through other countries, with other languages.

City gave way to suburbia, which dwindled to vineyards, rural land, split-rail fences, and languorous cows. Tom had said it was a far-flung area. She'd called him from her kitchen, standing in that same wedge of light, right after she'd hung up on Victor. The anger that surged through her had renewed her imagination; all scenarios seemed possible. Celeste had been considering making that call for years. Tom's deep, gentle voice resonated with everything she knew about him. She conjured a mental image of the man and held it close, so many years gone since she'd last seen him. At forty-four, she was finally making her way back to Tom.

At another gas station stop in another sweaty, isolated town, the girls chose brightly-colored candies. Celeste let them; even junk food seemed an acceptable, welcome distraction. She was a different mother than she'd been. The transformation had been accomplished in that nanosecond in her kitchen, the old husk splintered, her goals rearranged.

After their stop, Sophie shimmied into the backseat, sliding into the only open space that wasn't stacked with belongings. Her beloved stuffed animals tumbled around her, spilling over luggage. "Mommy." Celeste's eyes shifted from the road to the rear-view mirror; Sophie was trying out her best impression of a forlorn face. "I can't find Miss Cushy!"

"She's there, sweetie."

"Mom," Alexa pulled out one earbud, leaking the faint rhythm of bass. "How long do we have to stay? You said I could go to the dance party next week."

"Yes, but that was before this trip." Celeste glanced at her honey-skinned daughter; every striking physical trait her girls possessed contrasted with her own pale collection of freckles and unmanageable red hair.

"Mom!" Alexa threw her hands in the air. "You promised."

"Sometimes things change. We're on an adventure. How exciting is this?"

"Not." Alexa snarled.

Mother and daughter scrutinized one another, then Celeste reached out, touching her arm. "Sweetheart, it'll be okay." Alexa shrugged her off and glared at the rolling hills.

Sophie's head popped up. "Mommy, I found Miss Cushy."

"Good job, sweetheart." Celeste checked the time. In Los Angeles, Victor must have already slipped his key into the lock and discovered their empty house. Just imagining her miscreant husband caused a gut twist. As she drove, she crafted a list of things that would bring him pain, a growing inventory that afforded her a wicked smile and some moments of blissful relief.

Countryside whizzed by, space widened between vehicles, and Highway 101 contracted from broad, nearly empty freeway to two-lane, twisting narrows. When they finally arrived in Garberville, the sky was spread with the mottled streaks of sunset. The town swarmed with cars, trucks, and people. It resembled other small towns they'd driven through, but here the largest sign on Main Street displayed a bright green marijuana leaf with the words "Hemp Connection" painted across it.

Celeste drove around for a while, unable to find a parking spot, which struck her as comical in a remote country town the size of a postage stamp. At last, she pulled in next to a purple-painted school bus with two goats tethered to its front bumper. She killed her engine and slid out of the car into the torrid heat, her flip-flops slapping the broiling pavement. The muscles in Celeste's back and neck had seized up, solidifying like cement. She did a jitterbug on the sidewalk to shake off the crimp.

"Mom! Stop!" Alexa hissed.

"I have to move." Celeste rolled her neck from side to side. "Do you need to pee?"

"Mom!"

"No one's listening, Alexa." Dreadlocked youths milled around the school bus, and farther away a mangy group sprawled across the sidewalk with dogs on ropes and a jumble of backpacks. Alexa retreated to the shade of a tree, far enough away to pretend she wasn't associated with her mother and sister, still close enough to monitor the conversation.

"Mommy." Sophie clutched Miss Cushy. "I have to pee. And I'm hungry."

Celeste picked up her young daughter, kissed her, squeezed her tightly, and then pointed across the street. "They've got to have a bathroom."

Inside a crowded gas station mini-mart, an over-whelmed-looking cashier tipped his head toward a back aisle when Celeste asked about a key. They joined the line in front of the bathroom door; Alexa and Sophie gawked at the assembly of women with tattoos, untamed hair, skimpy clothing, and multiple piercings. Celeste didn't want to draw attention by telling her girls to stop staring; but finally, she couldn't stand it anymore. "Hey," she said softly, trying to communicate with her eyes.

"What?" asked Alexa, as the bathroom door swung open.

"Go, go." Celeste pushed them forward. When they returned to the sidewalk, Sophie pointed at the sign with the giant marijuana leaf. "What's that?"

"Well, sweetie," Celeste said, buying time. "It's a kind of plant." She tried to cobble together some benign answer. "Used for many purposes, for clothing and rope, and other stuff."

Alexa rolled her eyes. "Yeah, other stuff . . ." She wore a look of defiance that was establishing a home on her thirteen-year-old face.

What would Alexa know about weed? They'd never discussed it, but Celeste couldn't appear flustered. "Let's stretch our legs." She used a loud, jaunty voice that sounded artificial even to her. "Then I gotta call Aunt Greta."

Sophie tugged on her mother's T-shirt. "I'm hungry."

"Okay, we'll find something." She fished her cell out of her purse and checked the time—not more than a half-hour in this town. She still had to locate Tom's place in the hills.

"Mom," Alexa said, "I'm not gonna like anything Sophie picks."

"Honey." Celeste placed a hand on her daughter's arm. Alexa pulled away, stung by the touch and strode off. "Alexa!" Taking Sophie's hand, Celeste followed after her, shocked to realize that from the back Alexa no longer looked like a girl at all, but like a young woman with long, golden legs.

Down the sidewalk, she and Sophie stepped around people

lolling on the Hemp Connection's front steps. A plump woman wearing a short dress of stitched-together Crown Royal bags gripped a kitten draped over her shoulder. Sophie stopped to look. Celeste pulled her along and called out, "Wait up." Alexa, about to cross a side street, stepped back into the shade of an awning, waiting until they caught up.

The heat was sweltering and thick, not at all like the thin, dry, polluted air of Los Angeles. "Mommy." A tear rolled down Sophie's cheek. "I miss Tinker."

"Oh, I know, sweetie." Celeste wordlessly cursed the woman with the kitten.

"I wanna call Grandpa's about Tinker Kitty."

"Okay, honey." Celeste's stepmother was the only one home when they'd dropped off their cat, before they left the city. She'd been thankful for that. The last thing Celeste wanted was to see her father. When she'd called to tell him that they were leaving, he'd been furious, and then belligerent when she wouldn't tell him where she was going. In her father's mind, Victor was the blood relative. Musicians were like that, always sticking together.

They approached a square with a clock tower—the time stuck at about a quarter after four. An older man with unkempt hair waved at passing vehicles as he chanted, "Impeach Bush!" Some cars honked in response. Around him a few other people held signs. "No Blood for Oil" and "Bush is the Terrorist!" Vans pulling tent trailers cruised Main Street; giant pickup trucks rumbled by, stinking the air with diesel fumes, as pit bulls circled and barked in back. A truck with a "Support the Troops" sticker went past and the driver shook his fist out of the open window, yelling, "Crawl back in your hole, you ungrateful bastards!"

Celeste and the girls huddled together on the sidewalk. "Let's cross." She tugged Sophie's hand, Alexa followed them across the street. A barefoot, dreadlocked white man, wearing only a short skirt, strolled by, his arm wrapped around a woman who held a naked baby. A cluster of older hippies, gray-haired and pony-tailed, chatted and laughed.

These denizens seemed to have all the time in the world. Celeste was used to the indifferent, fast-moving multitude in the city; here, there was an easy familiarity, no one was in a hurry. Strangers on the sidewalk looked at her and smiled or nodded in acknowledgement. Some even said hello. Celeste turned away, startled and confused, wondering if perhaps they mistook her for someone they knew. They walked the few blocks of storefronts cornered by gas stations; behind Main Street were rows of clapboard houses. Garberville reminded her of a Wild West-era town—no stoplights, no fast-food signs. Nestled against dry yellow hills with creases of dark green forest, it would have appeared quaint if not for the peculiar antics.

Next door to a movie theater advertising a film they'd seen the year before was a restaurant. She reached out to open its glass door. All the people inside turned to look. Celeste felt exposed, suddenly on stage, as if the audience inside was able to see her raw state of crisis. In the door's reflection, mixed with all those swiveled faces, she saw her own disembodied face—a ghost of herself in this alien place.

Sophie cried out, "No, Mommy!"

"Not here," Alexa said.

She let go of the door and turned away. Alexa motioned to a smaller café across the street, where through the window a row of pinball machines was visible. Ignored as they entered, they settled at a window-front table with hand-written signs taped to the glass. *Restrooms for Patrons Only. Cash only, no credit cards. You sit you order!* Inside was cooler than out yet inexplicably muggier; the heavy smell of fried food hung in the air. In a far corner, a few kids in baseball caps leaned over one of the pinball machines, swearing and whooping. A Stephen Marley tune, whirring fans, plus the loud buzzing from a drinks cooler produced a rhythmic backup to the players' outbursts.

"Can I have a chocolate milkshake?" Alexa asked.

Sophie chimed in. "I want one too."

Suppressing her immediate reaction, Celeste mustered a relaxed-sounding tone. "Sure." She needed to make calls. *Everything's okay;* she repeated the silent incantation as she had for the last twenty-four hours. *Everything's okay.*

After they ordered, Celeste pulled a wad of paper napkins from the dispenser to wipe down the dirty table. Then, gathering more napkins, she blotted perspiration from the back of her neck. The humidity affected her hair, turning already unruly curls into red frizz, which she tried to pat down.

The waitress set the milkshakes on the table. Alexa took a slurp, jumped up, and stood in front of Celeste, her hand outstretched. "Quarters."

"Please." Celeste sat still, hands in lap, waiting for Alexa to say it before she would rummage in her purse.

"Yeah. 'Please'."

Celeste raised an eyebrow, and then gave in, unwilling to fight on a point of attitude. There was too much happening for that. Every quarter from her wallet went into Alexa's outstretched palm. "Be nice to your sister." Alexa turned away, but Sophie stayed. "Wanna play, sweetie? I can get more change." Sophie shook her head. "Okay, give me a minute, please. I have to call Aunt Greta." Shrugging, Sophie crossed to where Alexa was dropping quarters into the pinball machine.

Greta's number went straight to voicemail. A blessed reprieve. "We're on the road. Love you." She clicked off her phone and closed her eyes, then tapped in her dad's house number. "Oh, Ruth . . ." Celeste sighed, relieved her father hadn't answered.

"Where are you? The girls okay?"

"We're good. How's Sophie's cat?"

"Already killed a bird in my yard."

"Sorry, Ruth." A crowd had formed at the sidewalk table

in front of the window where she sat. Celeste watched a man outside nonchalantly light up a joint and pass it on. She shook her head and tried to concentrate. "Is Dad home?"

"At rehearsal. Victor was here, real upset. He's got a private investigator looking for you. Celeste, he has a right to know where his daughters are. Your dad agrees with him."

A private investigator! Celeste recoiled, drawing back into the rickety chair. Of course her dad would agree with her husband rather than defend her. Nothing could shatter that fellow-musician bond. "Actually, Victor's lost his right." Outside, the woman holding the kitten joined the rabble at the sidewalk table. Celeste turned away from the window, wondering why she had even called her father's, tapping into what she was attempting to leave behind. "Tell Victor we're safe. I can't deal with him now. I need time."

"Did Victor have another affair?"

"Oh Ruth. Ask him!"

"Celeste, come home; it'll be better." Ruth drew out her words, "They can find you from this call."

"How?" Celeste's head jangled. The impulse to throw her phone as far from herself and her daughters as possible gripped her—she resisted. *Everything's okay.* Since they'd left L.A., she'd been vigilant, paying cash for everything, including gas, so she wouldn't leave a trail. She'd bought a phone without her name attached. Yet her new number showed up on her father's phone and, possibly, Ruth was willing to share it. Her father certainly would, believing Victor was a good dad. In comparison to her father Victor was a good dad—except for being gone on tour all the time, his numerous affairs, and of course his most recent admission. "Ruth, don't give Victor this number. Please."

"Don't hang up. No, don't . . ."

Ruth's tiny voice whined as Celeste clicked off the phone. She brought a glass to her lips; her hand shook so badly she spilled the water, darkening the front of her T-shirt. Her whole body broke into a sweat, as if the heat had been upped by ten degrees. Across the room, Alexa and Sophie stood next to each other, transfixed by the pinball game, ensconced in faint electronic noises.

Sophie turned, looked at Celeste and then walked to her. "Mommy, I wanna talk to Tinker Kitty."

"Sweetie." Celeste tried to smile.

"I want to talk to Ruth," Sophie said.

Wrapping her arms around her young daughter, Celeste rested her clammy cheek on the fragrant cloud of Sophie's chestnut-colored hair. "She wasn't home."

Sophie raised her shoulders. "Who were you talking to?"

"Well, I did talk to Ruth. For a minute, but she had to go."

Sophie pushed out of her mother's embrace. She seemed to try to make sense of something tangled up.

"Ruth said Kitty's great. He loves Grandpa's backyard."

Sophie's doe eyes misted over, her head tipped to one side. "You promised."

"Sweetheart, Ruth didn't have time." Celeste had to look away.

"Why?"

Every cell in Celeste's body felt as if it would explode or implode, or continue to pulsate between the two. "I don't know."

Alexa appeared in front of Celeste with her hand out. "More quarters." Then, registering the peculiar hush, she glanced from Sophie to her mother. "What happened?"

A fan rotated weakly above their table. The music paused between songs. Celeste focused on a second-story loft at the back of the café, jumbled with empty boxes. She attempted to regulate her breathing. Turning back to Alexa and Sophie, she thought of how changed their lives were going to be. "Remember what I told you at the motel? Daddy and I can't be married anymore." She took in a sharp breath and reminded herself she would not disparage her husband to their children.

The harsh facts did not need to be spelled out, not yet, but Celeste could feel it building on her tongue, forming bitter angry shapes that would cut as they came out. If she told them herself, they'd blame the messenger.

Stepping from the café onto the scorching sidewalk, Celeste, tugged on her daughters' hands, slicing through the crowd and the pungent clouds of pot smoke.

※ ※ ※

On 101 North, she accelerated up the grade, watching her odometer compulsively for seventeen miles before taking an exit that spit them west. She crossed a bridge spanning a flood plain where a silver river snaked, flashing the last colors of sunset. This was the point where the directions she'd scribbled grew hopelessly confusing. Her phone continued to read: "No service." It was almost dark. The curving two-lane roadway narrowed. Mammoth redwoods with pithy bark lined the road on either side like sentries. Music turned to static and Celeste punched the radio off. The raspy, grating noise of the air conditioner chafed her nerves. She opened the window and a blast of sweltering heat blew into the car, quickly replaced with the cool tang of forest air as they went deeper into the woods. Ferns and emerald moss, glowing like lanterns, reflected the last strands of low sunlight; in the depths of the forest, night had already fallen. Celeste sucked the moist, aromatic air into her lungs and imagined their car dwarfed, a wind-up toy under the giant trees. Then, abruptly, the forest ended. The terrain opened up and the road curved like a black ribbon through yellow hills, shrouded in now-violet air.

She picked up her phone—still useless—and tossed it in the cup holder. The fierce energy she'd coasted on the day before had dwindled to hollow fatigue. In the intensifying gloom, the road grew more treacherous and remote. There'd been only a couple of cars since she'd gotten off the highway. "Please help me," Celeste murmured.

Alexa took out her earbuds. "What?"

"Look for a pile of rocks stacked on the side of the road." Celeste lifted her chin to the right.

"Why?"

Celeste didn't respond. She tried to make out any roadside shape.

"Mom, how long do we have to stay?"

"Look for the rocks. Please."

She'd called from Garberville to confirm this rendezvous, but without a working phone, without streetlights or address numbers, possibly lost in the boondocks and reduced to searching for a landmark of piled rocks, it suddenly felt beyond absurd. Then, after a dangerous curve, there it was: a pile of deliberately placed, large rocks and a dirt road that climbed a steep grade.

She saw a truck flashing high beams parked at the turnout and pulled behind it. The driver's door swung open. Celeste drew in her breath as a shadowed figure got out. A man's silhouette walked toward them. He was tall and well built. When he entered the beam of her headlights, she gasped, doubting—rejecting even—that this could be Tom. Then a large hand folded over her open window. "Celeste!" he exclaimed.

"Tom?" She began shaking. Words disconnected from her feelings tumbled out of her mouth. She switched on her car's interior light, which lit Tom's wide smile and revealed the gap of a missing tooth. Crouching by the driver's door, he loomed close, reaching in to touch her shoulder. A strong odor of sweat and something soapy and herbal overwhelmed her. He wore overalls, no shirt, had a long, braided beard, and was balding with a horseshoe band of hair that straggled to his shoulders.

"You look the same, Celeste. Beautiful as ever."

"Thank you." Shock and disillusionment slapped her memory. She felt numb as if she weren't really there at all. This was a movie she was watching, or had watched, and was now imagining. It was only Tom's voice she recognized; the reality of flesh and bones erased her cherished image. In her fantasy, she now knew, he wore shining armor, as if at this late date he would abandon his own family to heal her broken life. She fidgeted, unable to control her visceral reaction, rustling through items in her purse, her palms clammy. "Really," she barely managed to speak, "this is beyond anything I could expect."

Tom lifted his hand from her shoulder. "Well, hell, what are old boyfriends for?"

Celeste blinked and stared at him again. He smiled, displaying the dark chink of his missing incisor. She looked at the braided, gray beard lying flat against the bib of his overalls, then turned toward Alexa, who sat stiffly, the earbuds in her hand emitting a distorted bleating.

"We got the cabin cleaned up some," Tom was saying. "Still funky."

"That's fine." Celeste pictured her clean, light-filled house in the city. I made a mistake, she thought bitterly. "Funky's no problem," she said.

"Okay then, you came to the right place." Tom chuckled, then quieted. On his leathery face, with his wiry eyebrows raised, was an expression of inquiry. It was her turn.

She forced a smile. "Alexa and Sophie. This is Tom, a very old friend."

"Hey." Framed by the car window Tom nodded toward the girls. "Instead of 'old', let's just say 'good'."

"Oh, yes. 'Good'," Celeste repeated. "I mean, a very good friend."

Tom laughed. Pointing toward his truck, he said, "Follow me." He straightened up and slapped his hand on top of her car, making Celeste jump.

Off the pavement, the steep gravel road was riddled with potholes. In front of her, Tom's truck bounced in a dust cloud dense and luminous in her headlights. Even with the windows closed and air conditioning on, she could feel the grit of dirt in her teeth.

"Mom, was that guy really your boyfriend?"

"Yes. My first, really."

Alexa groaned. "How long do we have to stay?"

"We'll see."

"Mommy," Sophie whined from the backseat. "I have a tummy ache."

"Me too," said Celeste. It seemed impossible that anyone would live so far out on a practically inaccessible road, miles and miles off the pavement. Unseen potholes violently jolted the car. There were no flickering lights from houses or any other visible sign of human life. They drove into the murky abyss, the sound of rock fragments hitting the car's under-carriage. Finally, after turning onto another dirt track, Tom's truck bellowed up a hill and stopped. Celeste pulled next to him and cut her motor. Exhausted and trembling, she dropped her head to the steering wheel, closed her eyes, and wished she were anywhere else.

lost

Celeste heaved her overnight bag up the hillside. Indents in the dirt meant to be used as steps were neither stable nor consistent. She kept slipping as small rocks rolled like ball bearings under her flip-flops. Four big dogs jostled around her, sniffing, barking, and impeding the way. "You're sure the dogs are nice?" she asked again.

"Totally. You're okay," Tom responded.

The headlamps Tom helped them fit around their heads—bands with a small light stuck at the center, like a third eye—cast rays of odd, crisscrossing light as they ascended the hill. The band around her head was uncomfortably tight. It hadn't occurred to her that they might need to bring special equipment, like hiking shoes, flashlights, or headlamps. "Could you move, please?" Celeste asked a dog, as its wet nose vacuumed her bare leg.

"Trinity likes you," Tom said, reaching his arm out. "Give me your bag."

"No, it's okay. Thanks for hauling Sophie's." Besides the headlamps, the only other light was from Tom's house, which glowed at the top of the steep hill. "Don't you have any neighbors?"

"Unfortunately, yes."

"You can't see them?"

"Oh, they're out there." Tom swept his arm at the shadows.

The heat hadn't abated with nightfall. Celeste was sweating and breathless. "It's so dark."

"It's called the Lost Coast for a reason. We're eighty-plus

miles from the nearest traffic light. There are advantages. Look up."

Celeste arched her neck and gasped. Against the vast vault of inky velvet, bright configurations of stars glittered. Spellbound, she stopped climbing. "Oh, my fucking God."

"Mom!"

"Sorry, Alexa. It's incredible."

"So cool." Even Alexa couldn't help exclaim; they were accustomed to the opaque night sky of Los Angeles.

"It's even better if you don't have a lamp stuck on your head," Tom said with a laugh, and started back up the hill.

As they approached the crest, Celeste helped Sophie up the last of the dirt steps. Flashes from Tom's headlamp shone on plank stairs leading to a rustic-looking cabin. A faintly visible footpath connected the cabin and the house on the ridgeline they shared.

Suddenly, before them, two tall, willowy forms materialized on the path. "Welcome." Glancing light from headlamps illuminated a Black woman with a mane of dreadlocks. Gliding forward, she enveloped Celeste in a hearty embrace, eventually stepping back. "I'm Luna," she announced. "So good to meet you after all these years."

"Thanks for having us." Celeste said, trying to catch her breath.

Luna smiled. "That hill will whip you into shape."

"I bet." Celeste breathed. Tom had never mentioned that Luna was Black. But, of course, Celeste realized it would be unlike Tom to even think of telling her.

"You'll like the cabin," Luna was saying. "Good energy. We lived there for years while Tom finished the big house."

From behind Luna, the other figure stepped forward. Celeste extended her hand. "Are you Jonah?" He nodded. Taller than his mother and lighter skinned, he had the same bulky volume of dreads. His angelic face gave him the innocent appearance of a child. "How old are you?" was out of Celeste's mouth before she could contemplate whether it would bother him.

"Sixteen," he responded quickly, meeting Celeste's gaze without hesitation.

Luna slipped an arm around her son. "He'll be seventeen in November. Hard to believe."

"He's a keeper," Tom said, smiling proudly. Tom's free hand landed on Jonah's shoulder. Oh, I remember those huge hands, Celeste thought. Standing at the top of his hill beside his wife and son, it was obvious Tom had become the family man she had known he would. The hurt of her own shattered union with him rose, then ebbed.

"Whaddaya think?" Luna strolled toward Alexa and Sophie. "Let's go to the big house and get some dinner?" Celeste's daughters turned toward their mother; their headlamps shining out like desolate beacons reminding her they were still so tender and young—even insolent, teenaged Alexa.

Celeste tried to sound reassuring. "You go with Luna. I'll get our bags to the cabin." Her girls didn't move.

Tom reached for Alexa's bag. "I got it," he said, as he hoisted it away from her.

Luna threw her long arms around the girls' shoulders. "Good plan," Luna declared as she herded them away.

"Be there in a few," Celeste called out. In the distance, the rattling sound of a diesel engine was getting close. It sounded like one of the logging trucks they had passed on the highway.

"That's Jake," Tom said. "My older son, from my first marriage. Drives one of those hella loud trucks." Outsized headlights pulled up the driveway below them, the engine noise echoing in the hills. When the motor quit, doors opened, then slammed. "Hey." Tom yelled down the hill, "Jake, bring the luggage from that Subaru up to the cabin."

"No!" Celeste cried out. "We have everything we need.

Really." She only wanted their overnight bags in the cabin, in case she decided to leave in the morning, but couldn't say that to Tom.

"Hey," he said, waving her reluctance aside. "Take advantage of these healthy young men while you can."

"But, I don't know how long we're going to stay," Celeste protested, as voices, a man's and a woman's, called out something unintelligible from below.

"Thanks, Jake." Tom called back.

"But Tom . . ."

"No worries." Tom went up the porch stairs to the cabin door. "I'll show you the light switches." Celeste paused before stepping inside; she gazed back at the house with its softly lit windows where Alexa and Sophie had disappeared, then looked down the hill into the shadows where their possessions were being handled.

Inside the cabin, Tom aimed his headlamp at a switch. Celeste flipped it on. A bare bulb came on weakly, building strength with a slight popping noise. "We're off the grid," he said. They stood in a narrow, plywood hallway. In the bright light, Celeste fought against the reality of seeing Tom as he was. "Mudroom," he said. Still slim with muscled arms, he waved toward a side door. "Bathroom has a composting toilet." Tom opened the door to the main room and she followed him in. The odor of mildew was overwhelming. Celeste coughed, clutched at the headlamp and ripped it off her head. "Yeah, kinda musty." Tom said, as he went about opening windows.

A blackened wood stove occupied one corner of the cabin. Nearby, a Formica counter held a kitchen sink with shelves above and below. At the back of the room, a wooden ladder leaned against a sleeping loft. Celeste envisioned her house, its sparkling airiness and gleaming wood floors, the way the white curtains billowed in the breeze. She thought of her daughters' muffled sobs as she drove them away from the only home they'd ever known. She closed her eyes and took a breath to gain composure. At last, her gaze rested on Tom. "So, you built this place yourself?"

"Just for me and Jake. Then I met Luna, and soon Jonah came along. Cramped, but it got us through. Took me a few years to build the big house."

"Well, this is nice." She gestured at the tree trunks that supported the floor of the loft. "No pretensions."

"Exactly." Tom grinned. "So good to see you. After all these years. When was the last time? San Francisco, right?"

Celeste knew exactly when. She could still visualize the corner where they'd met; the woman on the sidewalk selling fragrant bunches of violets, which Celeste wanted but didn't buy. It was before Victor. Before Luna. She'd been accompanied by her lover—they'd broken-up just weeks later. Tom and Celeste's life pauses had always been out of sync.

The sound of things being knocked around came from the direction of the mudroom. The door swung open and a man carrying what appeared to be her entire carload of luggage stumbled backwards—his cargo wouldn't fit through the doorframe. He laughed as he careened from side to side, finally lurching into the room, pitching her suitcases, bags, and bundles over the floor.

"Shit, lady." He straightened up, standing over the pile. "You moving in?"

Celeste leapt toward the mound, pawing through her things, wondering if anything could have broken.

"Celeste," Tom said. "This is my son, Jake."

"Oh, sorry," she said, embarrassed. "Thanks for getting our stuff." She peered up, extending her hand, and froze. After a momentary confusion, she felt herself flush. There were the moss-colored eyes she used to know so well. The big hands, the strong jaw, the ruffled, shiny hair—all the same. Everything felt still and connected. Then, gradually, like light dawning, she became aware of an uncomfortable silence and forced herself to drop Jake's hand. "Nice to meet you," she stammered.

※ ※ ※

The big house consisted of one rambling octagonal room that held kitchen, living, and dining areas. A hallway branched away on one side leading to a bathroom and, Celeste surmised, bedrooms. After dinner, Celeste and Luna cleaned up in the kitchen, moving around a cramped space hemmed in by countertops. About half the walls in the octagon didn't have drywall, instead, puffy, pink insulation bulged between wall studs. Patterned rugs lay scattered over rough, dirty plywood floors. Prayer flags hung from the top of windows at either side of French doors leading to a deck; an old Bob Marley tune played in the clammy air.

Across the room, Harmony, Jake's girlfriend, clattered plates together at the dining table. Celeste plucked a tomato out of a basket on the kitchen counter. "Homegrown?" she asked Luna, as she brought the asymmetrical fluted tomato to her nose and inhaled.

"Yep, that's a Cherokee Purple. I grow about ten heirloom varieties." Luna turned toward her and smiled, tucking a dreadlock behind her ear. "Smells like summer, right?" There was an effortless elegance in Luna's movements, in her long-limbed leanness and the rich gleam of her ebony skin. "Tomorrow I'll show you my veggie garden."

"Nice." Celeste said, becoming uncomfortable, as Luna continued to gaze at her.

"So, Tom told me your trip was a last-minute thing."

"Oh . . ." Celeste tensed; a sickening rush of emotions overwhelmed her.

"That bad, huh?" Luna laughed, waving away her question. Still smiling, she turned back to the sink. Celeste exhaled, almost moaning in relief, unable to imagine explaining her circumstances, especially to someone she didn't know.

Carrying a stack of plates, Harmony glided across the room, her long blond hair swinging heavily against glossy shoulders as she moved. All eyes followed her. Even Alexa, on the couch with Jonah and Sophie, looked up to observe her passage toward the kitchen. Harmony was young, curvy, full of her own allure, aware of her power to hold the focus of a room. *Time diminishes that power, slowly and steadily in uneventful moments,* Celeste thought. She recalled believing youth was her personal state of being; sure it would never abandon her. It defined who she was. Yet, without looking in the mirror, Celeste could swear she was that same seventeen-year-old girl who had fallen in love with Tom. Twenty-seven years earlier.

Harmony deposited plates next to Luna at the sink, emitting the same cold detachment Celeste had felt when she sat across from her at dinner. Jake sat next to Harmony at the table; its lacquered, irregularly-shaped burl surface had reflected a collection of lit candles; standing fans at either side of the room blew the candle flames in a hypnotic rhythm. Celeste tried to keep her eyes off Jake, but it was as if an invisible cord tugged or a magnet drew her to him. Even his voice sounded just like his father's. He'd hurtle through a story, which she couldn't follow, about drunken shenanigans with friends at the river, his language crude, swear words punctuating every sentence. "Then he goes, 'Dude, keep your fucken feet in the kayak!'" He'd thrown his head back and tousled his hair, laughing, looking so intimately familiar. She had been mesmerized; it was all she could do to not fly over the table. He hadn't seemed to notice, but his girlfriend had. Whether Harmony was unfriendly because of the attraction Celeste was trying to repress for Jake, or if it was her nature to be aloof, was unclear. But Celeste was stunned that Tom, the sweetest man she'd ever known, could have such a brute for a son. Jake was obnoxious and insufferably self-centered. He wasn't what her inner compass was responding to. He wasn't young Tom. It wasn't twenty-seven years ago. Yet, slugging down her second beer, Celeste felt herself dizzying, memories merging with the people in front of her. She began to lose track of what was past and what was present. She wished she could openly stare at Jake, without the dynamics, without his personality interfering, so she could quench herself without being subtle or secretive.

"So where do you live in L.A.?" Luna asked.

"Uh . . ." Celeste was frozen in thought, midway through wiping a plate dry. She turned to see Harmony reaching in next to Luna, scraping leftovers into a compost bucket. "Our house is on the Westside," Celeste answered as Harmony pivoted out of the kitchen, her long blond hair flying like swirling fringe. From across the room, Jake's voice thundered. He seemed to be standing next to Celeste, yelling into her ear, making it impossible to concentrate.

"Tom tells me you teach at a Waldorf School." Luna's hands sunk deep into soapy water.

"Well," Celeste said. "I just quit."

Luna turned to her. "Oh, baby, you are full of surprises."

"Yeah, quitting isn't something a Waldorf teacher should do. I love my students. I'm ashamed."

"Oh hell, it's summer." Luna flashed a smile, and then laughed. "Those kids don't know you quit, right? So put off feeling ashamed until fall."

A sudden pungent burning odor hit Celeste; Tom had lit up a joint at the table. She scanned the different areas of the large space, looking for Alexa and Sophie. "Do you know where the kids went?"

Luna stared at her for a moment and then responded, "Jonah's room?"

"This way?" Celeste asked, pointing as she headed toward the hall. Luna nodded.

The door to Jonah's room was open. Inside was a separate world from the bohemian decor of the octagon. Here, electronics ruled. On a long desk against the wall, gutted computers and other cannibalized electronics lay in disarray. In the far corner, a laptop played the opening scene from *Breakfast at*

Tiffany's. Sophie stared at the screen, transfixed. Neither Alexa nor Jonah watched. They both scribbled in journals, sprawled on the floor, their backs to Celeste. *Moon River* played, and they wrote. Celeste watched from the doorway. Audrey Hepburn, in sunglasses, got out of a cab, gazed at a jewelry display window, took a bite of her Danish and a sip of coffee. Sophie watched intently. Alexa and Jonah kept writing, so absorbed that Celeste went entirely undetected. The teenagers were in absolute sync with one another. Jonah's long dreads bobbed slightly as he wrote. Celeste could tell Jonah was intelligent, yet mercifully seemed to lack the angst and sarcasm that Alexa threw regularly, like daggers. Jonah and Alexa had obviously bonded—almost instantly. It was worrisome—her recent everything-you-should-know-about-sex conversation with Alexa had not gone smoothly. Celeste took one last mental snapshot, then left the doorway.

Back in the octagonal room, Tom, Jake, and Harmony sat at the table. As she approached they watched her intently. "Tom, can I talk to you for a second? Please."

"Sure." He held out the joint to her.

Celeste flexed her palm. "No thanks." Tom brought the joint to his mouth and inhaled slowly. Staring at her, he sucked a few extra sips, and held the smoke in his lungs. Jake and Harmony seemed to examine and evaluate Celeste. She flushed, grew feverishly hot, then broke out in a sweat. They were a panel, and she was standing before them for some kind of judgment. "Can we go out?" she asked, tipping her head toward the French doors that led to the large deck.

Tom exhaled his lungful of smelly smoke. "Okay." He passed the joint to Jake and rose from the table.

The screen door slapped shut behind them. Outside was shockingly hot and silent, except for an occasional owl hoot. Celeste scanned the horizon for lights from other homes, but saw none. She could just make out the ascending and descending waves of hills and mountains that surrounded them. Bundling together the sweat-soaked hair stuck to her neck, she twisted it away and gathered her courage. "Tom, could you please just for tonight, not smoke weed in front of my daughters?"

"Shit." Tom's mouth fell open. "You're kidding."

"We'll leave in the morning. Early."

Tom seemed to scrutinize her. "Do you still smoke?"

"Not in front of my kids."

"Funny how you had no problem enjoying beer in front of them."

"Oh, come on. That's legal. Please, it's just this big, confusing issue to explain to Alexa at an age when . . ."

Tom interrupted, "Smoking pot is practically legal in Humboldt County, growing pot maybe not so much. Celeste, we keep no secrets in this house."

"I didn't think it through when I decided to come."

"That's an understatement," Tom grunted. His jaw tightened. "Welcome to SoHum." Celeste saw a brief flash of exasperation cross his face as he flung his arm at the night. "We grow weed and we smoke it. That's what we do. What'd you think I was doing in Southern Humboldt for the past twenty-five years?"

"You told me you were building houses."

Tom tilted his head toward the house. "True." He paused, studying her. "Remember when you first moved to L.A. and found out your dad lied to you about smoking pot?" She nodded. "Remember how the hypocrisy made you crazy. You're doing the same thing. If everyone was truthful . . ." He shook his head. "Man, it's the mind space that keeps it down." Taking his eyes off her, he looked up at the glinting stars. "Man, I thought you were planning on hangin' with us a while. Doing some summer months."

"I have no idea what the fuck I'm doing." Sweat rolled down her neck. She swiped at the drips. "Damn it. Doesn't it ever cool off here?"

Tom glanced back at Celeste. She could feel the burden of the past tug at her. It seemed as if, until this moment, she'd lived her life at breakneck speed, zooming to this standstill, where she stood skinned of her own pretense in this ridiculously far-flung place. With her ties to home cut, she imagined all she had now were threads connecting her with her daughters, the three of them loose and orbiting in this hot, alien black space.

It was quiet outside. There was no traffic noise. No sirens. No car alarms. No streetlights. Celeste caught sight of Jake through the screen door. He and Harmony were laughing. Jake glanced over at her. He appeared thoroughly entertained. Assuming it was at her expense, Celeste shot back what she hoped was a poisonous look. Actually, when she considered how she'd ended up in Humboldt, even she found it almost amusing. In her blind leap out of her quagmire, she'd inadvertently delivered her children into this most inappropriate territory. After thirteen years of carefully weighed and meticulous parental decisions, it had somehow come to this. Celeste lowered her voice. "Tom, if you grow pot, is it safe here?"

Aping her, Tom whispered back, "I feel safe . . ." He appeared exasperated. But after a moment, he spoke quietly in measured tones, "In fact, just a few minutes ago I was feeling kinda relaxed." His fingers grazed the length of his braided beard. "Shit, Celeste. You call me outta the blue and tell me you gotta get outta L.A. right away. So, here you are. Decide about this place for yourself. But if you stay, there's some adjustments you have to make."

"If you don't want us here, just tell me."

"Hey." Tom touched her elbow. "I told you on the phone, you can stay as long as you need to. One thing that's never changed: my word is gold. Especially in this business, where there's cruisers and collaborators. . ."

"What?"

"Cruisers and collaborators. It's about personal integrity. You gotta be able to tell the cruisers from the collaborators."

"Okay. What adjustments are you talking about?"

"Just know how to be quiet. No big deal. Luna'll have the conversation with you and the girls. But you can trim for us and make some money. We always need help."

"Actually, I'm out of here. I can't see exposing my kids . . ."

"If you're here," Tom declared, "one fucking day, Luna's having that conversation."

Celeste stepped back and leaned against the deck railing. She threw her head back, took in the sweep of the Milky Way then turned back to Tom. "What do you mean 'trim'? If I look for work, it would be a teaching position."

"Schools are laying teachers off here." Tom went to the railing, next to her. "Trimming is cleaning weed. You just take off leaves, shape up the bud. Jake has his indoor ready to go. We'll be harvesting our light dep soon. After that our outdoor will be ready."

"Oh," she said, "that's not happening."

Tom was silent for a moment. Then he smiled and ambled away. Pulling the screen door open, he turned back to her, "Get over it, Celeste. And stay for a while, for Christ's sake."

breathing

Celeste sat up with a gasp. As her dream receded she shuddered and fell back in the sheets. The next time she opened her eyes, the cabin was bathed in light. From outside came the low buzz of insects accompanied by bright birdsong.

The futon she lay on put her inches above the dirty floor. Everything seemed even more dilapidated than it had the night before. She shook her head and wondered why she'd left her home. She could have made a stand there, it would have been the rational thing to do, what any other woman in her place would have done. But she would have had to see Victor and be scrutinized by family and friends as she sorted through the vestiges of her marriage. Thinking about that made her nauseous. She recalled sniggering groups, falling silent as she came near. She'd had enough of that already—her disastrous affair at school had made a mess of the best job she'd ever had. Celeste reminded herself not to brood about that failing.

She needed to get stuff organized and get back on the road, but she also needed to catch her breath and figure out where to go. Her sister had that lead on a place to rent in Idyllwild. She thought about Tom's offer that she stay awhile, but couldn't justify taking refuge with a pot-grower. She wasn't going to expose her children to illegal activities and put them at risk. Besides, Tom wouldn't have offered if he'd known that a private investigator had been dispatched. Marijuana growing and PI's—oil and water.

The girls were talking above her, in the loft where they'd slept. Their words weren't distinct through the floorboards, but their voices wove together melodically the way children's voices do without adult interruptions. It occurred to her that her daughters probably hadn't been alone with each other for a long time. At home in separate bedrooms, they'd led separate and antagonistic sibling lives. Not since Sophie was a toddler had Alexa been happy to play with her.

"Good morning," Celeste said, as they climbed down from the loft.

Sophie slipped between the sheets on the futon, and Celeste hugged her, burying her nose in Sophie's thick hair.

Alexa stood over her looking irritated. "Mom, I have to pee, bad."

"Well then, go."

"But, Mom, it's so gross, that combustible toilet, yuck."

"Composting, not combustible. That wouldn't be good at all."

"I can't use that thing."

"Alexa, you have choices: go to the house and use their bathroom, pee outside, or use the composting toilet—which happens to be the closest."

"Oh, God!" Alexa stomped out, slamming the door to the mud room, and then the door to the toilet room.

Sophie peered up at Celeste. "Mommy, I wanna go home and see Daddy."

"Sweetie, I know." Celeste stroked her daughter's soft arm. "But how cool is it that we're having an adventure?"

Sophie pushed herself into her mother and whimpered, "I wanna go home."

Celeste suddenly felt an uncomfortable feverish-heat descend, and that same annoying twitch under her eye returned. Holding onto Sophie, she scrambled up, leaning against the window sill and pulling air deeply into her lungs as her heart pounded and she began to sweat. "It's already so hot."

Outside the window, a dragonfly lighted on the screen, sun-light shimmering over its blue-green iridescent wings. "Look, Sophie." Celeste pointed, and then a realization dawned—this was a new day.

** ** **

Stepping into the spots that Luna's feet vacated, watching her strong leg muscles flex, Celeste tried to match her stride as they followed the path through the sprawling vegetable garden.

Luna pointed at a slumping plant ornamented with mottled greenish and dusky-pink tomatoes. "Cherokee Purple, my new favorite." She reached out to another plant and pulled off a stem heavy with little tomatoes, bunched like bright red grapes. "But for snacking in the garden, you can't beat this." She handed the bright stem to Celeste.

"Umm," Celeste murmured, as a cherry tomato burst open in her mouth, popping sweet, sharp flavors. "Like candy."

"So, Celeste, tell me what brought you here?"

Shocked by the question, Celeste realized she had been in a pleasant sun-warmed bubble, enjoying the tastes of the garden, only worried about stepping on a squash flower. Suddenly, the stink of lilies rotting on her kitchen counter came to her, and she was back there, on that crazy day. If she talked about what had happened, she'd be thrown down a well she couldn't climb out of, but Luna's dark marble eyes held hers. With her crown of dreadlocks, twisted high on her head, Luna appeared regal and commanding. The queen had asked a question and Celeste felt compelled to answer. "My husband told me that a woman is six months pregnant with his child."

Luna's eyes widened and her shoulders stiffened. Strangely satisfied by her reaction, Celeste continued, "He'd promised he broke it off with her. Victor's a sound engineer, she's a back-up singer and they're on tour together. He's always on tour. Hardly ever home." She looked past the garden fence, past the clearing and gnarled oak branches, out to the mountains and deep, vibrating blue sky. To the west, only a dozen miles away, was the end of the continent. She could almost taste the ocean and its saltiness.

Celeste cast her eyes back to Luna's unflinching gaze. Without a word, Luna opened her arms and Celeste fell into her embrace. The first tears loosened, and then a deluge came as Luna patted her hair and said simply, "It's tough." They stayed like that, Celeste being hugged like a child, in the middle of the vegetable garden. Luna enwrapped her without the stickiness of judgment, or pity. The sun burned down as a backlog of tears poured out. Celeste let the complication of her own dalliance float away, unsaid. It was an ugly detail, and didn't need to be spoken.

Tom appeared at the garden gate, surrounded by the gaggle of dogs. He waved and yelled in a jovial voice, "Guess I don't have to worry about you two gettin' along!" then followed up in a concerned tone, "Hey, everything okay?"

Luna and Celeste unlocked themselves and Luna called out, "She'll be fine." Then they went single file to the gate where Tom stood. The midday heat quickly dried her tears, leaving a taut, salty residue on her face.

Tom looked cautiously at Celeste and spoke in a hushed tone, as if she'd just awakened. "The girls want to ride. Sophie can ride the pony." Celeste nodded at Tom and tried to smile. Then the three of them tramped up the hill, the dogs orbiting around them.

※ ※ ※

Taking up the halter, Luna guided the pony—with Sophie riding—out of the barn as Alexa, mounted on the reddish mare, followed Jonah on his horse into the corral. At least, Celeste thought, the horses moved slowly. "You're sure it's safe?" Shaky from her crying episode, Celeste tried to weigh her concerns rationally. "They've never ridden before."

"Well, Alexa's on my mare. She's mellow, perfect for a beginner." Luna turned to the pony and rubbed the white strip blazing its muzzle. "Oh, and this baby loves kids. People joke that they choose me as their midwife 'cause they get free pony rides." Luna laughed; her laugh came easily and had warm rolling tones.

"Tom told me you're a midwife."

"I worked as a nurse in Chicago, where I'm from. Worked at a hospital for years. Raised my family there."

"So, you have other kids?"

"I have grandchildren older than my Jonah." Luna gazed back at Jonah, as he and Alexa made their way across the corral. "Jonah's my sweet hill child."

"He seems so smart," said Celeste.

"Smart and sweet. Loves his horse, rides to the river every day. Bonding with animals is so great for kids. Animals demonstrate truth; they aren't handicapped by reason like we are. Excuses are useless with animals." Celeste fell in step next to Luna who unhurriedly guided the pony around the corral. She continued, "Jonah wanted his own horse, so it's his sole responsibility."

"That's a big animal to take care of," Celeste said, staring at the imposing horse Jonah rode as he went through the metal gate and started down a path.

"Stay on the trail," instructed Luna. "Don't be gone too long."

"No problem, Mom."

Alexa, atop the red mare, followed behind Jonah. "Love you!" Alexa flashed a wide smile as her long dark hair swung in perfect sync to the horse's gait.

"Love you too. Be careful, please." Celeste stared, amazed at this radiant young woman, so distinctly unlike the petulant teenager of that morning.

"You're a natural rider," Luna called out. Tom emerged from the barn, joining them as they watched the horses pass out of sight on the path.

"Oh, Mommy," Sophie cooed, beaming from her position of pony-rider.

"Wow, look at you." Celeste patted the pony's forehead and it turned its head toward her, fluttering lashes which closed over bulbous shiny eyes. "Thank you for taking such good care of my girls." Celeste looked toward Tom, and then Luna. "I really appreciate it."

Tom smiled. "It's easy when they're sweet."

Suddenly feeling spontaneous and impish, Celeste asked, "So, Tom, where's your garden?"

Tom's eyebrows rose. "What garden are you referring to Celeste?"

"The other one."

"Really? After that bullshit last night?"

Celeste's smile faded. In the face of their warm hospitality, she'd pushed the only hot button. The whole weed thing was a whopping good reason to have already gotten back on the road. But since morning had dawned, one event had melded into the next. Her daughters were happy. And as she always realized in bright intervals with her children, when they were happy she was too. Besides, she couldn't stomach driving out to the highway not knowing whether to turn north or reconsider going south.

Tom wagged a finger at Celeste. "Luna's gonna have that talk with you and the girls."

"Tom, stop scaring the girl," Luna said, grabbing Celeste's arm. "Don't worry."

"Just a reminder. That'll be today." Tom winked. "Come on, I'll show you the light dep."

"Actually." Celeste touched her young daughter's back. "I need to stay with Sophie."

"I've got her," Luna said. "When the kids get back, Jonah and I can show the girls how to cool the horses down. Heck, we'll even show them how to muck out." Luna's warm laugh welled up again.

☀ ☀ ☀

Tom and Celeste took the trail the horses had taken, but instead of hiking down, they traipsed up a forested hillside. The dogs followed Tom, like four loyal shadows. After an arduous hike, they emerged at a wide meadow and crossed bare, dry land under scorching sun, until three long greenhouses came into view. A pungent odor swelled the air as they approached the structures.

Tom drew back the flap of opaque fabric. Celeste followed him inside a brilliant emerald realm. Rows of plants almost as tall as Celeste stretched out of sight. The closeness and skunky stench was suffocating—it seemed stronger than the horseshit smell, and almost more animalistic. Fiercely moving air, pushed by whirring fans, created a sort of wind tunnel. "Hey. You have electricity here, to run the fans."

"Solar, we're off the grid."

"Right. Off the grid." Celeste repeated the phrase. "I didn't realize plants got this huge." The light inside the "hoop house", as Tom called it, was diffuse and bright without shadow. Inches from her face, a leaf the size of a plate rhythmically waved at her, its serrated edges and iconic shape unmistakably recognizable. "Well, your plants seem healthy."

Tom was bent over, poking around the base of a plant. "Indoor ain't nothing compared to good ol' organic sun-bud."

"Aren't we inside?"

"This ain't indoor, light deprivation plays a little trick on nature. We actually withhold sunlight."

"What?" Celeste asked, confused.

Tom smiled knowingly, and, without answering, continued in his element, examining his plants. Standing up, he pulled a top stem down, inspecting a fat bud that sparkled as if sugar had been poured over it.

"See the crystals? Super-sticky. When those white hairs turn color, it's time to harvest." He studied another bud. "A few more weeks, these girls are ready."

"Then what?"

"Then we harvest. This is farming."

"Gotta be a big job." Celeste gazed at the endless rows.

"Oh, man, hope so. Means I did good." Tom smiled wide. Celeste stared at that empty spot in his mouth where a tooth once lived. The smell in the greenhouse seemed to be getting stronger. She flushed. Fumbling at the flap, she stammered, "I have to get out." Tom bent to sweep open the fabric, and then they stepped out into the hot air, which now seemed refreshing. Celeste inhaled deeply and lifted her arms skyward. "Air."

The dogs ran from the far side of the meadow to Tom's side.

"So." Tom pulled his braided beard and rocked back on his heels. "Now that you've seen my grow, I'll have to kill you." His eyes twinkled, and he burst out laughing.

"Jesus. Fuck. That's not funny."

"Well, what are you so afraid of?"

"Just the whole thing."

"Look, I'll tell you what to be afraid of—walking on paths or roads that aren't on our property, wandering up some random driveway."

"Okay," said Celeste, still stunned. "But, Tom, that wasn't funny."

"Sorry." Tom gave her a quick hug, meant to reassure her, she assumed.

Behind him the greenhouses loomed, stinking and animate with whirling noises, alive and breathing like hulking beasts.

river

Luna and Jonah brought a tray of lemonade to the cabin porch. It was late afternoon, and everyone seemed worn down by the heat. Celeste dropped into a broken-down wicker chair. She was nervous and unsure about the "talk," but also so hot and exhausted she was glad just to sit for a while.

In the long view past the driveway, distant mountain ridges layered themselves against the sky in greens and grays, brightened in spots by sunshine or darkened by folds of thick forest. To the west a fog bank spread lengthwise, suspended between mountains. The dogs sniffed around. Trinity, the fluffy black dog, nuzzled Sophie, then turned a tight circle and collapsed next to her with a sigh. Sophie leaned back against his mat of fur and dangled her legs off the porch.

Luna poured lemonade, then came around ceremoniously handing everyone a glass with a smile. She settled next to Sophie, but gazed at Alexa. "So, what do you know about the Constitution?" Alexa shrugged, she swiveled with a shocked glance toward Celeste, clearly feeling sabotaged by some sort of unwelcome lesson. Luna glanced at Jonah, who took a step back and leaned against the rough wood siding of the cabin.

Luna continued, "You know the Constitution is the document our government is based on?" Both girls looked unnerved, but they nodded obediently. "What if I told you that there was an amendment to the Constitution that said it was against the law to drink wine and beer and any other alcohol?"

Alexa shook her head. "No. There's not."

"Okay. What if I told you that it used to be law, but now it's repealed. "

Alexa looked back at her mom. Celeste raised her shoulders. "That's true."

"Sometimes the government tries to mandate what people should or shouldn't do," said Luna, her voice calm and steady. Sophie stared at her.

"What's 'mandate'?" asked Alexa.

Luna took a long contemplative sip of lemonade. "Force, by law. Like in 1920 when the government mandated that drinking was against the law. Beer and wine are legal to drink, right?" Alexa nodded. Luna focused on her, and Alexa's eyes darted sideways as if she were looking for a place to hide. Celeste had the urge to sit near her, protectively, but then Luna turned to Sophie. "Cannabis is a flower that people smoke to relax. It's also called marijuana, or pot, or weed, or ganja. Or lots of other names." Luna looked back at Alexa. "People smoke ganja for the same reasons they drink wine, or other alcohol. But, and this is important, cannabis doesn't just relax people: it has very important medical uses too. Native peoples and ancient cultures have always used it. Eventually it will be legal. And it will be recognized and revered as an important medicine that has many uses."

Luna put her arm around Sophie. "Here's the important part that you need to understand." Sophie gazed up at Luna, who continued, "Because it's not fully legal yet, you are not to talk about it with anyone. Ever."

Luna looked back and forth between the girls. "Do you understand?"

Alexa nodded grimly and eyed Luna. Sophie turned and patted her hands on Trinity's dense fur. Celeste looked at Jonah, who pushed some stray dreads from his face, smiled shyly, and met her gaze.

✻ ✻ ✻

Women sat facing each other as their hands whizzed expertly. Celeste felt as if she were surrounded by the incessant beating of birds' wings. It reminded her of olden times—something like a quilting bee or a sewing circle, but in this case, the circle of women was manicuring marijuana bud.

"Anything smaller than your pinky nail goes here. We don't trim the little buds. That's what we smoke." Luna and Celeste sat close together, clippers in hand, piles of dried cannabis stems before them. They'd been trimming since early morning. Celeste's hands weren't working in sync with her brain. She balanced a cardboard flat on her lap; her hands moved in slow motion.

Luna's Fiskars moved deftly, the plastic container on her tray filled quickly with perfectly shaped buds. Leaves and stems were dispatched into separate bags near her feet.

Midday turned to afternoon, sweltering heat overwhelmed Celeste. Even her hands were perspiring. She itched from the dry plant duff that flew everywhere and stuck to her moist neck and exposed skin.

"Don't cut so close, Celeste. Remember, we want those crystals. Just clip the big leaves from their base. Keep those little sparkly ones." Celeste's competitive juices were flowing, yet a refrain kept repeating in her mind: *What the fuck am I doing?*

"Luna, I'm just no good at this."

"Are you kidding? Next week you'll be clipping a pound a day with your eyes closed. Your fine-motor skills are great. You'll be fast. Don't worry."

"Okay." Celeste resisted rolling her eyes. Suddenly she understood exactly how Alexa felt when she rolled her eyes. It was a specific, overwhelming expression of: "*Like I care.*"

How had it come to this? Celeste wondered. That the goal she now aspired to would be trimming a pound a day. College education be damned. This activity was mind-numbing, unimaginable for one more day, even one more hour.

"How long will you be trimming?" Celeste asked.

"Oh, we trim on and off all year. Jake's got his indoor, that's what we're working on. When we finish, our light dep will be ready. Then our biggest harvest, our outdoor, will be done. How long it takes all depends on our crew. If we keep this group I'll be lucky." Luna raised her head and smiled.

A disorganized chorus responded: "My favorite place to work." "Keep it local." "Love you, Luna."

"You're Union, Dude." A pregnant woman, who had introduced herself as Anya, pointed to her T-shirt. The phrase "Clippers Union" was printed over an official-looking, bogus emblem. Everyone laughed. Celeste swept a quick glance around the trim shack. Harmony sat at the far end of the circle, and she looked up at Celeste. Then, immediately, their eyes disengaged, just as if they were old foes.

In the corner, on blankets scattered with toys and books, two children played, occasionally clamoring for their mothers' attention. A constant drone of conversation hovered over the circle and sometimes drifted off into mumbled digressions. The women talked easily with one another, their voices interlaced around Celeste. Every time she looked up to see who was talking she'd stop clipping, and when she looked back down she'd have to evaluate where she'd left off, which would lead her to once again wonder, *what the fuck am I doing?*

But sometimes she just had to look up, at least for a second. A woman with a raspy voice was talking. Deja was her name. ". . . the perfect penis, I keep hearing about it. But no one can tell me which brother has it. One does and one doesn't."

Celeste cast her eyes back down to her task. Her fingers had a dark coating of resin on them and the buds she was clipping were sticking to her.

"Which brothers? The ones whose mother lives up Chinook Creek?"

"No, no, these dudes are hot. Big growers in Blue Cove. Surfer dudes. One has longer hair and drives a bigger truck."

"So he's got the small dick."

Celeste looked up again. Anya was snickering at her own quip. She had long blond dreadlocks and arms covered in tribal-design tattoos.

"I didn't say 'big dick;' I said 'perfect dick'," the woman named Deja responded.

"Hey, Celeste, you married to that bud?"

Celeste startled. "Excuse me?" The woman who had spoken had a long face and dirty-looking lanky hair. Celeste had no idea what the woman meant but understood it was said in less than a warm-hearted way.

"Lay off, Sipotty," Luna shot back, then turned to Celeste. "What she means is that you don't want to cut on a bud too much. Keep moving. Don't get obsessive. I see that's your tendency. It's okay; you'll learn. Just remember, you're not married to one bud. We pay two-fifty for each pound you trim, so it behooves you to be fast."

"Okay." Celeste stole another peek at Sipotty.

"We all had to learn, Sipotty." Luna seemed irritated.

"What do you want, Luna?" Sipotty responded, "You want me to keep quiet while she's butchering your buds?"

Luna's hand movements stopped. She looked up. "Give it a rest, Sipotty."

"Whatever you say."

Sipotty sounded American born and bred. Celeste knew it was impolite to ask, but she didn't care. "Is Sipotty your given name?"

Sipotty stiffened upright in her chair. "It is a name of choice, given to me as a gift."

There was a sudden, pregnant, absence of conversation. The din of metal blades slicing in rapid motion continued, accented by an occasional pinging sound when a flying piece of cut stem hit something hard. And now another layer of background noise, the local radio station, could be heard. KBUD Radio was playing to a captive audience. Celeste barely made out the lyrics in the song, "Smoke two joints before I smoke two joints, then I smoke two more . . ."

"So, anyway," Deja interrupted the hush, "one of the brothers—the one with the smaller truck, by the way, Anya—anyway, he flirts with me every time I see him at the post office. I know a girl who went to North Fork High with them. Next time I see her I'm gonna ask which brother is the one."

"But, Deja, what *is* a perfect penis?" Celeste could tell it was Anya talking, even without looking up. She had a deep voice and a teasing attitude. She continued. "Whadda ya gonna see when you're head-to-head with perfection?"

"Dude," said Deja. "There's only one way to find out."

Laughter joined the droning engine sound of an approaching all-terrain vehicle. It stopped outside the trim shack. In the morning the ATV had carried the workers to the trim shack, two at a time. It easily scaled the steep hills of Tom and Luna's property, like a supercharged golf cart with truck tires. Jake pulled back the screen which draped the entrance and stepped into the shack. Tom followed him inside.

"Hi girls. Whatup?" Jake flashed a smile.

The men in charge. Celeste's blood started to boil. Men coming to check on their worker women—this was the counterculture. It seemed trimming was designated women's work, probably because something was being cleaned. Celeste couldn't help shaking her head.

Tom waved in the direction of Luna and Celeste. He was wearing overalls without a shirt, again. It looked like the same raggedy, dirty pair she'd seen on him the first night they'd arrived. Even in this incarnation, Tom was as she recalled: steady, sweet, unflappable. And although she would have never recognized him as her handsome ex-lover, his horrible doppelganger son proved her memory hadn't lied about his former attractiveness. Jake had the jaw with cleft indent that Celeste remembered Tom having—and probably still had, under the wacky beard. But Jake had a solid, larger build and Tom didn't have tattoos. Inked curling lines extended from underneath Jake's T-shirt sleeves. Celeste couldn't help watching as Jake moved toward Harmony. He bent down to her; she whispered to him.

Since Celeste had arrived in Humboldt, her past and present seemed to coexist in a dream-like way, as if the whole of her time in Los Angeles, including her years of marriage, were sealed off from her life before and after. She felt she was slowly waking from a long comfortable nightmare. Even with her concerns about exposing her children to the pot culture, she was glad to have escaped the shambles of her marriage—and her job, after the affair with her coworker. And, although at first she was nervous and unsure about Luna's talk, Celeste felt, days later, that it was good to have everything in the open. She'd lived with deceit too long. It was rejuvenating to put the truth out there, on the everyday slab, to be witnessed by all, adults and children alike.

Tom crossed the room and bent down to give Luna a kiss.

"Are the girls with Jonah in the corral?" Celeste asked.

"They're eating lunch at the house." Tom picked up Luna's paper grocery bag of trimmed-up weed. "Then they're gonna watch *Breakfast at Tiffany's* for the millionth fucking time." He reached his hand into the bag and pulled out a bud, examining it closely. "Hey, Celeste, the girls are getting good at mucking out. And, Sophie, man, she loves that pony. All by herself, she hosed Kiwi and brushed her down."

Tom took Luna's bag over to a table, putting it down next

to a scale. He began to adjust weights on the metal scale and then turned back to Celeste. "So, the kids've been working on me to take 'em to the river to cool off."

"Uh, wait. If the girls are swimming," Celeste said, "I'm going too."

"Okay. I don't know if I have time. I gotta weigh up and finish some other stuff. But they'd be safe with me. I'd make sure of that."

"Thanks, Tom. But if they go, I want to go too." Celeste and Tom looked at each other. Then he walked over to her and picked up her bag of finished buds, peering down into the almost-empty bag.

"Man, you're not getting much done."

Luna jumped to her defense. "She's learning, Tom."

"Fine. Fine." He put her bag on the floor and walked back to the scale.

Celeste tried to get back to focusing on refining a bud into a pine-cone-shaped form. Anya was saying, "My daughter's teacher is burnt-out. Been teaching for, like, thirty years or something. The principal knows she's fried but says there's no money in the district for new teachers."

"If her teacher's overwhelmed," Celeste felt compelled to speak, "maybe it would help to have a parent in the classroom as a teacher's aide. California schools are broke. And your local schools don't get any of this money," Celeste said, pointing to Anya's bag of trimmed buds. "Right? Property taxes are probably low here?"

"Yeah, but growers are generous in our community," Luna said. "We have fundraisers for our schools, and the Bear Ridge Volunteer Fire Department is thriving. Although I will say, the younger growers don't contribute the way the older Mom and Pop growers always have."

"Yeah," Deja shouted. "Hipnecks suck."

"Hipnecks?" Celeste repeated.

"When a hippie and a redneck breed." Anya explained. "The new generation of grower—a hippie without a conscience. They only care about getting their boy-toys, the biggest truck with the biggest tires." Celeste glanced up; she wanted to see Jake's reaction. Anya had just described the truck he drove. But Jake and Harmony were standing near the opening of the shack. Jake leaned toward Harmony as a breeze flapped at the screen, and kissed her neck.

"Hey, Luna," Tom called from across the room, "where're the turkey bags?"

"Should be about a dozen boxes there, under the table."

A glass pipe was making its way around the circle.

"Okay . . ." Celeste asked, "what's a turkey bag?"

Tom was sipping on the pipe, and he laughed, choked, and then recovered. "Man, I got the turkey bag story for you. Our little store, Busy Bee Grocery, they . . ."

Sipotty interrupted, "Tom, please weigh me up. I have to go. You can pay me later."

"Oh-Kay." Tom enunciated deliberately. Celeste could see Tom was surprised and irritated, the same way Luna had been with Sipotty. Everyone looked up as Sipotty stood and brushed off the bits of dried ganja stuck to her loosely-woven, beige sleeveless dress. It looked like burlap and hung listlessly on her bony frame. Celeste felt itchy just looking at it, and then realized she could see through it; Sipotty was not wearing underwear.

"Jake, can you take Sipotty back to her car?"

Straightening up, Jake said, "Sure, Dad." Harmony went back to her chair, and soon Jake and Sipotty ducked under the screen curtain. The ATV started up and took off. When the buzzing of the engine faded in the distance, the circle exploded into gossipy bits. "She wears only fabric that she spins and weaves herself. I think it's admirable," Luna was saying to Deja.

"The whole idea of not using anything that's manufactured is ridiculous." Anya went on, "She's using clippers to trim. They're manufactured. It's a selective approach, like any religion."

"What's her name about?" Celeste asked.

"Her guru gave her the name so she could practice humility," Luna responded.

"They could've just called her 'Shit Face'," Tom yelled from across the room.

Luna continued as if she hadn't heard Tom. "Her people live in Oak Prairie. The whole group gets up at sunrise to walk in the woods together, holding hands. I respect what they're trying to do."

"Okay, but see, you say 'group,' I say 'cult,'" Anya continued. "I think it's disingenuous to say they use nothing that's manufactured. How can you completely avoid plastic, for instance? There are other ways to focus your energy. Being neurotic doesn't help save the planet. How 'bout toilet paper? That's manufactured."

Luna practically whispered, "They don't use toilet paper."

The whole circle let out a collective groan.

"No toilet paper? Okay," Deja said, incredulous. "Wait, what do they use?"

"They use their hands. She says it keeps them in touch with themselves."

"Yeah, in touch with what assholes they are," Tom interjected. "Luna, why do you keep inviting her to clip?"

"For one thing, she's the fastest trimmer I know. Also, she's an interesting person. She's intelligent, just a little intense." Ripples of laughter went around the circle.

"Which hand do they use?" Deja asked. "I'll never shake hands again."

Celeste stood up and stretched. Her whole body was stiff, tense, cramped. She'd been sitting for hours. When the blunt or pipe was passed, she hadn't partaken but she felt like it had gotten to her anyway. She was punchy and sweat dripped down her back. Around the circle others had glistening faces and sweat-stained clothes. The stink of perspiration intermingled with the intense scent of freshly clipped pot.

Celeste went to pour herself some juice. Organic munchies were arrayed on the table where Tom was loading up a thin plastic bag with buds and weighing it on a metal scale. She watched him move little slides on the scale until he seemed satisfied. He jotted numbers on a slip of paper, then looked up smiling. "My trusty 'triple beam.'"

"Nice," she said. She picked up a folded paper bag to fan herself.

"So, this is a turkey bag." He held up the plastic bag filled with buds. "They keep the smell down. Our local grocery sells more turkey bags than anywhere else in the nation. Out of our little town of Garberville. Population, nine-hundred, although that number doesn't count the thousands in the hills, like us. Anyway, I heard our market is the only store in America that receives turkey bags on pallets."

"Wait." Celeste was befuddled. "What are turkey bags really made for? Are they supposed to be for turkey?"

Tom looked at Celeste. "Yeah, you're supposed to bake turkeys in 'em."

"Bake a turkey in a plastic bag?" Celeste took a sip of juice. "I can't imagine that."

"How un-American of you," quipped Anya.

"Sipotty's worst nightmare," Deja added.

"Last year," Tom continued, "the turkey bag manufacturer sent a rep to SoHum to collect recipes from the locals, 'cause they're thinking we're major into baking turkeys. This rep checks into the motel and in the morning he's having breakfast and strikes up a conversation with a waitress. He tells her why he's in town, and she tells him the real reason for the high sales."

"That's funny." Celeste put her empty cup down and went back to her seat next to Luna. "Who told you that story?"

Tom tied the top of another bag full of buds. "The manager at Busy Bee, as he was restocking the turkey bag display. Apparently the rep came into the store demoralized."

"Funny," Celeste said. She returned to her cardboard flat and Fiskars, back to trimming, amazed that every marijuana bud was crafted this way.

She was getting faster.

✹ ✹ ✹

Wild anise gave off a licorice scent in the heat as they brushed against the ferny shrubs crowding the path. They hiked down the steep embankment in the late afternoon heat. At the bottom of the hill, hard earth gave way to soft, fine dirt, and Celeste could hear the sound of water. Tom held back dense foliage and they jumped off a low cliff, landing on the river bar. Celeste helped Sophie down, and then looked around, dazzled. "Wow."

"Yep." Luna smiled.

Alexa was already at the shore, shimmying out of her shorts, letting them fall to her feet. She ran to the river, waded into the water, dipped under, and emerged glistening.

The water was silver on its surface, reflecting the low afternoon sunlight and fragmented images of oak, madrone, and fir growing up the far slope. The vast, flat floodplain and river that flowed through it forged a passageway, dissecting the surrounding steep hills. Celeste couldn't move for a moment as she quietly took it in, then she and Sophie tramped out on the pebbled gray surface where Luna was laying down a blanket.

"Mom," Alexa yelled, "it's awesome. Come on."

Sophie pointed. "I want to go."

"Let's get this off." Celeste helped Sophie wriggle out of her T-shirt, and then admired the frills on the back of her daughter's swimsuit. She peeled off her own dress and stared down self-consciously at her body in its black one-piece suit.

"You know," Luna said, "people don't usually wear anything when they go swimming here."

"Oh." Celeste exclaimed. "Guess I'll have to work up to that."

"Tom," Luna said. "Keep your shorts on." Luna's loud, rich laugh rolled out.

"Mom!" Alexa called from the water.

They eased into the river and when Sophie could no longer touch bottom Celeste swept her up and they floated together, hugging each other. Small silver fish darted through ripples of light. Sophie pointed up river to a recessed grotto in a steep bank where a waterfall cascaded over a rocky outcropping.

Celeste smiled. "Wanna go?"

"I'm staying here." Alexa swam toward a boulder on the side of the rapids.

"As long as I can see you," said Celeste.

The grotto smelled green and fresh and had a low rock ceiling. Sophie and Celeste climbed over mossy rocks, until they were crouching in the small cave behind the waterfall's downward rush. In the mist, they gazed through the curtain of water in front of them.

"This is a secret place," said Sophie, as perfect glassy drops fell from her long dark eyelashes.

"Feels like it," Celeste agreed.

"Mom!" Alexa yelled.

Climbing out of the grotto, Celeste saw a horse and rider coming up the fringe of shoreline.

Alexa waved her arms, shouting, "Jonah!" She took off, swimming to the beach and then sprinting down the river bar toward him.

The two teenagers were almost always together. Often alone. It was worrying. Although Celeste didn't see any of the grasping affection of new lovers, it seemed inevitable that they would eventually experiment sexually. She'd talked to Alexa about using protection, and urged her to speak to Luna as well. But Luna's take surprised Celeste, confounded her. Although Luna agreed that, obviously, Alexa and Jonah had bonded, she said, "I know Jonah. He'd tell me if he was going to do something."

Luna and Tom lounged on a large rock in the river, one of a cluster of boulders protruding from the water. Celeste and Sophie clambered onto a bowl-shaped boulder nearby. The stone was burning hot, and the wetness on Celeste's skin evaporated immediately. Celeste practically had to shout so she could be heard over the din of rapids upstream, "You'd think there'd be other people here on a hot day."

"Probably were, earlier," Luna responded. "But there're tons of great river spots. This is our favorite, though." Luna grasped at some loose dreadlocks, tucking them into her tall crown, and then lay back on the rock. Tom pulled himself up on his elbows. His broad shoulders were markedly tanner than the rest of his body, with lighter lines where his overall straps usually were.

"This place is called 'The Crossing,'" he said. "It's where Jonah rides everyday." Tom still had a boyish body, narrow at the hips with long legs. The only difference Celeste noted in his shape from when she'd known it intimately was a slightly softened belly. Her belly had also softened.

Jonah and his horse, Tatanka, were approaching, ambling through the shallow edge of river. He rode bareback. With a start, Celeste realized Alexa was on the horse too, her arms wrapped around Jonah's waist. "Is that safe?" Celeste called out to Tom and Luna.

Tatanka changed course suddenly, heading into the swimming hole. Water rose up its hindquarters, and the horse whinnied and reared.

"Tom!" Celeste cried.

"Yeah," he responded. "Right here."

Tatanka neighed and reared up again. "Tom, the horse is in the water!"

"They're playing," Luna said, sitting up. "Jonah knows what he's doing."

"You're not in the city anymore." Tom laughed.

Celeste watched, shocked, as the horse continued to whinny and rear up. Obviously Tom and Luna didn't think it was dangerous to ride bareback on a horse cavorting in the river. She wondered how long it would take an emergency crew to arrive if something happened, then remembered that her cell didn't even get reception.

Jonah and Alexa laughed as Tatanka thrust his head up and down into the water. The horse reared again, with his front legs tucked up in the air, Alexa and Jonah slid down the back of the horse, as if they were young kids on a slide. They splashed into the water, one after the other, and Jonah reached out, grabbing the horse's tail. Tatanka charged forward, pulling Jonah, and Alexa, who clung to him, through the water.

When the horse got to the shallows, Jonah let go of his tail. Tatanka came out of the river, nonchalantly plodding across the beach to a shaded area of short stems, where he pawed at the ground, plucking grassy plants out of the sand with giant teeth.

Alexa and Jonah swam to the boulder where Celeste and Sophie were and hooked their hands on the stone. "That was the bomb," Alexa said, as she treaded water. "Did you see?"

"I did." Celeste tried to steady her voice. Jonah looked up at her. She felt Jonah's incandescent eyes beaming from his coffee-and-cream complexion, taking in her alarm.

"Tatanka loves the water," Jonah said, as if that was the explanation she needed to feel safe as his horse lobbed her daughter around the river.

"Well, I didn't know horses were like that."

Jonah smiled, but didn't say anything more. He stayed where he was treading water, and seemed to be waiting for her to release him. Slowly Celeste's trepidation and fear melted away in Jonah's light, and she gathered herself and was able to smile. At last, he let go of the rock and swam to the shore, joining his horse in the shade.

Alexa pulled herself up on the boulder, fitting herself into the contours of the stone. Celeste scooted over to make room. "Mom, that was totally cool, really."

"Well, it looked really scary."

Alexa's wet body made dark drips on the colored surface of rock, and Celeste traced the patterns with her finger until the marks evaporated. Then she leaned back on the warm slab. With her eyes closed, Celeste could hear the breathing presence of the river; her body nodded down, calming and softening into the smooth, warm stone.

Falling asleep briefly, she woke refreshed and sat up quickly, her gaze found Tom and Luna. Reclining on his rock with Luna by his side, Tom looked over at her. After a moment they smiled at each other. A shiver came up from the bottom of her spine, prickling over her scalp.

Instantly, Celeste knew they would stay in Humboldt. Not because a trimming job was available, and despite the fact that marijuana was being grown. Not because they had settled into the cabin. Not because she'd seen the girls active and content, connecting with people and animals and the beautiful land. Not because she couldn't think of anywhere else to go. It wasn't a decision weighed rationally or influenced by available teaching jobs or great schools for the girls, or anything reasonable. But there it was: a knowingness in her bones and her blood and in the squiggly cells that made her who she was.

teenager

Celeste parked under the dense shade of a redwood tree. "Stay in the car. Be nice to your sister."

"Geez." Alexa rolled her eyes and went back to reading her book. Every time they weren't with Luna, or Tom, or Jonah, Alexa instantly reverted to her impossible teenage self.

Sophie pleaded, "Why can't I go?"

"I won't be long. Read your book." Celeste kissed Sophie and closed the driver's door, checking the locks. The windows had to be open because of the sweltering heat. She considered restarting the engine, switching on the air conditioning, and leaving the girls inside the running car, but she was less comfortable with that option.

She walked towards an old structure with a substantial mortar and stone foundation. In L.A., small homes were being razed and replaced with new houses in this same Craftsman style. But this shabby, rambling two-story building was authentic. A stand of redwoods towered behind it and a loud creek gurgled in some nearby gully. The building could have been mistaken for a once-grand house, except for the dirt parking lot spiked with tall weeds and a crudely painted sign that sat on the side of the deserted country road: *Redwood Tavern, Restaurant and Bar*. In the middle of nowhere. How could tourists find the place? The business had to depend on locals. A "Closed" sign leaned against the window. She pulled the handle on the massive, carved wood door. It was unlocked, and she entered a vestibule lined with red-flocked wallpaper.

An antique mirrored cabinet faced her from the next room. Celeste bent, and tried to flatten her red hair; it looked unkempt, grown out of the short, convenient style she'd worn for years. Her sleeveless cotton dress was wrinkled; she ran her hands over the seams.

"Can I help ya?"

"Oh!" Celeste jumped and her hand flew to her heart. "You startled me. Sorry. I didn't see you there."

"Hon," a short woman responded in a raspy smoker's voice, "yer the one startled me." She appeared to be in her mid-sixties and everything about her looked dried-out. Above the waistband of her yellowed pedal-pushers—made of what looked like prehistoric double-knit polyester—a triangle of withered skin was exposed. A knotted red gingham shirt attempted to cover her bosom—the only large thing about her except for a teased, whipped topping of blonde hair. Celeste suspected she'd worn this look for decades.

"Lookin' for a drink?" the woman asked.

"Oh, no. No." Celeste shook her head vigorously. "A friend of mine, Luna, thought you might have a waitress position available."

"Luna. Well. Love that lady. She was midwife for my daughter. Brought my grandson into the world without a scratch. God bless her." She extended her hand. "Name's Delores."

"I'm Celeste. Amazing place. Is it yours?"

"Been taking care of the tavern for ten years. Live above." She pointed to the ceiling. "Place got real history. Used to be a bordello. Rooms upstairs still have the brass numbers on the doors. Ya know, where they did the deed." She winked and stepped close to elbow Celeste. "We got pitchers in here."

"Pitchers?" Celeste was confused.

"This way." Delores led Celeste out of the vestibule. A wide bar spanned the room. Tables and mismatched chairs loitered in disorganized groupings. Behind the bar, bottles of colored liquor glowed on shelves softly back-lit by a stained glass window.

"See," Delores said, pointing to rows of ornately framed sepia-tone photographs.

"Oh," Celeste exclaimed. The top row showed crowds of men posing on top of giant stumps of felled trees. Their stance was that of victor; they had won the battle. The opponents—redwood trees—lay prone, splayed across the broken forest, otherworldly in their size. In one photo, the tree was so enormous that a man mounted on a horse stood inside the wedge of the first cut.

"History. Real history." Delores smiled, her orange-frosted lipstick cracked and frayed into wrinkles at the corners of her lips. "Here's the ladies." She pointed to the last row of photographs, seemingly from the same time period. Uneven, tattered edges of photos were crushed under glass. Women in long white dresses, their hair in buns, stared straight ahead unsmiling with gazes that were strangely vacant. With a start, Celeste realized the photos had been taken in the very room in which she stood; there was the long bar, the pattern of stained glass, the dark redwood-paneled walls.

"What year was that?"

"See there," Delores pointed to the bottom of a photo. "1912" was scrawled in faded ink.

Celeste stared, transfixed, momentarily distracted from her mission and suddenly unclear why this peculiar woman was standing so close, breathing stale cigarette breath over her. Celeste focused. She thought of her daughters, waiting outside in the heat. "So, do you have any waitress jobs available?"

"Tell ya what—ya ever waitressed before?"

"When I was in college."

"Shit, hon. Why ya lookin' for a waitress job? Did ya finish?"

"College? Yes. I have a teaching credential. But yesterday I went to all the local schools and they're not hiring. Seems the best I can hope for is being called to substitute."

"Schools here get worse and worser. Weren't no gems to begin with." Delores gestured. "Have a seat." On the chair closest to Celeste was a disheveled stack of newspapers. Celeste lifted the stack and, without thinking, straightened the papers quickly into a neat pile on another seat, then settled cautiously into the wobbly chair. When she looked up Delores was staring at her so intently she became self-conscious.

"Well, hon," Delores said, "I got three waitresses. Tell ya what though, I need a bartender. The girl who works now," Delores made a slicing motion across her throat. "On her way out."

Celeste shook her head; the thought of serving drinks at a bar was abhorrent. "I have no experience."

"Did I say ya need experience?" Delores had a fierceness about her, and she gazed unflinchingly into Celeste's eyes. "I can teach ya to pour in ten minutes. Shit, the customer can tell ya what to pour. Yer pretty and smart. Hon, ya already ahead of the game. Tell ya what, lose that schoolmarm get-up." Delores poked a finger at Celeste's chest. "Get yerself a push-up bra, somethin' low-cut." Delores slid the back of her orange-painted nail over the cotton floral that covered Celeste's bust. Celeste recoiled. Delores continued, "Some tight jeans . . . shit, hon, we talkin' biiigggg tips."

"No thanks." Celeste stood.

"Whatcha afraid of?"

Celeste reminded herself that this was Luna's friend and she needed to stay courteous. "For one thing, I don't want to deal with drunks."

"Ya have kids?"

"I have girls, two girls."

"Believe me, dealing with a drunk ain't nothing compared

to kids. They both need affection and discipline, and, ya know, an occasional beatin'." Delores laughed. The laugh deepened into a smoker's cough and then spiraled out of control. Celeste felt sick. Delores pounded her chest with her open hand, and her giant breasts quaked like Jell-O. Celeste had to steady herself: she wanted to run. Finally, the coughing died down and Delores went back to her chatter. "Shit, ya don't even have to get the drunk ready for school in the morning." She laughed again, and Celeste cringed.

"I'll think about it." This woman was keeping her from her kids.

"Hon, there's some fine tips to be made here. A good bartender can take home more than my waitresses."

"Well, please keep me in mind if you have an opening for a waitress."

"Now ya listen to Delores." She stood, her smoke saturated aura coming too close to Celeste. "First, if ya bartend, ya still gotta waitress 'cause we got the bar menu. So, ya got yer precious waitress job right there. Second, in case ya haven't noticed, Humboldt ain't like other places. Like, in 'Frisco, apply for a job, ya gotta have experience. Up here, ain't that way. People make big money doin' somethin' else. Know what I mean?"

Celeste nodded her head. After two weeks in SoHum, she knew.

"So," Delores continued, "no one wants to work a real job. Damn, they don't know how to work real jobs no more. Been bred outta 'em. Second-and third-generation pot farmers don't know what a job is. So, hon, I get stuck with the dregs, or, like, they only wanna work one day a week. If they git a good clipping job, then, ya know, they're calling in sick." Delores smiled at Celeste. "After harvest season, the locals have wads of money to burn. Some tips are big bills. Even hundred-dollar bills." Delores' orange-painted nails flitted about as she spoke. "They call 'em 'Humboldt Twenties' and keep 'em in fat rubber-band rolls. I say we try it. Ya need a job, and I need someone responsible. For a change." Delores sucked her teeth and shook her head. "Whadda ya say?"

It seemed the only way to honor Luna's contact and leave gracefully was to humor her. "What would the hours be?"

Delores leaned in. "Night hours. Shit, hon, ya could still substitute teach. What time can ya get here, four, five?"

"Honestly, I don't have a babysitter. We're staying in a cabin and I can't leave my girls alone at night."

Delores's eyes lit up. "You at Luna and Tom's cabin?" Celeste nodded reluctantly. "Well," Delores said, "I'll just give Luna a call. Leave it to me." She smiled, looking satisfied, as if she had just landed the fish she'd been trying to reel in.

✷ ✷ ✷

Celeste picked up her cell phone and smiled thinking of all the things her sister would hate about SoHum: the thick dust that covered her Subaru and every other car and truck, the giant yellow/green banana slugs they'd—so far—avoided stepping on during walks in the redwoods, the funky cabin where they were staying, the state of Celeste's finger nails, which no matter how hard she scrubbed, always had dark crescents of cannabis resin from trimming.

It was too hot to make calls in the car or on the street in Garberville, so they ended up in the same café they'd gone to when they first arrived. Celeste had an iced tea and a sad-looking scone, and the kids ate grilled cheese sandwiches before Alexa ensconced herself at one of the pinball machines at the back wall, with Sophie next to her.

Greta answered immediately, "Celeste, Jesus shit."

"Hey." Celeste laughed.

"Where the fuck are you?"

"I told you, Humboldt County."

"Still? Why haven't you called me back?"

"Greta, there's no reception at Tom's."

"So lame. And your voicemail is always full."

"Because I've been trying to reach Victor so he'll call off that private investigator, but I always get his voicemail. And then when I'm in the hills—without reception—he calls me over and over, leaving endless messages, which I don't get until the next time I'm in town. It's so frustrating."

"Ruth says that Victor's back on tour, and in a bad way. Celeste, we need to go somewhere, just you and me. Cocktails and a pool. While there's some summer left. Let's enjoy your freedom—before you take that undying loyalty of yours and stick it somewhere else."

"Greta, remember last year, after 9/11, how we promised ourselves we'd move out of the city 'cause L.A. would be next? I did it. The kids are happy. It's totally different here. The girls are outside playing, running around all the time, like kids used to do. We go to the river to swim every day. They're even riding horses."

"Okay, but Celeste, your house. You know, that house you worked so hard to own. You could lose it, everything you made so beautiful. Come on, be rational. Besides, I need my nieces near me."

"Greta, I gotta go."

"No. Celeste, we need to talk. Don't—"

"Sorry." Celeste clicked her phone off. The best part, Celeste thought to herself, was that her big sister couldn't show up tonight at her door waving a bullet-point how-to-improve-your-life list at her.

Celeste drew a deep breath. She tried Victor again, and again, but his phone went to voicemail. The next morning she and Luna planned to drive to Eureka, as Luna put it, to the closest stoplight—eighty miles north—where they'd do major pantry/staple shopping: rice, flour, tamari—things that didn't grow in Luna's garden. They'd arrive in Eureka before midday and there would certainly be cell reception. "Victor, I will be available to talk after noon tomorrow. I'll be where there's reception. I'll call you. Talk to you then."

Victor's threat of a private investigator hung over her, sticky and invasive like the humidity in SoHum. She felt reasonably safe at Tom and Luna's, it was remote, seemingly impossible for an outsider to find, but every time she ventured to town she'd obsessively check her rear-view mirror and cast a protective net of vision around her children.

Celeste and her daughters left the café and went down the sidewalk in Garberville, passing a variety of foreign accents—so many that Celeste stopped trying to identify them. The trimmigrants had arrived. Tom said every year there were more of them, making the small town of Garberville an international gathering spot. Arriving from Europe and South America, they all came to trim. There were also American trimmigrants who generally looked scruffy and homeless, colonizing street corners with signs that read "Will Clip for Food" or "Fast Hands." European trimmigrants and those from other parts of the world seemed more likely to have connections, trim jobs they'd worked previously, or some contact that got them off the sidewalk. Although once, driving into Garberville, Celeste had seen a group along the road holding a sign that read: "Germans = Good Workers," and just past them was another group holding a sign that said: "Italians Do It Better."

When Celeste questioned Tom about the likelihood of a grower hiring a stranger to trim, he told her he'd heard of growers who blindfolded prospective trimmers, drove them to a job site, had them work for days or weeks at the unknown location, and when the job was done the grower re-blindfolded them and delivered them back to town. Celeste asked, "After paying them for the work?"

"You would hope . . ." Tom responded.

Garberville teemed with odd characters socializing, clusters of people hugging and gossiping on the sidewalk. Pickup trucks on steroids thundered up and down Main Street. Since Celeste had heard that big trucks and big tires were status symbols for the big grower, she couldn't help but wonder why a grower would want to identify with an illicit stereotype? It was so brazen. If it were true, the town was full of growers on display, along with their barking pit bulls in the truck bed. There was also talk at the trim shack about the successful big grower having the obligatory girlfriend or "potstitute," usually a good-looking woman with, as Deja had said, "a new set of bolt-ons." Apparently breast-augmentation was the mandatory look. Luna had referred to specific stores in town as "potstitute" shops, but Celeste couldn't remember which ones she'd named.

As they passed The Hemp Connection, Celeste hurried her daughters away from the ubiquitous crowd lounging on its steps. Halfway down the street, Sophie looked up at Celeste and whined, "Mommy, I want to go home." Celeste dropped down to Sophie's height and touched her cheek.

"But, sweetie, isn't it nice when we're at Tom and Luna's?" Sophie nodded. "Look." Celeste pointed across the street to the painted-up school bus that always seemed to be in town. Tethered to a pole nearby were the two goats. Sophie silently stared at them.

Celeste announced, "Okay, so, you both need new outfits, and I need a pair of jeans. Let's try that store and see if we find anything."

Alexa tossed her head and strode ahead of them to the shop. Inside, a green-haired woman slouched behind a counter, nodding her head in greeting, as they entered.

"Hello," Celeste said. She approached a clothing rack, and pulled out the tag on a pair of jeans: Size 4, $160. "Do you have any larger, lower-priced jeans?"

"Actually, that's about the lowest price on the jeans we carry." The woman smiled thinly, dragging her fingernails through her snot-colored hair.

"Oh, okay, thank you." Celeste wanted to get the girls out quickly. She put a hand on Alexa's shoulder, but Alexa shook her off.

"Mom." Alexa was immersed in a rack of halter tops. "I wanna look."

"Let's check the shop across the street. Come on."

"No. I want to try this on." Alexa pulled out a hanger dripping with skimpy strips of fabric covered in sequins. She'll wear that over my dead body, thought Celeste. Grabbing the tag, she stared at the price in disbelief. The salesgirl came out from behind the counter.

Celeste murmured, "Alexa, it's a hundred and forty-nine dollars."

"I have way more than that in my savings account." Alexa held the hanger up to her body. She went to a mirror and swayed from side to side in front of it.

"Your savings account is in L.A.. There's no branch in this town."

"You have money." Alexa cradled the hanger and walked in the direction of the dressing room.

"Come on. We're leaving."

"Mom!" Alexa responded in a voice drenched with contempt, "I said I'll buy it with my own money."

"Alexa, you don't have access to your account."

Whirling around, Alexa glared. "Whose fault is that?"

Shocked, Celeste clasped Alexa's hand and tugged her in the direction of the door. But Alexa pulled out of her mother's grasp and sauntered into the dressing room. A surge of adrenaline pumped through Celeste. She wanted to pick up her uncooperative child and haul her out of there, under her arm, like she would a toddler having a tantrum. Celeste imagined throwing the curtains of the dressing room open. But Sophie had wrapped herself around her mother's leg, and Celeste could see a partial reflection of Sophie's pitiful body language in a far mirror.

From outside Celeste felt the reverberations of a diesel truck downshifting to a low rumble on Main Street. She took a deep breath to regulate her pounding heart, then bent down and gathered Sophie in her arms. "Everything's okay."

Alexa pranced out of the dressing room, wearing the halter top triumphantly. The glittering material crisscrossed her chest, clinging to her developing breasts, exposing their shape. The ties wrapped around her waist and framed her belly button, exposing her midriff.

"It's so awesome." Alexa twirled in front of the mirror.

"You are beautiful, Alexa. Let's see if we can put it on hold."

"No. I want it."

"I know. Let's just leave it here, on hold, so we can think about it, while we look in some other shops."

"But Mom, I want it." Suddenly Alexa looked innocent and young, like a silly demanding child. "I can pay for it myself." Alexa stomped her foot on the floor. "With my own money."

Celeste had to resist a hysterical smile from forming on her lips. "If you really love something, I will buy it for you. But when you're spending that kind of money, it's important to think about it first." After a few more rounds of negotiations, Alexa, returned to the dressing room and then reluctantly handed over the halter top to be held. The saleswoman took it with barely concealed contempt. Before an hour was up, Alexa had let go of her dream of the skanky halter top. At a thrift store at the far end of town, she'd been appeased with a purple bikini, three pairs of shorts, and a cotton sleeveless blouse with a skull-and-crossbones pattern, all for a sliver of the price of the halter top.

At a decidedly un-hip hunting store, Celeste came out of a makeshift dressing room. She stared past mounted deer heads into a dusty mirror. The jeans she'd pulled on were a size smaller than the jeans she usually wore. Her regular jeans, her favorite pair, had become bunchy. She'd assumed from too much wear, but now she realized she'd lost weight—quite a bit of weight—on the wreck-your-life diet. Her appearance had not been given much attention lately. In the cabin there was one tiny mirror over the kitchen sink. She'd entirely abandoned her use of lipstick and mascara. The places she'd frequented were the river, the veggie garden, and the trim shack. Celeste came closer to her image. An expanded dusting of freckles crossed her nose, and in her out-of-control hair were new silver strands. It was surprising to see her hair so wild, like it used to be. Maybe it was more attractive that way, despite being too curly, too frizzy, and too red.

Walking around Garberville, she'd garnered attention from men. She'd forgotten what it felt like to turn heads, the way she had when she was young. L.A. was populated with a glut of magazine-pretty young women; she'd long ago gotten used to being invisible. In SoHum, Celeste noticed that, unlike the potstitutes, the hippie women eschewed makeup and allowed their hair to go gray. When she'd first arrived, she'd noted that the women over forty seemed to look older than their men. Slowly, it dawned in her that she was used to city women, with their dye jobs, small nips, smoothing injections—requisite procedures for the aging process in the city, even in her social circles. In the country, women were growing old naturally. Women, like Luna, weren't looking backward at youth.

Celeste turned in front of the mirror, admiring the way the denim hugged her sleeker-looking silhouette. She thought of

Delores telling her to get a push-up bra and a pair of tight jeans—it was crude and sexist and, maybe, smart.

hot flash

Luna's dreadlocks fell like serpents around her head, back, and shoulders as she drove. Celeste studied her profile, the landscape blurring behind her. Usually she and Luna were around the kids, surrounded by other women in the trim shack, or working side by side in the garden or kitchen. Usually, Luna's laugh came easily and Celeste soaked it up like sunshine. Today, Celeste could tell, was going to be different.

"Jake's road is just a few miles up." Luna gripped the steering wheel. "I need to drop by his place. He was supposed to help Tom in the hoophouse this morning, but didn't show."

"Oh," Celeste said, surprised, wondering how long that would take. Luna could've told her about this detour before they left Bear Ridge. Apparently she'd been hijacked, and Celeste had an important agenda today. She needed to contact Victor by noon, to convince him to call off the private investigator. As long as they stayed in the hills, there would be no cell reception. Celeste was tempted to reveal her predicament to Luna, but stopped herself. Mentioning to a pot-grower that she was being pursued by a private investigator wouldn't be an intelligent move. Celeste leaned back in her seat, her gut in a knot. She tried to relax; she tried not to think of all the potential repercussions from this spin of events.

"Tom and I were thinking that maybe you'd like to rent our house in Garberville."

"You own a house in Garberville?"

"Where Jake has his indoor grow scene: it's got a giant

garage, easy to light up, 'cause it's on the grid. A sweet little house."

"Luna, are you telling me that we should move out of the cabin?"

"No. We love your girls and having you there. It's great for Jonah to have friends on the land. It's just that this guy, Eddy, is living in the house, taking care of the indoor, doing a terrible job—even though he gets a cut of the profit. Anyway, we thought it would be a good opportunity for you."

"Thank you. I appreciate it. But I couldn't live somewhere with a grow."

"Like our place?"

"But that's your place. It's in the hills. I wouldn't want to have a grow in my own place, with my kids. I'm uncomfortable with that."

"Well, if you stay in SoHum that'll change. Although Tom and I aren't into indoor; we're all about organic sun bud. But Jake just had to light up that garage."

Celeste attempted to sip hot coffee out of her defective travel cup, a dangerous activity on a curvy road. "Guess Jake's a big grower."

"Jake? You kidding? He's not. A big indoor grower has underground bunkers with banks of lights as far as you can see. A big outdoor grower grades mountain tops and puts in irrigation ponds. Big is what the Romanian or the Mexican cartels do in remote areas of inaccessible parkland. They'll put in ten thousand plants, or ten times that. Those are big, illegal grows. Yet conscientious home growers get popped and go to prison while the environment is ruined by those massive grow scenes producing nothing but greed weed."

"Meaning you're small and legal?"

"We have 215's." Luna glanced at Celeste. "Proposition 215. California voters passed that in 1996. Medical marijuana. You know?"

"I voted for it."

"You should get one."

"I couldn't qualify."

"Of course you could. You just state that you use ganja for an ailment. Deja, who trims for us, got a 215 for carpal tunnel pain. She got carpal tunnel from clipping."

Rounding a blind curve, Luna braked to a stop. In the twisting, two-lane road, a large doe and two fawns held statuesque poses. Everything was quiet. There hadn't been another car on the road that morning. Abruptly the deer bounded off into the sun-dappled brush. Celeste watched as pointed tails bobbed out of sight.

"Things are changing fast," Luna said grimly, accelerating as if she hadn't just come to a full stop for a family of deer. "Every year it's less viable. News stories about the Emerald Triangle have created a green rush. Outsiders move here just to grow. They flood the market with greed weed, so the price of a pound keeps plummeting. Each season we grow more and make less. When it's legalized, corporations will take over and everyone local, big and small, will be regulated out. Then, just like wine grapes took over food crops in California's Central Valley, it'll be pot. Grapes and pot. Used to be growers were back-to-the-landers who accidentally fell into it, like us. Used to be SoHum was this remote bubble."

Celeste felt like retreating somewhere peaceful and soft, somewhere she could sleep awhile. She wondered who this woman lecturing her was? She missed the other Luna she knew—or thought she knew—the woman who was calm and supportive, someone she could lean on.

Luna turned to Celeste. "Ganja should be recognized as a medical wonder. As a drug that has never killed anyone. You can't say that for aspirin, or alcohol—but instead of acknowledging the truth, the government makes us the flower-growing enemy."

"How about lung cancer. Lung cancer kills."

"Smoking pot does not cause lung cancer. Bullshit. Obviously you've never read the studies. Ridiculously measly studies. Researchers are hog tied 'cause there are no funds to study an illegal substance. And even though American laws lock people up over ganja, guess who took out the patent for medical marijuana?"

"Uh. . ."

"Our government. No hypocrisy there. None at all."

Celeste was a bad candidate for a coherent conversation. She'd been up during the night with a weird fever and wasn't feeling particularly sharp. Besides, Luna's agitation worried her. Celeste inhaled the wisps of steam escaping from the lid of her cup. Her coffee had cooled, so she braved another sip, wondering if there was ever a day, or an hour, or so much as a minute, when there wasn't a cannabis-related conversation going on in Humboldt County.

"You know weed is the biggest cash crop in America?" Luna continued, "And clipping is a craft. One of the very last handicrafts. Every bud touched and shaped by hand. Made in America."

"Well, but, marijuana can't be a bigger cash crop than corn." That seemed impossible, although Celeste hadn't been paying attention to statistics—not like Luna and Tom, who always had the latest pot-related stats at their fingertips.

"Bigger than corn, or wheat. Yet politicians—most of them have smoked ganja themselves— perpetuate this hypocrisy."

"So . . ." Celeste said, "with all the problems, why don't you quit growing? Quit now while you're ahead?"

Luna shot back, "We know the risks." For a few minutes they didn't speak. When Luna resumed talking, her voice was softer and steadier. "It's about self-reliance, used to be even the smallest grows could support a family off the grid—if they weren't materialistic. The proliferation of big grows changed that. But Tom and I have achieved the dream, right? We don't labor for some heartless corporation, and we get satisfaction from filling a basic need. We're in the solace business. Plus, it's a family enterprise. For most of the old-school growers, two, three generations work together. And when we need money for something big, like a car, we don't go begging for a loan to some corporate entity whose mission is to exploit its customers and employees. We just grab our shovel and dig up some of the cash we've buried."

"You bury your money?"

"Bank of the Woods."

"Geez . . . No interest."

Luna smiled acknowledgment.

They passed horses swishing their tails in a pasture. On the passenger side a verdant band of foliage announced the river's presence. "I saw the moon last night," said Celeste. "It was full. I was out on the cabin porch and watched it rise. It was so bright it cast shadows like the sun."

"Tonight it'll be truly full. Usually one of my pregnant ladies goes into labor during a full moon. But Anya's not due 'til next month. That was my other call this morning. She called about her Blessingway. You're invited."

"What's that?"

"A baby shower is the easy analogy."

"You lead a full life, Luna."

"Yep, always. The good news is our light dep turned out so nice and gooey. You never know, some years are a disaster. During harvest, we slay ourselves to get it done. Then, in December, when it's raining, we take off for our house in Mexico and lounge around."

"A house in Mexico?"

"More like a hut, but it's paradise. Right now there's lots of work 'cause we're gearing up for our outdoor harvest. And the full moon's influence is making everything chaotic. Tide comes in, sanity goes out." As Luna turned off the pavement onto a dirt road with deep potholes, they were jounced violently in their seats. "Roll up your window," Luna said, turning on the air conditioner, "and prepare yourself."

"For what?"

As they rounded the curve a pack of snarling, barking dogs ran at Luna's car, attacking the tires. Luna stayed calm. "Ignore them." An expanse of mangled and rusted junk had come into view. Crushed, burned-out cars were stacked like pancake piles in the brush. A rotted school bus lay on its side, next to an upside-down couch extruding dirty stuffing. Plastic fertilizer containers and empty dirt bags were massed, degrading, near a rusted washing machine and other ruined appliances, large and small. Yet, behind the ruin a beautiful forest flourished.

"What is this?"

"The Broudy's property. Our next door neighbors."

"Jake lives here?" They passed a skeletonized red truck riddled with bullet holes, a slender tree trunk growing out of its window.

"No, this is the access road to Jake's. His house is at the back end of our property, but the best way to get there is this road. Jake calls it 'the gauntlet'."

"Scary."

"Grandfather Broudy lives in a cabin on the other side of the acreage. Oh, look." Luna lifted her chin toward a broken-down Winnebago. Cardboard and black plastic covered its windows. The hood was open, exposing an empty spot where the engine should have been. "I just saw one of the twins; they live there. Same age as Jonah."

Celeste was shocked. "How could anyone live there?"

"Hold on . . ." Luna pulled over, the pack of dogs circled the car, barking and growling. Without hesitation Luna opened her door, leaving the car running and air conditioner on. The dogs swamped her as she moved across the road toward the Winnebago. Celeste could hear Luna calling over the roar of barking, and then she was out of sight, behind the motor home. After a while, she reappeared, crossing the road, wading through the dogs again. She jumped in the car and took off quickly, accelerating up the incline. Celeste turned and watched the last dog trail off, disappearing into the dust.

"That was crazy."

"Yeah. Can't miss an opportunity to connect with those boys. They need it so badly. Jonah and the twins were born on the same day."

"I didn't see them."

"They only come out for me."

The road branched and they continued up the hill. Thick huckleberry bushes encroached on both sides, making it feel as if they were driving through a tunnel. When they came to a gate, Luna stopped the car. "Could you open the gate and lock it after I drive through?"

"Are the dogs really gone?"

"Should be. I've never seen them up here." Luna told her the combination for the lock. Celeste cautiously got out of the car, repeating the combination to herself as she spun the numbers until she felt the lock give way. It had gotten hot, and the storm cloud of dust around the car stuck to her sweaty skin. After locking the gate, Celeste jumped back in with Luna, glad the windows were closed and the air conditioner was on.

The terrain opened up and flattened out. Brush on the sides of the road had been cleared, shaved to the contours of the ground, leaving only a hint of yellow shadow. The landscape, dotted with few trees, seemed strangely bald. Celeste broke the silence. "So, last night I woke up with what seemed like a bad fever. But this morning I feel just fine. Except for being sleep-deprived. Fastest flu I ever had."

"You felt feverish? Were you sweating?"

"Profusely. Then I got really cold."

"You weren't sick."

Luna slowed the car. She took her sparkling dark eyes off the road and turned them on Celeste.

"What's the matter?" Celeste asked, alarmed, looking around, thinking she missed something in the road.

"Has it happened to you before?"

"What?"

"A night sweat. It's a menopause symptom."

"Come on. I get my period . . ."

Luna accelerated, and the car jerked forward. "When was your last period?"

A pang of nausea flooded Celeste. "I don't know; sometimes I skip."

"Exactly. And you've had emotional trauma, which affects your hormonal balance." Luna laughed. "Menopausal symptoms are a perfect reason for getting a 215." Luna's laughter, which Celeste had yearned for, now caused her to flinch. "Oh," Luna said, "and won't Tom be happy, living with two menopausal women."

"But I'm just forty-four." Celeste's mind whirled with fragmented facts about menopause that she'd never believed would actually apply to her.

Luna pulled up to a tiny shingled house bordered by a stiff line of rose bushes. In the driveway was Jake's monster truck, which made the house look even smaller in comparison. A pit bull bounded toward the car. Luna killed the engine. The dog bounced up and down next to Luna's window. Celeste stared out to the distant mountains. It seemed unnaturally quiet without the noise of the car engine.

Luna stared at her. "It's okay, Celeste. Peri-menopause is a symptom of hormonal change. It could be a year, or more, before you have another episode."

"Episode . . ." Celeste repeated it mechanically, but the hair on the back of her neck stood up—it was the truth: *last night I had a menopausal episode.* Even if she didn't have another night sweat for years, the border of menopause had been breached. She belonged to the other side.

Luna put her hand on Celeste's shoulder. The dog continued to bark and bounce behind Luna's window. "You know, you could view this as a positive change. There are empowering things about menopause."

Suddenly, Celeste saw everything lucidly. She had been trying to take control of her life, meanwhile her own physicality was out of her control. Her efforts were irrelevant. Ultimately, her body had its own plan, disconnected from the silly contrivances of her mind. Whether she and the girls lived in L.A. or SoHum, whether she taught school or tended bar, whether she contacted Victor today or never did, things, over time, would take their own shape.

The screen door slammed. Jake emerged on a shadowed front porch and yelled at his dog. Luna got out of the car; Jake stepped down into the harsh sunlight and Luna approached him. Jake stood motionless as Luna wrapped her hands around his forearms, which hung listlessly at his sides. There was a strikingly different quality about him. His voice was flat and low, and although she couldn't make out what was being said, she could see that Luna was focusing on every word.

The interior of the car was heating up. It was airless, claustrophobic, and the dashboard radiated heat. If she left the car, she'd be privy to whatever was being divulged. There was something going on. Celeste didn't want to be in the middle of another crisis, or have to pretend to be the polite guest, but before she developed heat stroke, she opened the car door and got out.

Luna turned, surprised, as if she'd forgotten Celeste was there. Jake glanced up, saw her and stared for a moment, before letting his head drop to his chest.

Taking Jake by the arm, Luna said, "Come on, let's get something cold to drink."

Celeste followed them up steps to the front porch, but then stopped at the door, wondering if there was somewhere else she could go. At last, she opened the door. Inside, the cool air smelled of pot smoke, with yeasty back notes of stale beer.

Her eyes took a moment to adjust to the opalescent blackness in the house. She found herself in a small living room with an adjacent kitchen. The windows were closed and shades drawn. Luna was rummaging in the fridge, which was funky and diminutive, even smaller than the one that Tom and Luna had in their kitchen, which she had explained was, "Propane powered." Luna closed the fridge door. "When was the last time you brought food into this house?"

Jake shrugged. He sat round-shouldered at the kitchen table.

"Hey, still got mint growing around your water spigot?" Luna moved through the tiny kitchen with purpose. She pulled an old-fashioned aluminum ice tray out of the freezer and took three glasses off a shelf. "Celeste, fill the glasses with ice and water, please. I'll be right back." Opening the door to the deck, Luna went out of sight.

Celeste picked up the ice cube tray. Instantly, her hands stuck to the frozen metal. She turned toward Jake, who was staring at the table, unmoving in his chair. "Uh, sorry, can you help me?" Jake looked up. She held her hands in front of her. Saying nothing, he got up, went to the sink, turned on the faucet, and grabbed her hands, pulling them under the stream of water.

"Thanks." She shook her hands, sending droplets everywhere. "Can't remember the last time that happened."

Jake stared blankly. Then, in slow motion, he gave a nod to the ice tray and said, "Hate that fucken thing."

When Luna returned with handfuls of aromatic mint, the ice and water were waiting in glasses. Luna rinsed the mint leaves, pounded them with the handle of a butter knife and stuffed some into each glass. "No limes, huh?" Luna asked.

Jake shook his head.

"Did I see a . . ." Luna pulled a lemon out of the fridge. "Yep." She cut it, squeezed juice into each glass, and added some maple syrup she'd rummaged from a cabinet. After a last stir, she handed out the glasses, frosty and bright green, set aglow by the slice of yellow. "Mojitos without the mojo.

We live on these when we're in Mexico." Luna leaned back against the sink and sipped her drink. "Of course, we put rum in them. And we don't use maple syrup. Or lemons. This is for sissies." She took another sip. "But it tastes nice."

Celeste was surprised: it was good. "You're the one who should bartend, Luna."

Jake looked up at Celeste and blinked. "What?"

"Delores wants to hire her," Luna responded.

Celeste had an impulse to tell the story of how Delores insisted she work as a bartender. She opened her mouth, but suddenly exhausted and overwhelmed, fell silent. Luna and Jake were staring at her. "I need a regular job. I can't just trim."

"Thought you were a teacher." Jake seemed slightly more animated than when they'd arrived.

"Guess all I can hope for is to substitute."

Luna came to the table and reached for Jake's large hand, which lay on the table. "So, when did Harmony call you?"

"Yesterday."

"Why didn't you tell us?"

He shrugged.

"Are you okay in front of her?" Luna tilted her head toward Celeste.

Jake looked at the floor and kicked something invisible. "I don't care."

Luna turned back to Jake. "Tell me exactly what Harmony said."

"She's in love with him, not me." He was almost inaudible, studying the floor.

"Is she going to stay in SoHum?" Jake didn't respond. Luna sighed, and then eyed Jake shrewdly. "Get your shoes on, dude, you're coming with us. Celeste needs to drop off a W-4 form at The Redwood Tavern. Maybe we can convince Delores to open the kitchen and feed you something."

☙ ☙ ☙

Jake sat in a red-leatherette corner booth at the tavern, and Delores aimed a long-nailed finger at him. Her bleached hair had been tortured into short pigtails that didn't move.

"How long I know ya?" she commanded. When Jake didn't answer, she turned to yell into the kitchen, "Ralph, an order of fried zucchini too, please." She honed back in on Jake. "Come on hon."

Jake's face was drained of color. "Uh, don't know. . ."

"Since ya was a baby, Goddammit."

"Uh," Jake grunted. He glanced desperately at Luna, who nodded, raised her eyebrows, and opened her mouth to speak.

"Now," Delores interrupted, "ya listen to me. I know about this crap. Been through it myself. I ain't gonna tell ya what a bitch that Harmony is. Yer gonna figure that out." Delores turned toward the kitchen pass-through. "And, Ralph, a plate of scampi for Luna."

"No, Delores, really," Luna said.

Delores waved aside her protest. "Jakey, Auntie Delores gonna tell ya how to heal-up yer broke heart. First thing—ya ain't gonna die. It feels like it, but yer tough, and it ain't gonna kill ya. Hell, yer a strong stallion. And a good-looker too." Her laugh slipped into a raspy smoker's cough, then built to a thunderous quake that shook the walls. As her long orange nails fluttered over her bust, the hacking wore down. Unrelenting, she continued, "Second thing is, ya gotta eat." She continued to slap her chest reflexively, as she spoke. "People, they stop eating when they get a broke heart. You gotta eat the fatty shit. The stuff they tell ya not to eat. French fries, cheeseburgers, bacon, all that shit. Lay off sweets. You can have beer, but no hard liquor. Not when yer hurting so bad. No drugs, but reefer's okay. They say smoking reefer helps." She took a breath and brightened. "Jakey, want a beer?" Jake perked up and nodded.

"Celeste, why don'cha get him a beer from the bar, hon. Good practice for ya."

Relieved to have a reason to leave, Celeste slipped into the empty barroom. Light fell through stained glass. She pushed against low-shuttered doors and entered the narrow aisle behind the bar. An old-fashioned brass cash register sat center stage, framed by shelves of back-lit, glowing liquor bottles. Below the bar, out of sight of the customer, were metal sinks, drainage areas, mysterious tubs, and a small refrigerator. Fusty smelling dish towels were draped everywhere. The bar top felt sticky. The glassware looked grubby. She walked the length of the counter; to her left, there was a door, which she opened into a long storage room. It was the other side of the stained glass, and Celeste saw the glass wasn't illuminated by daylight, but by strategically placed clip lights. On the floor were rows of metal canisters plastered with beer labels. Shelves that lined the walls held multiple bottles of every kind of liquor.

"Didja fall in?" Delores was suddenly behind her, bellowing.

Celeste jumped. "I was . . . looking around."

Delores attempted to cross her arms over her ample chest; she looked annoyed. "Take this long to bring a glass of beer to a customer, ya ain't gonna be seeing no tips."

"Actually," Celeste spoke slowly, trying to elongate and enunciate each syllable with conviction, "I don't see this working out for me."

Delores grabbed Celeste's arm and drew her close. "Ya just calm down, Missy." They locked eyes. Slowly Delores's orange frosted lips spread into an artificial smile. Celeste felt the polished smoothness of Delores's fingernails press into her skin. Then Delores released her arm and patted her hand. "This is the liquor room." She said it brightly, seemingly ignoring what Celeste had just said. "Usually it's locked. Shocking as it may be, some employees have been known to steal." Delores winked. "Bartender's in charge of keeping this room locked up."

"Really, Delores, bartending is not the right fit for me."

"Hon," Delores turned to face her, "yer not a quitter. Gotta give her a try."

Celeste shook her head, but found she was mute and dumbfounded in the force of Delores's dogged tenacity.

"Let's get little Jakey his beer." Delores demonstrated how to dispense beer into an iced mug from a lineup of taps. She handed the glass to Celeste, who looked down blankly at its foamy top, but then carried it dutifully into the dining room.

"Thanks." Jake took the mug with enthusiasm.

"And Jakey." Delores jumped right back on her soap box. "Ya gotta listen to those heart-broke-type songs. If y'all have a favorite, play the shit out of it. Men ain't supposed to cry, but hon, ya gotta cry it out, and those songs're gonna do it for ya. But don't stay home, alone. Ya gotta be around people. Gotta git out of the hills for a while."

The smell of frying food filled the dining room as Ralph, a large man in a dirty apron, backed out of the kitchen's swinging door with a steaming plate of scampi. He placed it on the table, which already held plates of fried zucchini, French fries, and a cheeseburger for Jake. After Ralph received a volley of thanks, Delores demanded, "Open, hon," and dangled a French fry between her shiny nails, waiting for Jake to open his mouth so she could drop it in. After a fleeting, furtive glance at Luna, Jake obeyed.

"You know." Luna put her hand on Jake's shoulder. "Maybe it's a good idea to stay at your mom's for a while, so you could hang in town with friends."

Delores lit up. "Jakey, ya can stay here. In room number 9. Upstairs we still got the numbers from when it were a whorehouse. Just don't be getting any ideas, 'cause that's one thing the tavern don't provide no more."

"No." Jake looked as if he'd had enough. "I mean, thanks, Delores, but . . ."

The restaurant's phone rang and Delores went to the entry

desk. When she answered, her voice took on a sing-song quality. "Redwood Tavern, your bar that's not too far . . ."

As soon as Delores was involved in the phone conversation, Luna turned to Jake. "It's not a bad idea for you to stay in town."

"Jesus. I can make my own fucken decisions."

"Okay." Luna quickly turned away from Jake.

Delores came back to the booth red-faced. "That was my bartender." She made quotation marks in the air when she said "bartender." "With another sorry excuse why she ain't gonna work tonight. I told her to stick it where the sun don't shine." Delores turned on Celeste. "Ya ready, hon?" She pointed to an antique-looking grandfather clock near the entry desk. "Shift starts in about two hours."

Celeste was stunned. She turned toward Luna, who laughed and said, "Well, at least you'll know what it's like."

"But Luna, your errands, my phone calls. What about the things we had to do?"

"Well," Luna answered, "some days just don't go as planned."

Delores stared at Celeste. "Whadda ya need so bad?"

"I have calls I have to make."

"Okay. We got the phone."

"I have a cell, but I need reception."

"Hon, we got reception—most of the time anyway. Yer welcome to room 9, for privacy."

"Delores, I don't have my car to get home." Celeste turned to Luna. "The girls aren't prepared. It just doesn't work."

"The girls will be fine, Celeste. I'll let them set up in the great room, and Jonah can fix up a movie. You can talk to them on our landline." Luna looked calm, amused even. "Jake drove his truck here. Maybe he'll drive you home?"

They all looked at Jake.

"I guess." Jake shrugged.

It felt like a conspiracy. Somehow, Celeste had come to entertain the idea of working at the Redwood Tavern without believing it would actually happen.

She realized she was holding her breath. She forced herself to gulp air as she heated-up, as a desert sun bloomed inside her. Suddenly acutely aware of the uncomfortable sensation of her arms hanging at her sides, of standing in the baroque, crumbly dining room, of the mounted animal heads which stared at her, their antlers like a desperate testimony of their death story. It was all closing in. She felt suffocated, isolated, betrayed, in a foreign-feeling body which sprung beads of sweat outward through her membrane of skin, onto her forehead and upper lip. She swiped at herself awkwardly, with a strangely numbed hand, trying to wipe it all away.

Delores came closer; she spoke softly. "Tell ya what: we get Jakey stationed at the bar. To watch over ya. That make ya happy?"

"How about training, Delores?" Celeste heard the ringing of her own whiny voice, "You said I'd work with the bartender for the first week."

"Best thing, doll, just jump in." Delores reached out her hand in a solicitous manner, touching Celeste's shoulder, leaning in close, engulfing her in a cloud of stale cigarette smell. "I'll be right here, hon, if ya run into any trouble."

⚜ ⚜ ⚜

Room 9 was small, with a high window and a single bed. Shuddering at the thought of its past, Celeste sat on the bed, pushing her back against the wall. Below the coverlet, the mattress felt thin and lumpy.

First she called the girls: Alexa sounded excited to be without her. Sophie was unhappy, but Celeste trusted Luna. "They'll be fine," Celeste said out loud, after her goodbyes. Behind closed eyes she watched bright forms move inside her eyelids. Her phone felt heavy in her palm. There were countless messages from Victor. Her voicemail to him the day before promised to call him by noon—she'd missed that deadline by about two hours.

"Hello."

"Hi."

"Celeste! Where the fuck are you? The girls. How are my girls?"

"Good." She was stunned to actually be talking with him in real time. It had been too easy to make the connection, as if even while she'd tried to escape he'd always been right next to her, invisible but watching.

"I have to see them." His voice cracked. "You said you'd call at noon, I'm going crazy. Where are you, Celeste? I miss them so much. You have no fucking right."

"You want to talk about what's not right?"

"I want to talk to my daughters." He sounded angry and demanding, just as she knew he would. "Now."

"They're not with me."

There was a pause. Then he insisted, "Tell me where you are."

"In the country. It's beautiful. The girls are happy. I think I've found a good school for them."

"Damn it. You just take them away and make plans without me. This is fucked up."

Celeste pressed her lips together so tightly it hurt. She had to stay mum, otherwise she'd start screaming. After a terse silence, Victor spoke again, but softly, in a wounded voice, "You have no idea what I've been going through . . ." Thick words pushed out between stifled sobs. "Please, Celeste, I fucked up. I love you. I love the girls. Please." His crying penetrated her and softened the edges of her convictions. She fought not to be seduced, not to melt into easy familiarity. She pressed her palm into her forehead, resisting tears—and forgiveness.

They'd met during her second year at UCLA, while she'd

been making phone calls for the English Department, seeking volunteers for a professor's research project. Victor was a music major with aspirations to be an arranger and composer. She'd been there when he came to the department office. He was tall, his skin a luscious dark caramel-color, his hair long, thick, black, and as shiny as lacquer. He was young. She was young. After Alexa was born, Victor took a sound engineering gig as a way to make money until his compositions sold and made him a success. But it never happened. He kept doing sound gigs. After the girls were old enough, Celeste went back to teaching. She urged him to stop working for other people and focus on his own music. He wouldn't. It wasn't because they'd have to live frugally; it was something else, something outside her understanding, something about his sense of being a man. The whole package of family life seemed to have quashed his creative potential. She always wondered if that resentment had festered inside him, laying a path to his infidelities. "Celeste? Are you there?"

"I hear you."

"You have to come home."

"You have to put the house up for sale."

"I'm not selling the house." He'd gained composure. "Where are the girls?"

"Safe. You can talk to them later. I'm working tonight."

"Tonight? What the fuck. You're working at night? What're you doing, Celeste?"

"Never mind." That was a horror show she hadn't considered: how Victor would react to her working as a bartender. Leaving the kids with someone else at night.

"Where are they?"

"I'm not going to get into it." She took a deep breath. "Ruth told me you have a private investigator looking for us."

"Fuck, man, I didn't know if you were dead or alive."

"Call off the investigator."

"When you tell me where you are. After I speak to the girls."

"I'll tell you, and we'll make a plan for you to see them. Then will you call him off?"

"After I talk to the girls."

"Okay, at noon tomorrow. Sorry I was late today. I've got to go."

"Celeste, you know I love you."

"I know." It slipped out, she hadn't meant to say it, and she wanted to take it back. "Doesn't change anything."

"You better fucking call on time."

"Tomorrow, Victor." She punched the phone off, threw it on the bed, pulled her knees to her chest and sobbed.

bear

Fragments of conversation intermingled with the sound of drink glasses, the chinking of ice, a yelp from the far end of the barroom. Stale beer and the rancid smell of a bar rag filled Celeste's nostrils.

". . . just can't get the price for outdoor these days . . ."

". . . he'll end up in the ground over that . . ."

". . . only Kush. Nothing but OG, or Sour D . . ."

The words came at her from every direction as Celeste flitted about behind the bar, trying to put together the newest request for a drink, a Cosmo. The faded red and gold book that Delores handed her at the beginning of the night, *Old Mr. Boston, De Luxe, Official Bartenders Guide*—Delores had described it as the "bartender's bible"—was open next to the register. So far it had listed only a couple of the drinks Celeste had looked up. She'd followed a recipe for a martini made with gin, and the customer had spit it out at first sip. "What is this? I wanted vodka."

She pawed through the book. There was no listing for a Cosmopolitan. In a possessed state Celeste wanted to know— even as the demands for drinks being shouted at her got louder—what year the book was published. There it was: "1946 edition". In disgust, Celeste threw the book on the back counter, determined not to pick it up again. She moved down the bar, ignoring new pleas for "One pitcher of Amber Ale" and "Just a Seven and Seven." Celeste held up her index finger without looking directly at the throng, as if she were that kind of teacher and her students were too loud or excited. *Calm yourselves.* But bar patrons weren't well-behaved, and the pressure was escalating. As Celeste passed where Jake was stationed, she caught a snippet of what a grizzled man with a massive beard was saying to him: ". . . a crucible, man. A broken heart is a crucible." Since her shift began they'd been hunched together in conversation.

At the end of the bar, the woman who had ordered the Cosmo was talking fervently to a tattooed, pony-tailed man wearing a kilt. He was draining his Crown and Coke. The woman was pretty, probably in her twenties. Her hair fashionably striped in contrasting brown and blond bands, she had big eyes that drooped and lips gooey with pink sparkles. She'd struck an exaggerated pose, with her nose in the air. "That bitch," she brayed to the ceiling, "she got what she deserved . . ."

Celeste took some pleasure in interrupting her. "Excuse me, do you know what's in a Cosmo?"

The woman paused her roaring and looked blankly at Celeste. "Why? Don't you?"

"No." Celeste felt she needed to give no further explanation.

"Well then, make me a Tequila Sunrise."

"Okay. Do you know what's in that?"

"In a Sunrise?"

"Yes."

"What the fuck!" The woman exploded. She scanned the area behind the bar and then became ferocious. "Where's the fucking bartender?"

Celeste pulled her shoulders back, lifted her chest and thought about stating, "I ate her." She resisted, and instead announced as calmly as possible, "Sorry, you're stuck with me."

Suddenly Jake was standing next to the woman.

Cosmo looked up at him in shock. "Jake."

"How ya doing, Shanti?" Jake loomed over her. "Got a problem?" For a brief moment, Shanti was speechless. She brought her hand to her breasts, which protruded, domed and unmoving, from her low-cut sequined top. Celeste took a second glace at the sequined halter. It was the same top Alexa had wanted so badly.

Shanti stepped backward. "Hey, I'm just trying to get a fucking drink here."

Jake placed his hand authoritatively on her shoulder. "Okay."

Mr. Kilt pressed forward. "No need to get pushy, Jake."

"It's all good." Jake smiled at Mr. Kilt. "No one's gettin' pushy here."

"Jesus. I just want a fucking Cosmopolitan." Shanti said plaintively, "Is it a crime?"

The pulse of the bar had changed. The deafening din of conversation and laughter had died out. Celeste could feel the hot breath of folks standing too close to her. She realized even the patrons on the bar stools had turned to watch. Noise from the dining room wafted into the bar and the shrill note of a jazz tune emanated from speakers above them.

"Cloud," Jake called loudly, "you still in here somewhere?"

"Yep." The response came from the far end of the room, where the tables and chairs were clustered. Celeste couldn't see the man, but then he rose, and she remembered him from earlier in the evening. He'd asked for the wine list and then ordered a bottle of Pinot Noir, locally grown, as he had pointed out. He had a thick German accent, and the top of his shaved head was tattooed with fanciful blue and white clouds.

"Okay, fun's over." Jake motioned for the crowd to move aside. Cloud glided elegantly forward, carrying a full glass of wine. He and Jake huddled briefly. Cloud nodded. Jake turned to Shanti. "Give us a few, Shanti. You'll get your Cosmo."

"Okay." Shanti's head bobbed. "OhmyGod." She looked unnerved. The crowd that had gathered slunk away slowly in disappointment.

Celeste went behind the bar, made a Seven and Seven, filled a pitcher with beer, took money and gave change. Jake hadn't yet told her the plan. She hoped Cloud would take over and she would go home to her daughters. But Jake and Cloud were taking their time settling, asking people already seated to move so they could sit together. At last, seated at bar stools, Cloud delicately swirled the red liquid in his glass, sniffed and took a sip.

"He used to bartend in the city," Jake said.

"So, okay, I'll talk you through it." Cloud smiled and asked, "Shall we start with a Cosmo?"

※ ※ ※

Around midnight, a few people clustered at the back tables; a few more hunched over the bar, including Jake and Cloud, talking in hushed tones. Requests for drinks had slowed almost entirely. Celeste wiped the bar with a dingy towel and wondered what a bartender's clean-up duties might be. It had been a long evening of sticky liquid pouring over her hands, ice cubes clattering as they were scooped, the tinkling sound they made when stirred in a glass, hundred-dollar bills foisted across the bar while she was quickly figuring out change. At the height of the action, she realized her tip jar was full. She emptied it once, then twice, stashing the bundle of bills in the cabinet below the register. Retrieving the wad, she counted it out: two hundred and thirty-four dollars. On a Tuesday night. Despite the fact that she had no idea what she was doing.

Celeste went to where Jake and Cloud sat on the other side of the bar. They stopped talking, which made her feel awkward and somehow uncouth. A wave of heat flushed over her, she tried to steady herself. "I'll split the tips with both of you."

"Not necessary," Cloud responded. "It's Jake you should thank."

Celeste glanced at Jake. "Thanks," she said.

He shrugged.

"Actually," Cloud gestured fluidly as he spoke, "I was about to escape when Jake called me up. But it turned into a stimulating evening. Takes me back."

"So," Celeste just had to ask, "How'd you come by the name 'Cloud'?"

"Well, my name's Claude, but people in SoHum always call me Cloud." He slapped his hands on his shiny inked scalp.

"You know what else they call you?" Jake chuckled. "Air Head."

"I refuse to embrace that." Cloud laughed, and his light eyes disappeared into squinty crescents. In the dim bar light, the scalloped shapes tattooed on his scalp appeared to be flattened ringlets of blue hair. Celeste searched his face for signs of irritation at being called Air Head, but he didn't seem offended.

"Are you from Germany?" Celeste liked him. She wanted to know how he came to tattoo his head, how long he'd lived in Humboldt, what had brought him to the place. And whether he was gay.

"I was born in Austria."

"What do you do for a living, Cloud?"

His face went blank.

"Hey," Jake looked up at Celeste. "Fucken never ask that. Especially if you want tips." Jake glanced at Cloud. "She just moved up from L.A., but my dad's known her for like twenty-five years."

"Twenty-seven." Celeste corrected.

"So." Cloud wore an ironic smirk. "In answer to your question: I'm in property management, landscaping, or carpentry . . . Just like everyone else."

"I only. . ." But she had no words. Cloud was interesting, she'd been basking in a kind of camaraderie she imagined they'd forged, but apparently some social niceties weren't acceptable in SoHum.

Delores entered the barroom, and a disheveled older man

at the end of the bar who had been quietly drinking "a shot of Bushmill with a beer back" came alive. He whirled around on the bar stool flung open his arms and began serenading Delores with "Volare."

Delores shook her head. "Broudy, nice ta see ya too. Keep yer hands to yerself."

Jake cocked his head in Broudy's direction. "John Broudy." Cloud and Celeste must have both looked blank. "Fuck brain that owns property next to me—the gauntlet. Skunk Twins are his grandsons."

"Oh." Cloud widened his eyes and stopped blinking.

"Vicious dogs and degrading trash heap?" Celeste asked.

"That's the one." Jake nodded. They all turned toward Broudy, his face florid and strangely elastic, as he continued to sing. Although he was too inebriated to hold the tune, he'd substituted Delores's name for the Italian words in "Volare." Meanwhile, over the speakers "Can't Get No Satisfaction" played. Delores waved at him dismissively. But he gained volume and spread his arms wide as he sang: "Del . . . or . . . es . . . ohhh. . .ohhh."

Delores stared him down sternly. "Broudy, it's been a long night." He kept singing. More harshly, she said, "Don't do it." She set her brightly manicured hands squarely on her narrow hips. "Cut it, or yer outta here, bud." Her bleached-fluff hair glowed in the light shining down.

Broudy spun on his bar stool and miraculously changed back into the quiet patron he'd been. Delores turned and strode across the room, greeting people as she made her way, smiling cheerfully. She sat next to Jake and Cloud, who were both chuckling. "Yeah. Broudy likes to rhyme. Go ahead and laugh." Delores slammed her hands down on the bar. "So, Celeste, busy night. Never did git a chance to check up on ya."

"Well, it's only thanks to Cloud and Jake that I'm still here. That bartender's bible is useless."

"Hon, I learned on that book."

"How many years ago was that?"

"Doll face, just 'cause ya did good don't mean ya can git cheeky." Delores turned to Jake and Cloud. "So, boys, ya helped out the new girl. Ya think yer all hot shit? What trouble ya git into?" Then Delores held up her palm and shook her head. "Never mind. Got no need to know." She smiled maternally. "Just tell me how many years I gotta comp ya."

※ ※ ※

There was no small talk in the cab of Jake's truck. The music was cranked up, and the background rattle of the engine filled Celeste's head. The moon hung plump and low in the night sky, seeming to dance from one mountain to the next as they traversed the curves of Bear Ridge Road. She was tired from a long first night working the bar. After they turned off the pavement, Jake turned the music down and broke the silence. "So, way back when, why did you and Dad break up?"

"We didn't."

He turned to her briefly, questioningly, and then refocused on the road before him.

"My mom sent me away, to live with my father in Los Angeles."

"So you met Dad in Colorado?"

"Yeah, I grew up there too. We were together for a while, but he was twenty-six. I was a senior in high school, not eighteen yet, when my mom found out about us." Celeste thought of her mother screaming *cradle robber"* in Tom's face. Her mother was convinced that Celeste's relationship with Tom was just another aspect of her teenage rebellion. After about age thirteen, when hormones had taken hold and jolted Celeste's core, she'd acted out—sneaking away to party after her mom was asleep, stealing her mom's car, crashing it into a tree. What her mother didn't understand about Tom was that he was the steadying hand. "One day, I was at school, my mom came and got me out of class. She had my bag packed and took me straight to the airport. Tom and I didn't get to say goodbye. I had to finish my last semester of high school in a new city. Kinda ruined my relationship with my mom."

"She's still in Colorado?"

"She died, from cancer, a few years later." Even after her mother's death, Celeste ruminated about how wrong her mother had been. "My mom thought she was protecting me. She kept telling me that someday I'd thank her."

"So you and Dad stayed in touch all these years?"

"We did, yeah." Celeste smiled. "He's a good friend." She leaned closer to the open window and let the warm wind soothe her.

"Best man I know," Jake said.

Well, she thought, we have that in common. Celeste stole a glance at Jake. She watched his hands on the steering wheel as he negotiated an especially bumpy curve.

Over the years, Tom had become Celeste's talisman. Whenever she was depressed she'd buoy herself with fantasies of him and invariably write him a letter. Even after she emailed everyone else, she was still writing Tom real letters, pen and paper, at least once or twice a year. Time would dissipate whatever crisis she was having and deliver his response, in the same handwriting she once pressed to her lips. When she first landed in Los Angeles, banished from home, disoriented and broken-hearted, she and Tom had spent hours on the phone hashing out schemes to be together again. Initially, he was going to drive out to California and steal her away. But, gradually, everything settled into the mechanisms of their new lives and the urgency waned. Yet, in romantic relationships Celeste had always looked to replicate the dreamlike quality she'd felt when she'd been with Tom. With him, it seemed things became safe and easy. He made her feel that her vulnerabilities were an asset. Tom was the first lover she'd had an orgasm with, the first man she'd loved.

The truck stopped suddenly, and Celeste fell forward, her seatbelt yanking her back.

"There's something in the road."

"What is it?" Celeste said, trying to lean toward the windshield, squinting at the dark.

"I think it's a fucken baby bear."

Celeste could hear a soft, high pitched yap. "Is it hurt?" she asked, but Jake had already opened the driver's door. She saw him round the front of the truck, moving toward an undefined furry brown animal. When he was a foot or two away from it, his head jerked up, and he flew out of sight. Then he was hurtling into the cab of the truck, yelling for her to close her window, as he threw the truck in reverse. They skidded backward, down the rutted road. Fast, too fast, until, finally slowing, Jake positioned the truck in a turnout. His chest heaved. "Holy shit." He shook his head.

"What happened?"

"I saw the mama. She was fucken coming for me."

"Jesus!"

"Yeah!" He put his hands on top of his head. "Can't believe I did that. Stupid, stupid."

Celeste was trying to make sense of what had happened. She'd never seen a bear before; actually she still hadn't seen much of anything discernable.

"Shit!" Jake said again. It was quiet for a moment, then he started to chuckle. Soon he pitched his head back and was laughing uncontrollably, and then Celeste was laughing too.

jake

Victor stood framed in the doorway of the hotel room, weighed down with packages and travel bags. The girls ran to him shouting, "Daddy, Daddy!" Celeste's first impulse was to throw her arms around him too, but the impulse died, replaced by a roiling rage. He looked at Celeste through the tangle of arms and legs that clung to him. As bitterness vibrated out of her the atmosphere chilled and the girls' squeals quieted. Alexa, still in her father's arms, turned toward her mother, then looked back to her father, then again to her mother; she seemed shocked, as if she understood for the first time that there was conflict. It shattered Celeste, seeing Alexa caught in their web. She bolted.

"Celeste!" Victor called out.

She wailed, "I need a moment," and slammed the bathroom door. Immediately, she realized she could have gone into the adjacent hotel room, her room, which she'd insisted on so she could have privacy. She'd fled so fast she didn't think, and now she was trapped. Plops of tears fell on the floor. Her head felt swollen. On the other side of the wall, she heard Victor busying the girls with the presents he'd brought.

She hated him for ruining her family, for ruining her daughters' lives. She was incapable of making everything nice like she always had as mother and wife. Celeste cried, and pressed herself against the tiled wall of the bathroom, one hand against her mouth. She stared numbly through a blur of tears at the repeating blue and white pattern of castles, a river, and weeping willows beneath which a family picnicked. A slimy, salty mess, she eventually managed to move to the sink and splash her face. She emerged from the bathroom puffy-eyed and disoriented, with no concept of how long she'd been gone. There was a note on the bed in Alexa's handwriting: "Mom meet us downstairs for lunch. love"

The dining room was formal and full of period detail that she'd considered charming when she'd first seen the hotel. Today it struck her as annoyingly pompous. Only a few groups of people were scattered about the large room. The girls waved to her from a round table near a bank of windows. Victor sat with them. Her daughters and her husband. They watched her, waited for her, their faces reflecting some emotion, maybe anticipation. A cold shiver shot through her. It was blazing hot outside, yet chilly inside the dining room. She thought of her favorite soft blue sweater left back in the room. It was a mistake not to have worn it.

"Mommy," Sophie said, reaching out her small hand. Celeste settled and tried to appear calm.

The waitress materialized, chattering gaily, "So, the whole family is here, what would you like to order?"

"You haven't ordered yet?" Celeste asked.

"We wanted to wait for you," Victor said. He smiled at her as if bestowing a gift. She seethed. They ordered and the waitress left. Celeste glanced out of the diamond-paned windows to the stone patio and bright lawns below. She felt Victor watching her and it made her squirm. Celeste wanted to scream. She wanted to take the gilt-adorned plates off the table and break them over Victor's head. And stab him with the salad fork. She laughed involuntarily. A short, mean laugh. They all looked at her, and she raised her chest in response to their stares, pulling in air and puffing herself up. Then she found herself meeting Victor's eyes. He regarded her warmly, smiling as if they'd had a small tiff and he was patiently waiting for her to get over it. She narrowed her eyes and scrutinized his T-shirt; it was red with intentionally faded, stamped words. Very stupid. Celeste hadn't seen it before and wondered where it came from. She hated the shirt. She hated everything about him: his full lips which curved at the edges and were so distinctly formed, his long, heavy, black hair, his earrings. Yet, she noted coolly, if she hadn't known him, she would've found him attractive. Even in her hate-filled state she had to admit that. But being in his presence was disturbing. When they'd made plans for his trip, she'd contemplated her daughters' need to be reunited with him and the necessity of being there to support them when he told them he was having a baby with another woman. But she hadn't considered her own reaction. He wasn't a bad father; he'd been more attentive than her musician father had ever been with her. Whatever happened between Victor and herself, she believed he would never attempt to take their daughters from her. Though she wanted him to think she didn't understand that, because what he had done made him, in every way unsafe. She had to treat him as the kind of a man she couldn't trust with anything valuable . . . especially her heart.

They ate their lunch, the tension hanging like thick smoke. Alexa and Sophie were quiet. Celeste pushed food around her plate. Everything seemed separated from reality: the pretty, almost fake-looking food was inedible. Looking at her husband's intimately familiar features, made her flinch; the overly air-conditioned dining room chilled her and, despite its size, made her feel desperately claustrophobic.

After lunch, they went out into the heat and down ancient-looking stone stairs onto the expansive lawn. Alexa and Sophie ran as if they'd just been let out of a cage, across the cleanly mowed grass down to the riverbank. A row of chaises fitted with pristine white cushions faced the river, which snaked, sparkling, in a half circle around the hotel. A stone bridge arched over the river, its underside reflected in the water, making it look like a perfect circle. It was a lush tableau, but Celeste ached to be back at Tom and Luna's—in the crude, simple cabin, or working in the vegetable garden with the pungent smell of tomato leaves, or clipping pot in a circle of gossiping women. She had come to like trimming; it was profitable and social, and she'd gotten good at it.

Victor stepped close to her and took her hand. "I made a mistake, Celeste. My relationship with Gina is over. All I've . . ."

"Stop."

She ripped her hand out of his and pushed him away from her, forcing an arm's length between them. Her whole body was shaking, as if she were trying to get his sticky words off her. She turned on him, spigot open, words spewing, "Your relationship with her isn't over. Jesus Christ. It's just beginning. You've got a baby coming! That's a fucking life sentence. Unless you do the wrong thing." Celeste glared at him and took a step forward, pointing her finger at his chest. "Are you going to do the right thing, Victor?" It was a schoolyard dare. "Are you?"

Except for the birds chirping in the treetops, everything was quiet. Behind him, she saw that Alexa and Sophie were watching them from the riverbank. They were out of earshot, but she knew there was no disguising body language.

Victor stared at her. His jaw muscle twitched, yet he possessed an eerie composure. "Yes, I'm gonna do right by the baby." His gold earrings glinted in the sunlight. "But my first obligation is to you and the girls, and what's best for them is for us to be together. In our home."

"Not gonna happen," Celeste said. "That house needs to sell. I want a divorce. I need the proceeds from the house to make a new life for the girls."

Slowly, in his envelope of imperturbability, Victor turned away from her, toward the shore where Alexa and Sophie were. What she'd said seemed to have washed over him without sinking in. He spoke slowly, "You have no idea what hell I've been through. Wondering if you and the girls were okay. I didn't know where you were." He turned back to Celeste, his face contorted now. She remembered once when he'd dislocated his shoulder and she'd driven him to the emergency room. He'd had a similar look then, a look of physical agony, but then she'd cared. He continued to speak in an oddly syncopated way. "I understand that you're angry at me."

Celeste's mouth fell open. Someone had coached him, she was sure of it. "Victor, psychobabble won't work here. I'm not having a tantrum."

For a moment Victor was quiet, and then he spoke again, softly. "Can you tell me that you don't love me anymore?"

"Go fuck yourself." Celeste walked away, but Victor came after her, putting his hand on her shoulder. She wheeled around to look him square in the face. "I don't love you."

He didn't react, but continued in his controlled tone. "Celeste, the kids need us to be together." His hand released her and then immediately, unnaturally, flew to his forehead. "I can wait this out. We're a family."

"No, Victor. Families live together. You haven't lived with us for years." Celeste walked away, going toward the river where the girls were standing, watching and waiting.

☀ ☀ ☀

In the hotel hallway, the four of them stood stiffly in front of rooms 204 and 206. "Well, what are your plans for the day?" Celeste forced herself to look at Victor.

He smiled wanly, then addressed his daughters. "What would you like to do?" There was what was being said, and then there was what was really going on. The kids were not fooled. Alexa and Sophie looked bewildered and upset. Celeste moved toward the door of her room.

"Mommy." Sophie grabbed her arm. Celeste was desperate to get away before she lost control. She could feel the wrath expanding in her gut. It was as if a disease had invaded her organs, permeating them with toxicity. She could barely breathe. "Where're you going?" Sophie asked.

"Just a little nap. In my room." Celeste put her hand on the door knob. "Here." Her hands were shaking as she used the old-fashioned key and opened the door, pointing into the empty room. "Right here." The girls stared. Victor looked on impassively. Her time as a functioning mother, before her cover was blown, was running out. Her gestures felt exaggerated and odd. It was all she could do not to rip the door off its hinges. "*Do* something." She tried to keep her voice calm. "Victor, go somewhere. You gotta have a plan."

"Mommy?" Sophie's doe eyes pleaded.

"Sweet pea," Celeste said slowly, "this is your chance to spend time with Daddy. You've missed him so much."

"But . . ." Sophie's words trailed off.

"Why can't you come with us?" Alexa asked. Celeste couldn't think of one acceptable, benign answer: because Mommy can't stand Daddy. Her mouth opened. Nothing she could say would make any sense to her daughters. Except the truth. But it wasn't time for them to hear the story about their impending half-sibling. Not yet. Not on the first day. Not on the first afternoon of their father's visit.

"See you after my nap, okay?" Celeste gave Alexa, then Sophie, a quick hug and went through the doorway, closing the door after her as softly as possible.

Alone in the room, the quiet enveloped her. The floral curtains were drawn, and the air conditioning was on, which made the room hauntingly dark and cold on the hot, bright summer day. Her hands and feet, her whole body, seemed numb, frozen, tingly. It had to be emotional, yet, for a moment, she indulged in a fantasy of giving herself over, collapsing, being diagnosed with some horrible disease, dying of it on the spot. Then this would all stop. Trying to repress her out-of-control emotions had only strengthened their hold. She felt like she'd become that vengeful, spiteful woman who dwells in the past, full of bitterness and rage, the kind of woman who isn't open to something better because she's busy being victimized by her past. Victor's mere presence had eclipsed Celeste's true self, or who she wanted her true self to be.

Ripping the itchy floral coverlet off the bed, she fell onto the cold sheets and closed her eyes. Soon she was dozing in semi-oblivion, floating between awareness and a dream. Then the dream grew. There was a jungle, a tropical tangle of vines and branches; ganja leaves waved in the air. High in the trees, monkeys held shiny oranges and made screeching noises. Alexa and Sophie played on the shore of a river. But something was wrong. Celeste looked down and realized she was covered in fur. She pulled at it, finding it was part of who she was: an animal-mother. She woke, gasping and disoriented, panicked. *Where are the girls?*

Then she remembered. She felt untethered and lonely without them. Her daughters were the grounding influence in her life. While Victor had the girls in Humboldt, she realized she needed to do something to occupy herself. She could go back to Tom and Luna's to clip; recently she'd trimmed two-pounds in one day. The trim shack had endless bins filled with dry plants, ready to clip, but Celeste couldn't imagine leaving the hotel and her children for a whole week. And it would be too strange to be at the cabin without them. Celeste grabbed her phone and called Delores. She had negotiated not working this week, as if in some deluded part of herself, she believed that she would participate in activities with Victor and her daughters.

"Redwood Tavern. Your bar that's not too far."

"It's Celeste. Turns out I don't need the week off."

"Can ya work tonight? Got no one to cover yer shift."

"I'll be there. Four o'clock." Celeste punched off her cell and stared blankly at it, setting it on the nightstand. Working would be good, she thought, no time to be an emotional wreck there. She got out of bed, stripped off the clothes she was wearing and let them drop to the carpet, then kicked the pile and considered burning them later. The clothes looked clean but had been soiled by the turmoil of the day. She'd never wear them again.

In the bathroom, she stood before a full-length mirror, barely recognizing her own reflection. Her weight loss had changed her body. Where she was once full and taut, in her breasts and her stomach, she looked empty. It was a used body she stared at. She looked drained, small, vulnerable. The babies had come, grown there, then vacated. That part was done. Turns out youth and fertility had been a passing phase. Switching off the overhead light, Celeste ran a bath and tried to draw the curtains framing the window. Still, a bright slice of sunlight beamed between the fabric panels. She stepped into the bath and sank into the warm water.

Within reach, she'd placed the tin container with joints Tom had rolled for her to give to Victor. Celeste wasn't sure that was a good idea, but Tom had smiled calmly. "Don't tell him who grew it, but believe me, Celeste, it'll help. He needs a taste of SoHum." She lit a joint and took a long draw. Floating in the cool, aqueous light, Celeste wondered if Victor and the girls had gone out yet. Motionless in the water, holding smoke in her lungs, she listened for them in the next room. She couldn't hear anything beyond the bathroom walls, just the small, tinkling sounds of water. She exhaled violet-blue smoke, and in the thin shaft of light that leaked between the curtains, the smoke performed—curling and twisting. Her mind wandered. The hateful emotions that had seized her began to relax their grip. Watching her toes break the surface skin of the bathwater, she thought about when she first stepped into the river at The Crossing. In SoHum the rivers all flowed north, like the Nile; each time Celeste watched the coursing river and realized that anew, it made her dizzy, as if the water's flow were defying gravity, rushing upwards to the sea.

Seeing Victor brought back the realization of what she'd given up, and Celeste felt a cloying tug of homesickness. The loss of her beautiful house was a cold stone inside her. Without the protective shell of her home and the life she knew—although she had deliberately and willfully fled from it—she was raw and exposed to the elements around her.

Seeing her husband made her crazy, and hungry. In some secret place, a tributary of lust formed. It felt shameful though, given the state of their relationship. She shouldn't have sexual yearnings for a man who had done so much harm to her and her children. In a world of perfect sweetness, when Victor appeared in the doorway and the girls ran to him, Celeste would have thrown herself into his arms too. His homecomings had become a ritual—a celebration of family but also a renewal of their intimacy. The first night was always the best. This night. Suddenly it seemed the hardest thing to give up. Unlike her other married friends, who complained about stale sex, for Celeste the passion had stayed hot, often fueled by jealousy or anger, and his unyielding declarations of love. Ironically, the reason she'd been so unhappy was the same reason she and Victor had maintained passion—he was almost never home.

She conjured the feel of Victor's hands smoothing her; the silken feel of his skin; his musky, oily smell; and the stark, sexy contrast of their skin colors against each other, defining their movements. Celeste took another toke and exhaled smoke over her breasts. She eased water over her hard nipples. Aroused by fantasies of being with my own husband—I have no imagination, she thought. Her mouth was dry, and she slid down letting the soft water enter her mouth. She wondered if maybe the sensation of being raw was the beginning, as everything old was stripped away. Turning the faucet on full, she glided to the bottom of the tub and positioned herself for pleasure from the flow. Celeste touched her breasts with one hand and coaxed herself with the other while the water flooded her, until a lavish climax granted her a fresh perspective and a series of soothing, blissful moments.

✳ ✳ ✳

"What're you doing here?" The door of the Redwood Tavern had swung open mysteriously as she approached, and Celeste peered around it, to see Jake holding the door open.

"Heard you were coming in."

She envisioned him in a doorman's uniform and laughed; the image was so out of place in the back hills of the country, and on Jake. "How are Tom and Luna . . . and Jonah? Miss them already."

"All good," he said, as they crossed into the barroom. "Who's got your daughters?"

"Their father. My ex . . . Or soon to be." Celeste shot him a smile. He knew Luna had taken care of the girls during the two weeks she'd worked at the tavern.

Jake had changed since the day she and Luna had ended up at his house. There seemed to be some kind of an unspoken pact—some kind of understanding—between the two of them, perhaps because she'd witnessed the depths of his emotional vulnerability.

She went to put her purse and sweater away and did a check of what liquor bottles needed restocking for the night ahead. Celeste could feel Jake's green eyes glued to her. "You want a drink. Your usual?"

"Please." He took a seat at the bar. "Never seen you in a dress before."

"Yeah." Celeste looked down, fiddling with her waistband. Her soft rayon dress, was a little too showy, but very comfortable. "Didn't pack my work clothes. I wasn't scheduled to work."

"That's what Delores said."

"My husband got in this morning and it was a rough day. Anyway, I decided it would be better to work than to mope."

Jake seemed intent, but didn't respond, so Celeste went to fetch a tub of ice, the first of many she would need for the night. She made Jake's rum drink and put it in front of him on a napkin, not quite irritated that she hadn't had a chance to wipe down the bar. She looked at the clock; there was enough time to prepare. The place was blessedly empty, except for Jake. The restaurant wasn't open yet, but Celeste could hear a commotion in the kitchen. Delores and Ralph were yelling at each other, not an uncommon occurrence. She turned the music on, loud, conducted a quick scan of the whiskeys and went to the liquor room behind the bar for a few bottles. Bending down to the bottom shelf, she felt the pressure of a hand on her hip. Celeste jolted up.

Jake hovered, and kept his hand on her. Taking a deep breath, he closed his eyes—as if waiting for an epiphany, or a beheading. When he opened his eyes Celeste stared at his moss-green irises. Then his mouth met hers. He tasted of spice from the sweet drink she'd made him. His hands were steady and warm, and knew where they wanted to go: inside her panties and inside her bra. Their bodies became a tight unit, instinctively searching for a vacant wall or something, anything, for support, as they cast themselves around the room. Jake broke their kiss, turned his head, glanced at the soda cases stacked on a battered wooden chair. He lifted the tower of cases off the seat, the whole stack at once, in what she deemed a herculean show of balance and strength. After placing the stack on the floor, he put his hand firmly on her waist. Celeste fixed her gaze on him, reached under her dress and pulled her panties off. He unzipped his jeans and lowered himself on the chair, drawing her forward. As she burrowed down, the rush scintillated, shifting rapidly as she descended until he was completely inside. Jake groaned. She pulled up, and sank down, and then paused, in an attempt to mete out and extend the buzz. But then, deliciously, she gave in to the urge, driven to increase her rhythm. In some far-off land someone called her name. Her body drew taut, every cell hummed; she moved up and down. Jake bit her nipples, trapped inside the bra that pushed them forward. He moaned again, and an intense swelling began to reverberate through her. Celeste heard a customer settling in at the bar, as her body thundered and shook. Then, immobilized, her head floated, she felt the suggestion of a headache. Tingling sensations fluttered, subsiding gradually. Jake didn't move. They were motionless, shell-shocked, still joined.

Finally, all at once, the world came zooming back and they separated, frantically attempting to put themselves together. Celeste stepped into her panties, which lay discarded on the floor. She patted down her hair. Jake zipped and gave her a quick kiss. The bus boy called for her from behind the bar. Jake turned, opened the door, and walked out of the liquor room.

lies

Celeste was mortified by what she'd done, yet every time she looked at Jake that night at the tavern, she became shivery and light-headed. He stood around, mingling with one group or another, when he wasn't sitting on a bar stool talking with Cloud. She swam through the sea of bar patrons and their demands. People chattered loudly, shoveled in food, and tossed down drinks, the whole of it delivered by her hands. In great socializing waves they entered, crushing and swarming and gossiping. Celeste could feel Jake watching her as she clattered around the bar, making and serving drinks, delivering plates of food from the kitchen. He sent sideways glances out to her. It was like being back in junior high, being a naughty teenager in class, except in this case, drunk and half-drunk adults substituted for students. And the man she had just fucked was nineteen-years younger than she was and the look-alike son of her ex-lover. What have I done? Celeste wondered, just how badly have I screwed myself? But, oh, she could still feel how delicious it was.

At one point he was speaking to her, surrounded by the crowd near the bar, his mouth close to her ear, their faces side by side gazing in opposite directions. They weren't touching; presumably she was trying to hear a drink order from a customer over the din, but Jake was whispering an erotic activity he had in mind, and she could feel the warmth and moisture of his breath in her ear. His voice and the secret they shared were sexually hypnotic. In the midst of the tumult, his words were like hands stroking her. Finally, she forced herself to back away from him, at the very last breaking eye contact. From the other side of the swinging doors behind the bar, Celeste saw Delores in the dining room. She was almost within touching distance.

"Delores," Celeste shouted, "could you spell me, please?"

"Sure, hon."

Celeste made her way through the busy dining room and up the stairs to Delores's private domain. In the bathroom, she caught glimpses in the mirror—of a woman. She stopped, and straightened up to take a look. Who was she? This woman was radiant, a wild creature, a participant in a random act of unprotected sex. Suddenly her dream from earlier in the day came back vividly. Shockingly real. She relived the distinct sensation, the body memory on her skin, of trying to pull at the thick fur covering her body. The strange ridiculousness of it made her shudder. *The animal-woman who needs sex.* Staring into her own eyes, she saw they had a new incandescence. The corkscrew tendrils of her hair looked as electrified as she felt, and there was an upwards bend at the corners of her mouth, as if she had tasted something tantalizing. A sly smile appeared. While she was out fucking a younger man, Victor was taking care of their children. Perfect symmetry.

Then Luna and Tom came into her mind. Oh, please, she said a silent prayer; let it stay a secret, a one-time mistake that will rest quietly between me and Jake. She dropped her head in her hands, embarrassed and regretful. As soon as my kids are out of my sight, she thought, I revert to an out-of-control teenager—even going all the way. She cupped her hands under a stream of water and splashed her face, realizing she hadn't even begun to obsess about the terrible consequences that could unfold.

But later, after she slipped back behind the bar and Jake beamed a smile when he saw her, she was shamelessly exhilarated again. Then Celeste wished that the whole tavern and its people would disappear and she and Jake could go somewhere alone and lie together, so she didn't have to be concerned about becoming the newest gossip tidbit.

Celeste muddled mint for a Mojito ordered by a man who had been flashing a fat rubber-banded roll of bills. He kept referring to her as "doctor," and as she poured the liquor for his drink, he continued to blather, "Doc, go heavy on the liquid yoga." He'd introduced himself as "Eddy." Eventually, something dangling from Cloud's belt buckle distracted him.

"One of the biggest plants I ever grew," Cloud was saying in his heavily accented English. He'd tied a rope through the hollow center of a chunk of cannabis stalk and threaded it on his leather belt. The specimen was green and fresh, larger than the span of Cloud's hands around it. "I'm making a pipe with the rest of the stalk, using a side branch for the neck."

"Fucking awesome!" Eddy said.

"Your Mojito." Celeste handed Eddy the drink.

"Doc, here's to you." He raised his drink to Celeste, then after a long swig, detached himself from his barstool and went to admire Cloud's stem up close. The top of Eddy's bald scalp reflected light, while the hair he still had left hung down his back in stiff dreadlock pads. Cloud's head, tattooed with cloud-shaped puffs, and Eddy's ratted coiffure met as they bent to examine the stem together.

Soon Eddy had launched into a monologue on growing pot, which began, "Back in the day," and ended, "after Vietnam, growing pot saved my life." He had a thick New Jersey accent, but his phraseology was pure California surfer-dude. Earlier he had bragged to Celeste that he owned a vacation house, "my winter home," in the same village in Mexico as Tom and Luna's; then he added, "Heard you're living in their cabin on the ridge."

"Yep," Celeste had replied while thinking: oh, a town too small.

"Lucky girl, to have Tom and Luna part the Redwood Curtain for you. Hope you know it."

"I do." Celeste had been bustling about, hopeful that he would notice she was too busy to carry on a conversation.

Eddy turned to Jake and Cloud. "Hey, you hear about the weed they found in an ancient Chinese tomb? The shit was still green."

Jake cocked his head. "What the fuck you talkin' about, Eddy?"

"I'm telling ya," Eddy answered. "They found like a pound, in a tomb with a mummy, in the Gobi Desert."

Jake rolled his eyes. "You gotta stop smoking crack, Eddy."

"Hey, I heard it on the radio. World's oldest marijuana stash."

"Absolutely true," Cloud asserted, nodding. "A spectacular find. A twenty-six-hundred-year-old tomb excavated near Turpan, China. It was a shaman's tomb, probably from the Yuezhi—they were fair-haired people who lived in Western China." Cloud settled on a vacated stool. "The climate there is arid, so the cannabis was well preserved. Found it in a wooden bowl—still had trichomes, but no smell. They identified it as a cultivated strain, not from a wild plant. Which is significant. Means they were growing."

Other people at the bar had tuned in and were gathering to listen to Cloud. "So, they know from chemical analysis that it was high-potency pot, cultivated for psychoactive purposes. But the researcher said that due to decomposition no one would be able to feel its effects today."

Jake burst into laughter, then said, "Yeah, right, and the researcher was like: 'I'll just take this back to my office for safekeeping.'"

That got a laugh out of Cloud, but he continued, "For sure it wasn't hemp cultivated for fiber or food, which, of course, gives more validation that ganja's been used for medicinal and sacramental purposes for millennia."

A Coors Light customer spoke up, "Yeah, but the U.S. government is sending the mummy to jail for possession."

Mr. Coors was one of the regulars at the tavern and seemed an unlikely participant in the conversation, with his Marlboro Man face, cowboy hat, plaid shirt, and big metal USA belt buckle. Maybe what Luna says is true, Celeste mused, that everyone grows, even the decked-out redneck drinking domestic light.

"No, no, the mummy's chill," a woman at the bar shouted. "He got hisself a 215."

Cloud gave a half-smile and went on, "The tomb is located near the Hindu Kush Mountains, the region where, in the nineteen eighties, the original Kush seeds of *Cannabis indica* were scored and brought back to SoHum. The researcher said that the herb they found was similar to what we're growing today."

As Celeste handed out drink orders to the barroom, the quips on the subject continued, causing shouts and ripples of laughter.

"Like some guy in a lab coat can tell me our shit ain't better."

"He hasn't tried my strain of OG. I'd be happy to bring a Cannabis Cup to his doorstep, then we can do some testing."

She heard Jake's voice. "Sorry, Eddy. Next time you tell me about some fucken twenty-six-hundred-year-old chronic, I'll believe you."

When Celeste got back to the bar with a fresh round of drink orders to fill, the crowd had dispersed. "It's indoor," Cloud was saying, "Cherry Pie Kush, just finished trimming it up. An AK47 and Purple Kush cross. Not real dark purple, but nice hard buds. Super fragrant. I've got clones."

"Hey." Jake jumped, excited and energized. "I'm looking for something for my next round in town . . ."

Eddy interrupted, "As long as it cures wet mouth and clear eye."

Cloud gave a snort of laughter. "Wanna go to the deck?" He slapped his chest pocket. "Got a fatty right here." Without hesitation, the three men got up and pressed through the room to the vestibule, just as a rowdy group of overdressed young women in high heels came in, posturing, flirting, as they made their way across the room, eventually settling into a corner table. After Celeste had taken their orders, Jake and Cloud came back inside. When Jake saw Celeste, he pushed through the crowd toward her but was waylaid by Mr. Coors, who was on his way out. Celeste finished her order and secured refuge behind the bar, sunk in the recognition that Jake had no concept of discretion.

Luna had described how the hills and mountains surrounding Garberville were full of every variation on the trim shack and grow scene imaginable. Although the actual miles between scenes and dwellings could be great, it was, she said, entirely connected by rumor and gossip. At the post office in town, there was always a long line as people bought money orders. One after another they stepped forward, taking the rubber band off their wad and counting out hundred-dollar bills—converting to a currency they could use to pay bills by mail. It was an errand everyone in SoHum did and, as Celeste discovered while waiting in line, the post office was gossip central. Celeste imagined the weaving of chatty scraps, the knotting of truths and untruths into the warp and weft of the larger community. She didn't want to be raw material for that fabric.

When, at last, Jake made it across the room and hovered in front of her at the bar, Celeste fluttered behind it, working as fast as she could so she couldn't be pinned down and exposed.

"Cloud's having a party tomorrow night. Wanna go with me?"

"I work."

"Celeste." He leaned his chest on the bar. "Come on."

She lowered her voice, "Don't you get it? We can't."

One of the women from the potstitute table sashayed up behind Jake. She threw her arm up to him and let her hand hang loosely at his shoulder. "Hey, Jakey. Wat up? Goin' to the par-tay tomorrow?"

"Hey." He shook her off and gave Celeste a swift, meaningful glance.

Celeste shoved the metal scoop into the ice bucket, tossed the cubes into the blender, and switched it on, making enough racket to drive a sound barrier between herself and the world. The next time she looked up Jake was gone. She began filling new orders, pouring measured liquors into glasses, when Cloud took a seat in front of her at the bar.

"What can I get for you, Cloud?"

"Actually, I had a question. As you may know, I'm throwing my annual summer party, and I was wondering if, perhaps, I could hire you to bartend?"

"Sorry. I told Delores I'd work."

"We talked to Delores. She has Cynthia working because you weren't scheduled."

"It's in the mountains, all the fucken way up Elk's Peak," Jake said, appearing behind Cloud. "You couldn't find it yourself." He smiled conspiratorially. "I'll have to take you."

"Oh." Celeste stopped what she was doing. "I guess."

※ ※ ※

As the night waned, the crowd at the tavern dwindled. Celeste felt herself slacken with exhaustion. The dining room emptied, and finally the last stragglers in the barroom left. Only Jake remained. As Celeste finished stacking clean glasses, he quietly watched her. Despite Celeste's fatigue, their connection kept her spirit whirling high and fast.

Delores entered the barroom and slumped on a stool, sighing. "Hasn't been this much business in ages. I'm bushed."

"Well, I'm out of here." Celeste hung a bar rag over the sink. "Guess I'm not working tomorrow night."

"No problem." Delores smiled. She looked from Jake to Celeste. "Got it lined up."

As Celeste grabbed her sweater and purse, she noticed

Delores watching her. Flustered, Celeste struggled to get her arm into the bunched-up sleeve of her sweater. Jake came to her side and made an attempt to help, and Celeste knew that her secret had already sprung a leak. Her face grew hot with embarrassment. She rushed out of the barroom unable to meet Delores's eyes, saying good-night hurriedly, Jake still fumbling with her sweater as she went.

Outside in the dirt parking lot, she took in a long breath. She and Jake laced the fingers of their hands together. The night air carried the clean aromatic balm of redwoods, and the sky was dense with radiant stars. Celeste drank in the fresh air; it quenched a deep thirst after her night in the stuffy bar. Jake put his arms around her, and she basked in his embrace; he smelled faintly like nutmeg. It dawned on her that she was starved for physical affection, possibly more than for sex. "So," Celeste whispered, "do you have any S. T. D.s ?"

"No."

"Can I trust you?"

"You already have."

Suddenly the tavern curtain was pulled open, casting a spotlight where they stood together. The light glared, reflecting off Jake's silver truck. Then the curtain closed hastily, and they were shrouded once again by night.

"Oh, shit." Celeste breathed.

"It's all good. No worries." He pulled her tighter.

"No, it's not good. We gotta keep quiet." She ran her hands through his hair. "It's important."

Jake gazed at her, then pulled her earlobe with his fingers and bent to whisper. "Stay at my place tomorrow night after the party."

Celeste's mind swam with possible scenarios that she'd use to explain why she wouldn't be sleeping in her room at the inn. "Can you promise to keep this private?"

Jake put his moist mouth on Celeste's neck and began to explore her clavicle. She had to talk to him about Delores, how she surely knew, and how important it was to be discreet, so no one else would find out. Yet, Celeste's need to smooth her hands under Jake's T-shirt, over his chest, as he worked his way to her cleavage with his mouth became all-consuming. They leaned against his truck, his hand under her dress. It would be so easy to climb into the cab of his truck.

"Wait," she said. "Tomorrow."

He caught his breath. He was a train moving forward at a good clip, and she'd derailed him. He reverberated as he slowed. He took his hands off her in an exaggerated motion. The crotch of his jeans protruded beguilingly.

"Nice," Celeste said, smiling.

Jake stepped away from his truck. "Pick you up at four, at the inn."

"No, no. Not the inn. We have to meet somewhere else."

"In town, then, in back of the grow shop."

"Which one?"

"Humming Hydro."

She was uncomfortable with a spot in town but couldn't think of another place. "Okay," she said, and they hugged briefly, then separated, got in their vehicles, and drove away from the tavern.

⚜ ⚜ ⚜

The next morning at breakfast in the grand dining room, at the same table they'd occupied the day before, Celeste watched happily as the girls ate waffles with syrup and melted butter. Today she was able to be civil to Victor. Her terrible secret was nestled delectably inside her. Initially, her daughters had seemed confused by her changed mood, but they'd relaxed over breakfast. Sophie was recounting stories about their adventures the day before: "I wanted the yellow kayak, but we got the blue one."

"Sophie, it doesn't matter what color the kayak was!" Alexa

was her usual short-tempered self when it came to almost anything Sophie said.

"Well." Sophie crossed her arms over her chest and turned away from Alexa. "I wanted the yellow one," she stated again, as if it were necessary to clarify.

Alexa rolled her eyes. "We know. Jeez."

"Alexa. Be nice . . ." Sunshine fell through the window warming Celeste's shoulders. "So, how far up the river did you go?"

"Probably a few miles," Victor responded. "We got to a spot where a creek joined up with the river." He seemed relieved to be with the woman he thought he knew. Oh, but he doesn't know me, Celeste suppressed a smile.

"We saw ducks!" Sophie nearly jumped out of her chair with excitement. "A mommy duck, and daddy duck, and lots of babies."

"They were cute." Even Alexa had to agree with Sophie's enthusiasm.

"Wow. How lucky." Celeste was pleased to see her daughters in high spirits. "It sounds like you had a really good day."

As Alexa turned to Celeste, her demeanor changed. "You should've come with us, Mom." She looked solemn and intense.

It seemed she was really asking the question: *Why didn't you come?* Alexa would not understand that until Victor told the girls. But not today, Celeste mused, because I have plans. Besides, Celeste rationalized, waiting another day or two, would only extend her daughters' innocence. Their knowledge would only serve to generate questions—probably enough questions to last a lifetime. Celeste put an arm around Alexa and squeezed her. "I had to work. Someday soon I want to go kayaking with you."

"Me too." Sophie said.

"You too." Celeste put her other arm around Sophie.

"And Daddy," Sophie said, nodding assuredly. It was quiet; Sophie looked wide-eyed at Celeste.

Victor broke the silence. "I hope so."

He smiled at Sophie and then looked toward Celeste. The waitress came over. Celeste was grateful for the interruption; it distracted her from the venom building in her gut. The waitress asked Victor if he would like to charge the cost of breakfast to his room. Celeste watched Victor's mouth move. She was anchored in her chair, but she let herself float. Victor spoke to the waitress as Celeste conjured a sense of Jake. His smell and sweet taste. His hands. A sexual buzz ran through her and chased away her irritation. Anxiety melted away. Celeste gazed at the beautiful faces of her daughters, and a sense of gratitude came over her; her daughters were glad to be with their father. They needed him; they had missed him, and now they could begin to reestablish their relationship. Meanwhile, she reflected, I have something for myself, a tonic of sex and passion. Then she thought of Delores. *She knows.* A jagged bolt of fear ran through her.

Victor got up from the table and opened one of the French doors to the patio. One after another, the family of four went out of the dining room into the fresh air. It was sunny and warm, and humid. The girls flitted in front of Victor and Celeste as they walked down the stone stairs to the wide lawn. Victor took Celeste's hand as they crossed the grass. Celeste was taken aback, but it seemed natural. It was easier not to protest. Besides, in that moment she harbored no anger towards him. He smiled at her, and something like a look of relief crossed his face. Could they ever be like sister and brother, she wondered: comfortable in each other's presence when together with their children, staying friendly as they grew older? Victor attempted to help Celeste get seated on the rock wall that led to the bridge. She turned to him and said, "I got it."

He settled next to her, and they watched the girls at the river's edge. Sophie took off her flip-flops and cavorted in the shallows, then pivoted to wave up at her parents. Victor laughed and waved back. Celeste threw a kiss. Far across the lawn, Celeste recognized the young couple who had been sitting at the table next to them during breakfast, strolling arm-in-arm near the river. As she looked toward the couple, she could feel Victor wanting her, and she became aware of the physical void between them as they sat next to one another. It would be natural for a couple to touch each other in some casual way. She would rest her back against his warm chest; he would wrap his arms around her, and they would while away time, conversing and watching the girls play.

"I like your hair the way it is, growing out wild again. Like when we first met." A soft breeze came up and rustled leaves high in the trees. "You look beautiful, Celeste."

She had seen it too. In the mirror this morning, there was a veil of glossiness, a spark lit from within.

A leaf drifted slowly, erratically, down, landing on Victor's head, balancing delicately on his dark hair. Celeste resisted reaching out to brush it off.

Victor leaned in and asked, "Why were you so crazy yesterday?"

Celeste stared at him in disbelief. "Are you kidding?" She shook her head. "You've got some fucking nerve asking me that." Things had been ticking along; she'd been feeling pretty generous. Now she went blank and cold, her happy attitude wiped clean.

"Oh. Okay." Quickly, he pulled away. "It just seems like you're back to yourself today. And hey," he raised his shoulders, "I'm glad."

"I'm sure you are." Celeste took a breath, then spewed out what she'd pondered how to say. "I'm leaving for work early, there's an event tonight that'll go late. I'm gonna crash at the tavern." Lying to him felt so satisfying.

Instantly, Victor's mood changed; his eyes hardened, his back stiffened. They stared at each other. The benevolence bred from familiarity vanished. "You shouldn't be working in a bar. Plus, it's not safe for the girls to be alone at night when you're working."

"What the hell? You're taking care of them."

"You know what I mean."

"I would never leave them if they weren't well taken care of." She took a deep breath, reminding herself to stay calm. "We're not having this discussion." There was a long silence. Then Celeste spoke in the most composed tone she could muster, "When I get back tomorrow, you tell the girls about the baby."

Victor's jaw muscles twitched: he looked away. "I'll tell them tonight."

"No. Victor. No. You wait for me. The girls need me there when you tell them. It's really important." Victor turned and stared at her. "Do what's right for them," she said. "Victor, I'll be back tomorrow night. Tell them then."

mushrooms

The dirt path crunched underfoot. A brief early-morning rainstorm followed by afternoon heat had created a dry mud crust. "I love that just-rained smell," Celeste exclaimed, breathing in the musky, fresh air.

"Yeah, but rain can fucken mold our plants," Jake responded.

"Oh," Celeste murmured, still with a smile on her face. Even the mugginess and what it would do to her hair didn't bother her. Being alone with Jake made her feel jubilant.

As they got further down the hill, she could see the tops of structures, clustered buildings with sloping tin roofs that reminded her of shanty towns she'd seen in Mexico. Soon, a clamor of voices came from below. She looked down and saw several men trying to move a heavy object with much grunting and cursing.

"Hey," Jake yelled to them, "whadda ya doin' with that fucken generator?"

Celeste could make out the indigo shapes on the top of Cloud's shaved head.

Cloud hollered up. "Jake! Dude, get down here, the big genny crapped out." Jake ran down the hill, leaping the last few steps cut into the dirt.

When Celeste got to the bottom of the path, she took it in: the place, the faces of the men—some of whom she knew from the bar and others who were new to her, all young twenty-somethings, except Cloud, who was probably in his thirties. Jake had become part of the huddle, absorbed into the group which hovered over a large block of metal with dirty, oily gears. The men talked excitedly and all at once, in a focused frenzy around the machine like wasps buzzing a piece of meat.

The ledge she stood on was cut into the steep mountain and cleared of the surrounding forest. There wasn't a proper house in sight, just a jumble of connected shacks, large and small, clinging to the mountainside. Celeste was disappointed by the squalid aspect of the place and felt uncomfortable in the midst of the alien, masculine group.

"Hi." The screen door slammed, and a sweet-faced girl emerged. She approached with her hand extended. "I'm Pippin. You Celeste?"

"Yes." Thankful for her courtesy, Celeste realized, looking more closely at Pippin, that she wasn't a girl, but a slight, pixyish woman. At first, Celeste thought she wore a shirt with printed sleeves, but soon realized tattoos completely covered the skin of Pippin's arms. She also had a silver bullring through her nose and large plugs in her earlobes. Still, her delicate, symmetrical features read as girl-next-door pretty.

Pippin gestured. "This way."

Celeste followed her inside and found herself on a landing with surprisingly high ceilings and a view of rooms without walls, larger and smaller, on different levels and connected by flights of stairs. She had the impression that she was looking at a series of tree-house platforms, each painted a different bright color. The stairs that connected the levels had no railings. Celeste felt as if she was inside a colored Escher image, disjointed and dangerous. It was dizzying and dream-like, with stairs going and coming. Before she could stop herself, Celeste said, "Interesting place." Embarrassed by her euphemism for "I don't know what to make of it," she added, "It's much bigger inside than it looks from the outside."

"Yeah." Pippin had gone into the kitchen, which was on the same level as the entrance.

"Who designed it?"

"Well, Cloud. But I wouldn't say he designed it; more like he grew it." Pippin was bending over, pulling bottles of liquor from a box.

"Is that where the bar will be?" Celeste asked.

"No." Pippin put the liquor bottles into a battered wooden crate on the bright turquoise counter top. "Cloud wants the bar outside. We gotta talk to him about it." Pippin had a soft little-girl voice. "The main genny broke, the one for the DJ and the light show, so Cloud's spun. He's freaking."

In a small, brightly framed mirror on the far kitchen wall. Celeste glimpsed her distant reflection. She was shocked by how straight, old, and out of place she appeared in her sub-urban-looking silk tank top and jeans. She wanted out, now. But she didn't have her own car and wouldn't have been able to find her way down the mountain by herself anyway. She drew in a deep breath and then exhaled, letting her shoulders drop. "How can I help?" she asked.

"Ummm." Pippin turned toward Celeste and pushed a clump of long chestnut-colored hair out of her face. "Let's see . . ."

"Mommm."

"What, Zarian?" Pippin replied.

Celeste walked to the end of the kitchen where a boy about Sophie's age sat at a table covered with colored pencils and paper. The table was one level above the kitchen, connected by a short flight of stairs.

"I'm hungry," he moaned.

"Just a minute," said Pippin. "I'll make a PB & J."

Celeste was stunned to learn Pippin was a mother. She looked so much like a girl. "I'd never guess you had a child," Celeste blurted out.

"I've got a twelve-year-old son too."

"You're kidding." Celeste stared at Pippin, and, despite herself, continued to say what she knew she shouldn't. "How old were you when you had your first?" Immediately she followed up. "Sorry, it's not polite to ask."

Pippin shrugged. "It's okay." She took a jar of peanut butter from the open shelf. "I'm used to it, really." She looked toward Celeste. "I was fifteen."

"Oh," Celeste said. "Couldn't have been easy."

"No. But it would've helped if my father wasn't such an asshole."

"Yeah, well, I know about asshole fathers. You know, Pippin, you look like you're barely twenty."

"Oh, I know, believe me, I know." Pippin nodded.

Celeste looked again at the boy. He reflected his mother's fine features. Celeste waved up to him.

"Honestly," Pippin said, "I'd rather have you ask than look at me funny, which is what most people do." She glanced up from spreading peanut butter. "You have kids?"

"Two girls. Thirteen and seven."

Pippin smiled. "Funny, our kids are about the same ages."

Celeste wondered why in Pippin's mind that would be funny. Still, Celeste liked her. She came across as genuine and smart: a graduate of the school-of-hard-knocks, but with a charming sweetness.

Clomping sounds from the level below came up unseen stairs. Celeste watched as a pink head of hair emerged from a cut-out in the floor, followed incrementally by the rest of the person. "Hi, Celeste."

It took a moment to recognize Deja, from the trim shack. "You look so different!"

Deja pointed to her hair. "I went pink!"

"What d'ya think?" Pippin asked from the kitchen. "We did it this morning."

Deja's bright hair topped her plump, young body which was squeezed into a short, shimmering dress, with purple leggings and clogs. "Nice," said Celeste.

"Thanks. So, I found the twinkle lights." Deja dumped two decaying cardboard boxes on the entry floor.

"That's the schizzle." Pippin clapped her hands together. "Can't believe you found 'em."

"Mommy," Pippin's son wailed.

"Coming . . ." Pippin slapped the sandwich on a plate and bounded up the stairs.

"What a mess," Deja said, pulling at the tangle of wires.

"Can I help?" Celeste asked. "I don't know what I should be doing."

"No one knows," said Deja. "And there'll be like a hundred people here in a few hours."

"A hundred people?" Celeste couldn't imagine where a hundred people would fit, and how that many people could negotiate the tortured, crazy, random-seeming roads required to arrive at Cloud's property.

"Last year it was more."

"Might be less than last year," Pippin interjected from the kitchen. "Light deps are being harvested, so that eliminates some of the tribe. The party's later in summer than usual. Still, I think we're okay."

"Fuck," Deja said, as she reached her hand into a box and pulled up a mass of jumbled-up twinkle lights.

"Let me sort through that," Celeste said.

"Awesome. Thanks. Supposed to be more boxes of lights downstairs." Deja hurried off.

Celeste looked around for a place to get comfortable, then sat on the dirty floor and began to untangle strands of lights. Occasionally, Deja would reappear with a new box and announce enthusiastically that things were coming together and that Celeste was progressing nicely. Then she would disappear again, going up or down, with that shock of pink hair always the first or last thing seen. Meanwhile, Pippin worked in the kitchen. She chopped garlic on a cutting board and threw it into a bowl.

"What're you making, Pippin?"

"Biggest batch of hummus ever. Except I need the genny for the food processor to grind it up. So they better fucking fix it."

"Pippin, are you and Cloud together?"

"Almost two years."

"But he's not Zarian's father?"

"No. Both my boys have different dads."

By the time Celeste was done uncoiling wires, she'd heard the story of how Pippin had become a tattoo artist and learned intimate details about the two men who had fathered her sons. Celeste draped the last strand of lights across a cardboard box. Her hands were grimy. She felt itchy from the dust and spiders—some dead and some alive—that were in the boxes. She brushed the grunge off her jeans, and went to the kitchen sink to wash up. Just then, Jake burst through the door.

"Fucken fixed!" he yelled buoyantly.

"Oh, my shit!" exclaimed Pippin. "So we can do the DJ station and the lights?"

"Yep." He smiled. "On it."

"That was close," Pippin said.

Jake ambled toward Celeste as she stood washing her hands at the sink. He leaned in, grabbed her, and bent her back for a kiss. She practically jumped out of his arms as Pippin, near them at the turquoise counter, looked on. Celeste's face felt hot—it was probably bright red. She rushed out of the screen door, wiping her hands on her dirty jeans.

Outside, the herd of men hovered over the grumbling, grimy generator. They were clinking beer bottles, congratulating themselves, emitting wisps of pot smoke, but now all their eyes swiveled toward Celeste. Jake opened the screen door. She scanned the flat strip of land for a place to hide, the yard afforded no privacy. She eyed the slope of forest, but took off in the direction of a stacked wood pile at the far end of the ledge. Jake caught up to her as she sat down on a tree stump. "You can't be so public, Jake."

"These are my fucken friends."

"But don't you see?" Celeste pleaded, "There'll be gossip."

"What's the difference? They know anyway."

Celeste's guts felt like they might fall out of her body into the dirt. "Why do they know?"

"Cloud guessed the other night." Jake threw up his arms. "Big fucken deal."

They looked at each other. It was so naïve of me, she thought, to believe I could have a lover, this lover, and keep it secret. She kicked the dirt. The wind had been knocked out of her, she struggled to breathe. *Everyone will know. Tom will know. Luna will know. What will they think of me?* And now she and Jake were having a quarrel, practically within hearing distance of his friends. She was making a spectacle of herself. Jake placed his hand on her shoulder. Broken rocks rolled unevenly under the sole of her sandal. "Where's the bar going to be?" she asked.

Jake laughed. He pulled her up and pressed his body into hers. She could feel his crowd watching—all those male eyes. Luna and Tom had been so good to her and her daughters. Celeste pushed away from Jake impulsively, even as she wished she hadn't.

He stepped back, looking at her quizzically.

"Look, even if everyone knows, I'm uncomfortable. You know . . ." She tipped her head in the direction of the men, took a gulp of air and surveyed the blanket of treetops covering the mountains around them. "I was with your dad."

"Yeah, I know." He turned and began walking toward the house.

"Wait."

He swiveled and stared back at her. Separated by distance, he seemed to be inspecting her, possibly seeing her clearly for the first time, maybe finding some unpleasant explanation for her behavior. He turned again, yelling as he walked away, "I'll find out where Cloud wants the bar."

✺ ✺ ✺

People began arriving as twilight passed into night. Celeste felt tense and out of place. She was there to work; the others knew one another, and were socializing and carousing. She was the stranger, the hired help, taking orders and pouring drinks, standing in the dirt, laboring outside in the dark. It was degrading in a way that working at the tavern had never been. As she poured and mixed, poured and mixed, she ruminated despairingly on how she'd gotten herself into this situation. How had she gone from being a teacher in the city to bartending on a plastic table in this far-flung spot on a mountainside. And now she was surely the target of gossip. She needed to escape. Again.

Even in the open air the pot smoke was thick, an amorphous curtain making everything appear spooky and unreal. Like most of her perplexing dreams lately, it all seemed impossible to make sense of. Her recent dream of transformation into a furry being haunted her. Had she become that woolly monster by following her base animal instincts?

A familiar, humiliating, suffocating, sense of dread spread over her as people crushed in thickly around the bar table. She was pouring nonstop, trying to keep up. The party was in full sway. Night had morphed the place; small lights winked in the trees tracing the path up the hill, and a light show of colors and distorted images beamed from the house windows into the dense forest beyond. The ground shook with the pulse of the music. Celeste glanced at her glass tip jar—it was filling up. She could see a hundred-dollar bill amongst the jumble of bills and other things, buds and some small dried mushrooms, some of which she'd eaten. Eddy had dropped the mushrooms in her jar, assuring her they were a "soft trip." She'd been trying to ignore him as he stood next to her, where she worked behind the table. For an interminable amount of time, he'd been making dull remarks and bad jokes, attempting to hit on her. But when he showed her a small plastic bag of *cubensis* mushrooms, she took notice.

Although it had been years since she'd tripped, Celeste hadn't forgotten the high from psilocybin—a happy, airy quality she loved. She and her high-school friend, Becca, would enlist someone with a car to drive along Pacific Coast Highway, then up into the sage-scented canyon to Topanga State Park to trip. Her memories of those times were blissful: lolling in fragrant meadows, balancing in the branches of scrub oaks, laughing and laughing. *A soft trip.* She needed to take a trip away from her current reality. So, when Eddy unclenched his hand letting a shower of little shrooms drift down into her jar, she waited until he wandered away, and then—*fuck it*—the dry mushrooms she pulled out tasted like bitter dust, and made her want to gag, yet seemed as innocuous as a wafer.

She hadn't seen Jake since he'd set up the bar. It seemed at least a couple hours had passed since then. Suddenly full of regret about the fierce—and now, it seemed, unnecessary—scene she'd made, she realized with stark certainty that all she really wanted was to be held and caressed by Jake.

The crowd around the table was a rising flood. Most of the party-goers seemed to be in their twenties. Only a few people were her age or older. A tattooed, bare-chested, nipple-pierced man was waiting for her to make him a Margarita. He was wearing a black-and-white, fuzzy hat that looked like a skunk sitting on his head, complete with a long fluffy tail hanging down his back.

Celeste's stomach was upset, and she wondered if it was from the mushrooms she'd eaten. Being slightly nauseated made it hard for her to concentrate and the portions of alcohol she was mixing were becoming more and more inexact. Celeste marveled at the liquor as it poured into the shaker in a viscous, thick stream. Contained inside the flow she saw glittering reflections of ambient light and color.

And then Jake was there. She could feel his presence before

she looked up and saw him. The crowd around them was chatting riotously and seemed to undulate. But Jake looked as peaceful as a clear lake. He stood in the center of the throng, yet somehow distinct, from the others. His smooth skin and strong jawline were lit by the shifting light show. He stared at her. Immediately she wanted to open her hands and fly to him, dropping everything—the plastic cup she held in one hand and the canted cocktail shaker in the other. She wanted to be enveloped by him.

"I'm sorry," she said, apparently loud enough to seize the attention of the raucous crowd around the table bar. The revelry quieted. The motley assortment of thirsty young party-goers, tattooed, pierced, sporting clothes that were a combination of circus and gangster, seemed to turn toward her in unison. She kept her eyes on Jake, but was aware of the crowd slowly drawing its focus from her to him, in a kind of exaggerated kabuki motion. Then Jake moved decisively. He cleaved through the pack and went behind the bar, took the shaker and cup out of her hands and placed them on the table. He tucked her tip jar under one arm, put his other arm around her, turned to the man in the skunk cap and said, "Make your own fucken drink." Knit together, she and Jake glided around the table through the parting crowd.

In front of them, a throng of dancing bodies threw animated shadows against the colored lights streaming from the windows and door of the house. As they made their way through the swarm, Celeste turned to look behind her. Through silhouettes of moving figures she saw the crowd pouncing brutally on the bar table as if it were fresh kill. She turned back to look at Jake. His form was surrounded by a trembling glow, like the air above a fire.

She pointed to the orange luminance over his head. "Wow," she said, giggling.

"What?"

"You glow."

"Okay . . ."

"I ate some shrooms."

"How many?" he asked.

"Some. Some of those." She pointed to the remaining mushrooms floating in her tip jar. Jake swept the jar in front of him and shook it, examining its contents.

"You're gonna have some fucken fun." He smiled.

Celeste nodded. Sounds and sights were amplified, naked, and pristinely clear, as if layers of dulling screens had been ripped away. There was a rainbow-like quality of color and light to everything she saw. Jake's voice was part of the music, part of the bass rhythm. Sounds moved around her freely, and then, very clearly, she understood his words, "Wanna go inside and dance?"

"Yes." She raised herself up on tiptoes and stretched her neck toward him. It seemed a great distance. He put an arm around her and swallowed her in an embrace, and a kiss, which she felt both as a feather and a tornado. Even with eyes closed, she saw colors and shapes, rose-pink to iridescent blue, pearlescent white to raw sienna, colors that perfectly expressed the language of her emotions, precisely displaying her excitement and relief at being with Jake again. She found the softness at the inside of his lips with her tongue. *Alizarin crimson.* Their mouths were connected and moving. *Iridescent pink.* Centuries passed, and they stood kissing and learning.

A voice near them echoed metallically, speaking Jake's name. Jake lifted his head and responded. Cloud was next to them, holding an elaborate bottle filled with green liquid, talking and smiling good-naturedly. The distorted choir of voices was funny. Celeste said, "Hi, Cloud," and when she spoke his name she had to laugh because she was speaking in perfect time with the pounding beat, and she also understood that Cloud's name fit him perfectly. Jake took her hand, and they followed Cloud in the direction of the house. She looked up at the stars in the vast, black sky that sparkled and breathed in and out. When they stepped inside the pulsing, expanding and contracting house, the music seemed fused with the walls and the floor. Jake took a plastic bottle of water from a glowing tub in the kitchen and put her tip jar somewhere unseen. They drifted down stairs, which floated off the lit dance floor.

Revelers played conga drums in a circle around dancers. The drum beat and the rhythm from the DJ booth merged and surged into a bright current that coursed through Celeste's sandals and entered her bloodstream. Jake led her through the bouncing, jostling center of the dancers, then out towards the edge of the crowd. Celeste took in the writhing arms, legs and hands, and the flashing, intermittent lights. Jake opened the water bottle and handed it to Celeste. She pressed the bottle to her lips and drank.

Pippin was next to her, smiling. "Having fun?" she asked. Celeste laughed and nodded. Deja was there, pink hair sticking out in crazy spokes of electric energy. Realizing she had to pee, Celeste asked Pippin where the bathroom was, but her voice was drowned out by the music. Pippin turned her head, angling her ear up toward Celeste, who found herself immersed pleasurably in Pippin's long thick forest of chestnut hair. Then Pippin was nodding, and Celeste knew she'd understood. Cupping her hands around her mouth, Pippin yelled into Celeste's ear. "I'll show you my secret place. Otherwise you gotta hike up to the Porta-Potty where the cars are." Pippin pointed toward a door, which seemed to have just appeared at the opposite end of the dance floor. Celeste was certain it hadn't existed before. The concept of secret doors appearing out of nowhere made Celeste laugh. Pippin moved into the crush. There was an impenetrable barrier of people between where they were and their destination: *the magic door*.

Celeste felt a hand on her arm. It was Jake. He spoke loudly in her ear. "Hey, where ya goin'?"

She turned toward him and, finding his ear, answered, "To pee." Celeste waited until a kiss was placed on her lips, just as she believed it would be. Jake was smiling. Celeste turned back to see Pippin being swallowed by the crowd. She swam through the mass and arrived just as Pippin opened the door, and crossed the threshold. Deja was there too, with her mesmerizing, vibrating pink halo, an electric-pink Medusa. Celeste must have stared at Deja's hair for too long because Deja was asking her if everything was okay. She nodded her head up and down, up and down, but there was some commotion which Celeste was only vaguely aware of at first, being so fascinated by the pink-hair-electricity manifestation.

"Get the fuck outta here, shitweasels." Pippin screamed in her high little-girl voice at a man and woman entangled on the bed. "Go find somewhere else to fuck. This is my bed."

The couple struggled out of the bed reluctantly and slunk out of the room.

"I hate that. Every time we have a party some dumb asses try to do it on my bed."

Celeste started to feel strange and fearful from the yelling. The unhappy people who'd been banished seemed to remain in the room as gloomy gray ghosts.

Pippin pulled up the sheets; Deja was on the other side of the bed helping her. "Cloud told me Celeste's on shrooms," Pippin said to Deja from across the bed.

"Oh, that explains it." Deja snickered. "She's staring at my hair." Deja struck a pin-up pose and fluffed up her hair.

"I really like it," Celeste said. "I really love it." she said again, this time throwing her arms out. Both Pippin and Deja laughed, and Celeste joined them. Their chorus of laughter trilled, echoed, and elongated, washing over Celeste in waves of cleansing euphoric happiness.

"You wanna pee?" Pippin finished smoothing the bedcovers. She slid open a glass door and stepped out on a wood deck. "I go out here." Deja and Celeste followed her. The air outside was fresh and tangible. Celeste felt she could reach out and grab it, or take a bite. There were sounds of people talking and partying above them, from the direction of the dirt yard.

"Be careful, this deck has no railing. It's a long drop, like twenty feet." Pippin was positioning herself at the end of the deck, turning around to face the bedroom while pulling her shorts down. "I just pee off the edge." She hung her butt over the cantilevered deck and began to pee, nothing between her ass and the great distance below. Deja did the same.

Celeste stood watching them, then turned around and pulled down her jeans and panties. With a great sense of relief, she peed and then peed some more. She could hear distant splashes as their three concurrent streams hit ground. "So far away," Celeste said, giggling.

"Yeah," Pippin responded. Celeste glanced up at Pippin as she stood up. Tattoos of pink and red roses covered the skin of her hip; it looked like she was wearing lingerie.

"So pretty," Celeste said. As Celeste watched, the pink roses split into little blocks, like mosaics, and then buzzed back together.

"Thanks," Pippin said.

Celeste pulled up her panties and then her jeans. Wishing she had toilet paper made her laugh at the futility of wishing that she had toilet paper. As she zipped up her jeans, she became entranced at the miraculous zipper and its animated interlocking metal teeth. There was some background noise of whooping and yelling coming from the direction of the dirt yard overlooking them. Pippin waved upwards and took a bow. Celeste saw a line of people, silhouettes, gathered above them on the yard. She recognized the table where she had worked the bar earlier in the evening. It stood abandoned, covered in empty bottles and unidentifiable debris.

Pippin, Deja, and Celeste faced the yelling and clapping crowd above them.

"Just smile and wave," Pippin said nonchalantly. "The

deck is still better than the outhouse, even if you do have an audience. It's soooo much better than the Porta-Potty. I hate the Porta-Potty."

Deja laughed. "Baby, there ain't nothin' better than a flush toilet."

"Yeah, you a spoiled bitch," Pippin said, and wagged her butt at Deja. Pippin looked at Celeste, "Feel better?"

"Much better," Celeste said. "Thank you."

"If you were drunk, I wouldn't have brought you out to my deck. Deja, remember when Sean broke his leg?"

Deja nodded.

Pippin pointed off the deck, down into the abyss. "Pissing right here, totally drunk. It took Cloud like two hours just to get him up the mountain so we could take him to the hospital."

Celeste shivered and peered down into the void.

"Gnarly, dude," Deja said. "Let's go back."

Celeste followed Pippin and Deja as they opened the door of the bedroom and threaded their way back through the throng, toward the drummers. It seemed to Celeste that they'd been away for hours and hours, days even, *journeying* . . .

The music, muted in the bedroom, now seemed too amplified. Celeste experienced the loud sound as if it were texture, scratchy and rough and too strong against her sensitive skin. She saw Jake dancing, light was attracted to him. He seemed to be riding the music, moving exquisitely among other average bodies. When he saw her he extended his arms and pulled her toward him.

Celeste realized that they were linked in ways that hadn't been obvious to her before. She suddenly understood their interconnectedness clearly, the power of it.

Lights were boiling and warping around her as she moved with Jake, in sync with the reverberation that came up through the floor, into her gut, and out through her fingertips. Without inhibitions, she was free and euphoric. Jake reached around her, drawing her close. Celeste felt an electric charge pass from where his hand touched her spine. The charge climbed each of her vertebrae, spread through her neck at its axis, and passed into her mouth which opened willingly, as she accepted him in his true form: *Tom.* In a revelatory moment, Celeste understood that everything expanded to meet everything else; she was able to turn the pages of time backwards and forwards. In Jake's face she saw a tender glow alive and swirling in his cheekbones. His were the same prismatic green eyes that loved her when she was a teenager. *It's you.* Jake bent to her, and his breath mixed with hers as their lips brushed together. They were connected by a never-ending chain.

skunk twins

The truck heaved, descending the mountain on a maze of dirt roads, everything pitch black except the bouncing twin beams of the headlights. Psilocybin swam through her system, but slowly now, like a fish would swim through muddy water. Sights and sounds were heightened and fizzy, but she'd lost the swiftness, the ease, the primal magic. It seemed a great loss, like the death of a loved one. She regretted not eating every one of the mushrooms in the jar.

At Bear Ridge Road, the slope began to level out and Jake steered the truck onto asphalt. "Oh, so smooth," he said. They sailed, and Celeste edged closer to him, imagining they were flying. The truck—so high off the ground, so loud, with a vague but pervasive diesel stink—seemed more airplane than automobile. Out the window, she could almost see the tops of clouds in a night sky.

"Still feeling the shrooms?"

"A little."

Celeste hummed as they whizzed by county signs marked "HUM." Jake turned hard onto another potholed dirt road. "Almost there," he said. In the jittering headlights, Celeste saw the junk pile and wrecked cars and knew where they were. Soon the pack of dogs rushed the truck. The fierce barking faded behind them as they turned up the narrow road hemmed in on either side by huckleberry bushes.

Jake accelerated up the hill, when suddenly, flying at them from out of a blind curve, a flash of spokes—a motorcycle airborne. Two faces, a driver and a rider, seemed to hover in the truck lights, fully illuminated, before they careened away.

Jake jerked the truck to the side of the road, spraying gravel, dipping down into a ditch with the headlights shining at a wonky angle into the dense underbrush. He pulled the emergency brake, which made a squealing noise. A dust cloud billowed.

In a strange lull, the pulsing of the engine felt like a heartbeat. Splayed, shadowed forms of the boys lay on the road, one still attached to the downed motorcycle. Jake threw open his door and leapt out of the truck. Celeste could see that the boys were moving. She slid to the driver's side; clambered out of the cab, and jumped into the gritty fog of dust. Jake bounded to the boy on the ground and reached out to him. The boy grasped Jake's hand and drew himself up. The other boy tussled with the motorcycle in the dirt and managed to stand, still straddling it.

"You all right?" Jake asked, letting go of the boy's hand.

The boy bent over, brushing off his ripped pants. "Yeah," he replied.

When the boy straightened, he looked toward Celeste—his eyes lidless and reptilian, a cold white-blue. Celeste stepped away, stunned. She tried to remind herself that she'd done mushrooms—she was seeing things that weren't there. From behind her, the other boy spoke. She turned, and a shiver went through her. They were identical, with eerie, pale blue, unblinking eyes that floated oddly in the night, weirdly disembodied.

Jake was shouting, waving his arms. "What in the fuck! Stop driving so fucken fast on this road. Didn't you see the headlights? Think for one fucken minute." Both boys had the same buzzed light hair. Jake went toward the motorcycle; at first Celeste thought he was going to attack it, but he examined its front wheel, touching it gently, as he continued to rant, "You're gonna get yourselves killed!"

The boys stared vacantly as Jake yelled. Then the boy on the motorcycle responded, slowly, in an uneven, sluggish tone, "Didn't think no one was out this time of night."

"Like four in the morning," the other boy said, with the same disjointed intonation as the first. When he stopped speaking, both boys shifted their gaze to Celeste, in perfect sync. She felt their frozen eyes on her and recoiled. She almost screamed.

Jake stepped protectively in front of her. "Listen," he bellowed, "Doesn't fucken matter what time. You can't drive that fast. You hear me?"

Celeste touched the back of Jake's shoulder. He turned sharply as if he'd forgotten who was behind him. She tipped her head toward the truck. He stared blankly at her, and then turned back to the boys, leaning menacingly over the one nearest him. "No more of this shit. Got it?"

The boy nodded slowly and Celeste wondered if he was just mocking Jake. The other boy didn't move.

Jake walked back to the truck, helped Celeste up into the cab, then climbed into the driver's seat and slammed the door. They sat in silence for a moment, watching. The boy who was thrown off the motorcycle remounted behind the other one, who then kicked his leg to start the motor. Celeste could see, despite the dim light a dark stain spreading around the boy's knee where his pants had ripped.

Jake shook his head glumly. He let out a long sigh, released the emergency brake and rumbled the truck forward through the dense brush, up out of the ditch. They passed the sputtering motorcycle and continued up the road.

"The twins?" Celeste asked.

"Skunk Twins. We paid big money for an easement through that junk pile. Been nothing but hell. Every one of 'em, dysfunctional fuckheads. Tweakers and thieves. Luna's always trying to help 'em out. Dad and I keep telling her: 'Stay away. There's something wrong there.'"

"She stopped in at that Winnebago to see them," Celeste said.

Jake shook his head. "She shouldn't. We try to tell her."

Just kids, Celeste told herself, yet she couldn't shake the creepiness of those two sets of reptilian eyes.

"They ride that fucken motorcycle every night. Way too fast, lose control on the curves. They're everywhere they shouldn't be. I caught them up on my land more than a few times."

"Where are their mom and dad?"

"Never knew the dad. Mom was a tweaker. Died when they were little—OD'd. Never got prenatal care. Luna kept going to their land, to the old house, trying to help when their mom was pregnant with 'em. Dumb, dumb, dumb. Or scared. Never took the help. Then one time, Broudy, the grandfather, came out to Luna's car with a shotgun, told her to get off his property. When Dad found out, he wouldn't let Luna go anymore. And she listened. Like a month later, one night, Dad, me, and Luna were eating dinner in the cabin—I was still a kid. Anyway, their mom comes banging at the door, in labor and, like, crazy. Screaming and swearing shit. Luna and Dad took her to the hospital in town. Thing is, Luna was pregnant with Jonah. Right there in the hospital, Luna went into labor, early. Anyway, Dad took her home, she had her home birth, and, ya know, like Jonah was perfect. But it turned out, Jonah and the twins ended up being born the same day. Same birthday. Just freaky. Maybe that's why Luna won't give up on them. She thinks they're linked somehow. Or like she has some kind of responsibility."

Celeste knew she should feel empathy for the twins, it was a tragic story. Instead, revulsion swirled in her, the same way it had when she looked at the boys' faces. Even at their young age, they seemed ruined.

Jake drove up to the locked gate, got out, opened it, drove through, then went back to lock it up. Back to bouncing along the dirt road, Celeste asked, "Does the gate keep those boys out?"

He looked her way. "Wish it could."

※ ※ ※

Jake's house was cramped and stuffy. She went to open the French doors in the kitchen and walked onto the large deck. Outside, the stars were beautiful, brilliant and endless, yet Celeste wanted to see the stars as she had before: breathing in and out. She could almost conjure it up if she concentrated, but it was more memory than miraculous vision as it had been earlier in the evening. Seeing those twin devil eyes—whether a delusion or not—had sucked the left-over marrow out of her delicious high.

Jake joined her on the deck, clapping a hand on her ass. "Come here." She leaned into his body, resting the side of her face against his warm chest. His heart was beating fast. *All he wants is to rut.* She remembered her revelation that conflated Jake with Tom. Now she couldn't feel it. Here, at his place, she was confronted with the things that defined him: the truck, the bachelor pad, the pit bull that waited anxiously for his return. The only thing missing was the potstitute girlfriend with bolt-ons—Luna had confirmed Harmony's breast augmentation. *He's got me instead.*

"Know what I'd love?"

"What?" He nuzzled her neck.

"A shower."

"Oh." He straightened up. "Okay."

"And something to drink. Maybe something to eat."

"Uh, don't know what I have . . ." They went into the kitchen.

A quick hard fuck would suit him just fine. It was the only intimacy they'd shared. And Celeste could still get a thrill thinking about their encounter in the tavern, but it had been spontaneous. Here, an uncomfortable sense of expectation penned her in and an obstinate rebelliousness was brewing inside her. She hated the idea that something, especially something sexual, was expected of her.

"I'll be back," she said. Going to the back of the house, she stood in the hallway and poked her head in the airless bedroom. She switched on the overhead light, a bare bulb in the ceiling. The room was just big enough for the bed under one small, closed window. Celeste sensed Harmony's presence in every crevice. After taking a quick shower, she stood in the bedroom again, dripping wet and staring into the closet. "Can I wear this Hawaiian shirt?" she called out. It was the only shirt hanging in the closet.

"Sure." Jake responded. "Luna gave it to me. Never worn it."

Celeste draped the shirt over her shoulders; it was soft against her damp skin. "It's nice," she said, although Jake couldn't hear her. Looking around the room, she decided definitively that she wouldn't sleep, let alone have sex in this room. As she came into the kitchen, Jake was opening his second bottle of beer.

"You think we could get that mattress out on the deck?" she asked. A bong was on the kitchen table and the room was filled with smoke.

"What? Why?" Jake gave her a long, hard look.

"So we can sleep outside, under the stars."

"Man, you're a lot of fucken trouble." He rocked his head from side to side. "Ya know that?"

"It's so nice outside, in the fresh air."

"Right." He put his beer down with a thud and went into the bedroom. She followed him, and together they dragged the unruly mattress outside, letting it flop on the deck under the branches of a large oak. Celeste tried to adjust the position slightly with her foot; the mattress didn't budge.

Jake gave her the look again. "Where do you want it?"

"A little to the left."

He pushed it slightly to the side.

"Thanks, Jake."

He shrugged his shoulders. "Want a beer?"

"Something. I want something." They went to the kitchen, and he opened the door of the small propane refrigerator and gestured at its contents. "Help yourself." Inside the fridge were a few bottles of beer, another six-pack, an open container of half-and-half and a gleaming white Styrofoam to-go container. She didn't want to know what was in that.

Celeste pushed the fridge door closed. "I see you entertain often." She opened the freezer. "Popsicles!" After clapping her hands together, she took a Popsicle out of the box, unwrapping the orange and red confection. "Perfect." Celeste leaned against the kitchen counter, letting the cold sweetness flood her mouth.

"Looks good," he said. The sugar revived her. When the Popsicle came out of her mouth, its bright swirling colors receded behind a white veil of frost, and her mouth was pleasantly numbed. Jake leaned toward her, they kissed, a blend of beer and sugar.

Jake broke away. "You're so cold."

"But sweet, right?"

He moved closer.

"Almost done."

He sighed and reached for his beer, draining it in one long gulp. His hand—just like his father's—was so large it almost enveloped the brown bottle. Celeste waited for him to place the bottle on the counter, then she took his hand, turned it palm up and squished what was left of the Popsicle inside the cup of his palm. She sipped the icy bits in the puddle of pink, and sucked the extra drips trickling down his fingers.

"I wanna fuck you," Jake said.

"You fuck me, and I'll fuck you."

Jake hoisted her up onto the kitchen counter and pulled off his T-shirt and jeans. Soon, she felt the push and plunge; a rooted buzz ran through her. Her head fell back. Jake pulled away and thrust again. She grabbed him, pulling him as close as possible—melding—she wanted to stay filled up and still. It felt exactly right. For a moment they stayed that way, drawn in deeply, quiet and merged on the outside, pulsing on the inside. Then Jake pulled back to plunge again.

"Stop moving," Celeste said. "Can we go slow?"

"What?" He sounded confused. "Stop?"

Celeste kissed Jake's ear. "It felt so good to be motionless like that."

Jake seemed stunned, and unsure. The feeling she craved slipped away, her rapture dissolved. "It's okay, Jake." Self-consciousness took her away; she tried to play catch-up to her body, but it was too late. Jake pushed forward, his speed increased. His back sweating and his breathing changed. Celeste attempted to put her mind to sleep as Jake began to come. He groaned and panted, and, finally out of breath, quieted.

✹ ✹ ✹

In the morning, she opened her eyes to sunlit oak leaves, forming a collage of light and dark green that looked like stained glass. Turning on her side, she scrunched the pillow under her neck and sank back into sleep. When she opened her eyes again, the sun was blinding. She squeezed her eyes shut and bright amorphous shapes drifted behind her lids. She threw her arm out next to her; Jake was definitely not there. Bravely facing the glaring day, she sat up.

"Coffee?" Jake's voice carried out from the kitchen.

"I'd love some," she shouted back, and got up to go to the house.

Jake was by the stove lighting a burner. He looked up at her.

"Good morning," Celeste said, as she migrated through the kitchen, to the bathroom. When she returned, she sat down and assessed her state of being: woozy and light-headed, not quite uncomfortable. There was that peculiar unfastened feeling of sleep deprivation. Jake poured coffee into a cup and brought it to her at the table.

"You're so sweet." She smiled. "How long have you been up?"

"A couple of hours. I didn't know if I should wake you."

Celeste stirred her coffee. "Why?" She registered that Jake looked a little stressed.

"I talked to Delores."

Celeste tried to make the connection; why would he wake her because Delores called?

"About what?" she asked.

"There were some calls on my voicemail from her. I didn't listen till this morning." Jake sat next to her. An uncomfortable heaviness settled. "What did Delores say?"

"Victor called . . ."

Celeste's body became taut, panic rose in her. Hearing Victor's name, hearing about an intersection between Delores and Victor, was shockingly wrong. Everything about it. She stood up, wanting to rip her way out of how blind she felt. Suddenly, Celeste realized she hadn't checked her cell phone since . . . since the hotel yesterday. "What happened?"

"Alexa's sick."

"Sick? How sick?"

"Delores said to tell you that Alexa's sick." Jake shrugged. "That's all I know."

Celeste ran to the bathroom. She couldn't remember where she'd left her bag. It wasn't there. She ran back to the living room and saw it on the couch; she had no memory of how it got there. Frantically, she rummaged through her purse. Eventually finding her phone, she pulled it out and turned it on. "Where is the best reception?"

"Left side of the deck. Hold your arm up."

In the harsh sunlight, she tried Victor's cell number. She raised her arm and stared down at the Hawaiian shirt she was wearing. A gift to Jake from Luna. The call dropped. She tried again, and then gave up. There were voicemails from Victor the night before. "Call me." She put the phone on speaker and found if she held perfectly still, with her arm over her head, she could hear fragments of messages. "Alexa's got a fever. Call me." He sounded angry and accusatory. Victor's voice, so familiar, so out of place. Celeste closed her eyes and saw colors, as she had the night before. This time they were a violent, muddy ugliness, not the beautiful symbols they'd been. A refrain, part prayer, part rant, all ache, played in her head: *Alexa, my baby, are you all right?*

She went back into the house and picked up her bag. "Could you take me to my car. Please."

"Yeah." Jake went into the bedroom and came out wearing a new T-shirt.

Celeste pulled her clothes on and threw the Hawaiian shirt on the couch. She went out the front door, down the steps, and climbed into the cab of the truck. Jake lifted the dog into the truck bed, buckling his leash to the inside railing. Beavis barked excitedly and ran in tight circles. After Jake climbed into the driver's seat, he looked at her as if he wanted to explain something.

"Can we go?" she asked.

Jake sat up straight, nodded, and turned on the engine. The night before, she'd equated the sound of his truck with a jet engine. And flying. Last night Jake had been the young Tom, and the puzzle pieces of her unfinished past had connected perfectly with the present. She'd glimpsed something valuable, an alternate field, a brief stepping out into a space without clutter or turmoil, where disparate fragments made profound sense. The epiphany about Jake and Tom carried an enchantment, although now it seemed preposterous. But none of it means anything, Celeste reflected, if Alexa is somewhere out of reach, in need. If only she'd checked her phone during the party, like a responsible adult—a responsible mother—she might have known. Although there couldn't have been cell service on that mountainside, but she hadn't even thought of her phone. She was stoned on shrooms—a condition not conducive to responsible parenting. It seemed there was no pleasure that wasn't tied, irreparably, to a transgression. No grace period. No animal-woman juncture when she could afford to leave the animal-mother behind, even briefly.

Phone reception came and went with each curve of the road. She understood from parts of voicemails a loose chronology of what had happened. Celeste stared unseeing out of the truck window, her mind occupied by memories of when the girls had been sick and Victor hadn't been home. Alexa had a bad case of bronchitis when she was eight. Sophie had recurrent ear infections when she was a toddler. She remembered Sophie sitting on Victor's lap at the pediatrician's, once. Mostly she was taking care of a sick child alone.

Jake drove steadily, in his consistent, plodding way. He was like his father in that regard, moving with calm, slow precise determination. Celeste was finding it difficult not to scream, "Drive faster." Her head felt heavy. She let it fall back, knocking against the cold glass of the back window. The sound launched the dog into frenzied barking.

Jake glanced at her. "Gonna be okay?"

She took a deep breath and tried to gain control. "It's not me I'm worried about."

"Look," Jake said tentatively, "sorry I didn't wake you. I didn't know what to do."

She wanted her response to Jake to be graceful and casual, but everything she thought to say was ugly and bitchy and full of her own self-recrimination. Finally, she just stuck to what she'd learned. "Guess Delores called Luna, and Luna called Victor at the Inn to check on Alexa." As she spoke, the shame of it overtook her. She'd lied like an arrogant, irresponsible teenager, even taking pleasure in it. And she'd been exposed. She'd violated her own moral code. Her life was a sham, again.

blessingway

Victor swung open the hotel door and snapped, "Where the fuck have you been?"

Celeste pushed past him. Alexa was in the bed. The television blasted a laundry detergent commercial; images of sheets billowing voluptuously filled the screen. "Honey girl, are you okay?" Celeste moved close to where she lay. "Do you have a fever?" She put her hand on her daughter's forehead. It didn't feel hot.

Sophie threw herself at Celeste. "Mommy, where were you? Daddy said you got lost." Celeste glared at Victor.

"Mommy," Sophie murmured, leaning her head against Celeste's breasts.

"Your daughter's been sick," Victor declared.

Celeste put her lips on Alexa's forehead. "I don't think you have a fever now. Your tummy hurt?"

Alexa nodded. "I threw up."

"Oh, sweetheart." Celeste pulled her close. "I'm so sorry."

"Where were you, Mom?" Alexa asked. She looked emotional and vulnerable, though not unhealthy. Her storm-cloud of adolescent affectation was absent.

"I was working."

Sophie climbed up into her mother's lap. Celeste hugged her and kissed the top of her head. "I was working up in the mountains; there was no cell phone reception, so I didn't get your dad's calls."

"But," Alexa asked, "why weren't you at the tavern?"

"I went to work somewhere else." The television blared.

Everyone in the room was quiet. Celeste tried to stand. Sophie clung to her. "Victor, could I speak with you?" Celeste set Sophie down and she whined something unintelligible.

"We'll be right back." Celeste bent down to kiss Alexa's forehead. She let her lips stay there an extra moment, breathing in relief. "Right back," she repeated, trying to sound reassuring and solid. But she felt fragile, like she was fraying—a tightly woven basket coming apart.

Victor walked to the adjoining room. Celeste followed him in. He closed the door and turned on her. "You lied to me." he sputtered. "You look like shit. Where the fuck were you?"

Spittle hit her face. She put a finger to her lips. "Shhhhhh, Victor." She didn't want the girls to hear. "Cool down. Just tell me what happened."

Victor's eyes narrowed. "Tell me where you were, God dammit."

"Please, Victor. What happened to Alexa?"

"Are you capable of being a responsible mother?" Victor drew his mouth down. They stared at each other bitterly.

Celeste inhaled, then said very softly, "Go fuck yourself." She dropped down to sit on the bed. Victor hovered over her. She took another breath, trying to gather herself and focus. Her hands trembled. *Stay calm.* "Don't try anything, Victor. You're touring all the time. Cheating on us for years. Go ahead and lecture me. But you better not try any fucking legal shit, or I'll make sure you lose everything. Everything."

Suddenly the hot, angry air seemed to leave him. He sat down heavily next to her on the bed. "I told them," he said.

"You told them what?"

"About the baby."

"No. You didn't. They needed me there. We agreed to tell them together."

"I never agreed." He laid back and stretched out on the floral bedspread, his mood completely changed. He acted strangely self-satisfied. "Celeste, you can't control everything." He spoke at the ceiling and crossed his arms behind his head.

"You made Alexa sick." Celeste was aghast. "Asshole. Don't you get it?"

"No! That's not it." Victor jumped from the bed in one swift movement.

"Of course it is." They stared at one another.

"Don't be ridiculous." he said.

"Don't you understand? Their whole world's changed forever. Of course Alexa threw up."

Victor seemed briefly confounded. "You're wrong."

They looked blindly at one another. It was useless to dispute anything with him.

"Not everything can happen according to your plans, Celeste." Victor closed his eyes and pushed his fingers deeply into his eye sockets, rubbing vigorously. It was something he did often. A bad habit. It used to make her so crazy, she'd shout at him to stop. But this time she just watched.

Now she understood: Alexa had digested the news that her father was having a baby with another woman; it made her sick, and she vomited the information. The damage had been done. Meanwhile, her daughters were alone in the next room. She got up to leave.

Victor reached out as she rose from the bed, grabbing her and pulling her close to his face. She could smell stale coffee on his breath. "Did you have a good fuck last night, Celeste?"

She yanked her arm out of his hand and turned away. "I'm going back to the girls."

☀ ☀ ☀

On the last days of his visit, Celeste and Victor stopped talking to each other entirely. It was the only way to keep things from escalating. Celeste actually felt freed by Victor's coldness.

She was able to join in family activities without feeling she was pantomiming. The truth was on the table. Despite Victor not explaining the situation the way she would have liked, at least the girls knew. Although, for Alexa, who was more able to comprehend the ramifications of her impending half-sibling, Celeste felt the ache of lost innocence. She wondered if Alexa would remember Victor's disclosure as a defining moment in her life.

The remaining core of contention for Celeste and Victor was their home in Los Angeles. In the morning, while he packed to leave and the girls were still asleep, Celeste approached him. "Please put the house up for sale."

"I'm not selling it," he replied flatly.

"Victor, I need money to buy our own place here. How can I do that if we don't sell the house?"

He zipped his travel case closed. "I want them in L.A.. The kids consider that house their home."

"Right. It used to be. But we need a new home. If you keep the house you have to buy me out. You don't have that kind of money. Besides, you're always on the road. It would be stupid for you to keep the house."

"Celeste, I talked to the girls about it." Victor tipped his head back and flared his nostrils like an angry bull, but he stayed controlled. "They love that house."

"Shit, Victor. Why would you fuck with them that way?" He was using the girl's feelings against her, when she'd been so scrupulous not to do that with him. A wildfire flamed in her. She had to tamp it down quickly before it spread. She unclenched her hands and tried to modulate her voice. "I know they want to keep the house, but it's impossible."

He turned his back on her and picked up his cell from the bedside. "We'll see."

"The kids and I will come down over the holiday break to clear the house out. Meanwhile, why don't you get a realtor on it?"

Victor spun around. "You're pushing me too hard. Back up."

"Should we do this with lawyers?" They stared at each other. "If we do it that way all our money will go to attorneys. Victor, we've seen it happen with every one of our divorced friends, right? We can just split everything and come out ahead." She reached out her hand and touched his forearm. "Victor, please. Let's just get it done."

Later, as he hugged and kissed the girls goodbye, she didn't say anything more about the house. He'd arrived thinking he was going to rescue their marriage. He left knowing it was over.

※ ※ ※

In the back hills of SoHum, they gathered inside a small dwelling near a pond. Women stood in a circle as children wove in and out of their legs, tumbling on the floor and running up and down the stairs to a loft.

"Mmmmmm," the chant began discordantly, until the voices unified and then lifted. "Mmmmmm . . ." Luna stood on Celeste's left. Pippin and Deja were nearby on her right. The trim shack women were there, including Sipotty. "Mmmmmm . . ." The chant gained momentum. The small house reverberated with the chant Luna had described as "the universal sound of mother." Mouths widened, as the sound filled the space and then shifted into a roaring vowel: "Aaaaaaa . . ."

One note oscillated around the room, echoed in Celeste's ears, merged with the sound she made, and then reverberated again, sustained for an impossibly long period; at last, in gradations, it died out, becoming a wild silence. A current of stillness throbbed the air. Celeste was breathless. Everyone stood motionless; even the children were mesmerized and calmed by the incantation, then slowly they grew restless again.

"Birthing is a radical sacrament." Luna looked around the circle.

Celeste counted twenty-eight women and estimated there

were twelve children, including Sophie, and not including some babies, as she kept noticing one more, and then another, pocketed into their mothers in slings and front packs. Alexa had elected to ride horses to the river with Jonah rather than coming to the Blessingway.

Sophie hugged Celeste's leg, and Celeste reached down and rubbed her back.

Luna continued, "We aren't taught to believe in the intelligence of our bodies and accept that we are the link between what is visible and what is mysterious and unmanifest." The room stayed hushed, except for the noises of children playing and the suckling sound of a nursing baby. "We are the vessel for the mystery of life." Luna turned to the very pregnant Anya. "Use your vessel often in these last stages of pregnancy, so you open easily for birth." After a few seconds, there was laughter. Luna smiled contentedly and continued, her voice strong, "We are reincarnated through our children. In pregnancy and childbirth we are reborn. In labor we can't deny that vibes are real. Being safe and comfortable when we're birthing is vital. Our bodies know innately how to birth, if we can provide the dignity and space in which to surrender." Luna stepped forward, toward her birthing assistant, Evie. "Should we do the cord ceremony?"

"Sure." Evie held a ball of silky looking purple cord. Luna reached her arms out. "Calling grandmothers everywhere. We call on the wind and the spirits of the East." She made a quarter turn. "We call on the wind and the spirits of the South." She turned again, reaching her outstretched arms higher. "We call on the wind and the spirits of the West." She made another quarter turn. "We call on the wind and the spirits of the North." She raised her arms toward the ceiling. "Above." She scooped down. "And below." Luna turned to Anya. "We are connected to you."

Anya smiled, and Evie led her to a chair, settling her into an elaborate throne. Earlier, Anya's feet had been bathed in a bowl with fresh lavender flowers and rubbed with cornmeal, as Anya's mother stood near. Luna continued, "As you enter the labyrinth of labor and birth, these women bless you." Evie handed the purple-colored ball to Luna, who pulled the cord and wrapped it around Anya's wrist. The ball went next to the woman nearest Anya, and Luna indicated that she should circle her wrist, which she did and then passed it to the woman next to her. "Birthing is your own labyrinth," Luna said. "No one can be inside that labyrinth with you, but at its center you will find your baby." Anya looked glowy and tearful. Anya's mother had twisted Anya's long blond dreads on top of her head; tattoos encircled her bare arms, and she wore burnished armlets and heavy necklaces.

Loops of the purple cord drooped from one woman's wrist to the next as the ball made its way around the circle. Sophie tugged on Celeste's skirt. "Mommy, can I have that, too?"

Celeste bent closer. "What sweet pea?"

"The cord."

"Oh." Celeste glanced at Luna who was close enough to touch.

"Luna," Celeste whispered self-consciously, uncomfortable speaking to her in the midst of the ritual. Yet when Luna turned toward her, Celeste saw no reproach in her shiny, deep eyes. "Can Sophie do the cord too?"

Luna smiled. "Of course." Luna reached down to Sophie and patted her gently. "I bet Anya would be honored."

Anya smiled. "I'd love that."

When the ball of cord reached Celeste, she wrapped Sophie's wrist first and then her own. Celeste passed the ball to Luna who circled her own wrist, and then gazed around the room. Every woman was tied, wrist to wrist, by the purple cord. Luna turned back to Anya. "We are linked to you." Anya swiped at a tear rolling down her cheek.

Luna reached for Anya's hand. "The image of the tree of life is on every placenta. Drawn with the life-giving veins that bring nourishment and oxygen. Proof of the interconnectedness of all things." Luna lowered her head. "The new baby you'll hold in your arms will, at first, be attached to the otherworld of the placenta. Respect that, allow time for your baby's transition."

Luna, holding Anya's hand, began singing, and everyone joined in. "We are the flow, and we are the ebb. We are the weavers; we are the web . . ." After the song ended, a moment passed before Luna lifted her chin and looked again toward the circle. "When the cord on your wrist falls off, contact a friend to ask after Anya. See if she needs support, because she'll be in labor."

Evie handed Luna a pair of scissors, and Luna cut and tied the cord around Anya's wrist. Standing before Anya, Luna said softly, "Thank you."

The scissors were passed, and women paired up, talking and laughing as they helped each other cut and tie the string around their wrists. After the circle of women loosened, the room filled with loud chatter.

Celeste couldn't help consider the impending birth of Victor's baby in a new light. Although Victor's visit to Humboldt had turned into a debacle, maybe he would soften up with a new baby to engage him. Babies bring fresh love, and Victor needed that now.

The Blessingway continued with a belly dance performance. Pippin and Deja pushed a couch against the wall. Glasses of homemade wine were passed. Celeste accepted wine gladly; Luna was driving. Sophie didn't know any of the kids; she clung tightly to Celeste, who was happy to hold her close. The room teemed with the clamor of children before the drumbeat began, blasted from two giant speakers. The first beat was slow and deliberate, as the dancers emerged in their regalia, every move accentuated by jangling ornaments. Anya was center stage, covered in thin scarf material, head to toe, her back to the audience—she didn't look pregnant at all from the back.

As the beat of the drum intensified, the dancers' hips jutted and their arms writhed above their heads, undulating snake-like to their fingertips. The music had a strong Middle Eastern drumbeat—in a stunning moment Anya whirled, facing front, stripping scarves off, exposing her big ball of baby belly. Celeste caught her breath. Someone screeched, "Hell, yeah" and the audience went feral, making distinctive high-pitched clicking and tongue-rolling noises while holding their hands in front of their mouths.

The beat made Celeste want to get up and dance too. But she watched, spellbound, while the dancers shimmied and swayed, punctuated with crisp hip thrusts and tight spins. It was as if they were put together without bones or tendons. Anya moved in distinct, darting, lizard-like—almost twitchy— motions. Her body internalized a slow beat with impossibly elongated, slow-motion movements, changing, when the tempo quickened, to rapid-fire moves, as if electrical currents undulated through her.

The rich, fruity wine made Celeste light-headed and content. What could have been interpreted as a base sexual aspect of the dance was transformed into an expression of fundamental female sensuality, by the feminine environment. It captured that same kind of pleasure that existed between a mother and her nursing baby. An older woman sitting next to Celeste and Sophie launched into a discourse about the history of belly dancing: how it began exclusively for women and girls, then evolved into what it is present-day, viewed as a titillating dance to please men.

Celeste found new reasons to admire Luna. During a break in the dance performance, she observed Luna surrounded by a gaggle of adoring women, all listening intently to her. Celeste felt envious of those women, looking so at ease, so happy and free with one another and Luna.

After Victor left and she and the girls had returned to the cabin, Celeste felt stiff and hyper-aware around Luna. When they'd talked, Celeste felt self-conscious, analyzing every word that came out of her own mouth. Maybe she was projecting something awkward that wasn't there. But a sense of shame settled in, and an interior voice continuously whispered: Luna knows I've slept with Jake, she knows I lied, and put my children at risk.

After the performance, Celeste watched as the dancers gathered up scarves, she realized one of the dancers was Shanti, the Cosmo potstitute from the tavern. On the way home from the Blessingway, Celeste told Luna about recognizing Shanti.

"Shanti's Anya's half-sister."

"Oh, jeez." Celeste shook her head.

"They have the same father. Sisters from another mother, as they say."

"Shit. It seems everyone is related or connected in some way."

Luna was quiet. She glanced at Celeste quickly then brought her attention back to the road. "A small community," Luna spoke slowly, "can feel claustrophobic to some people."

Claustrophobic. Celeste was overcome with an image of the mountains and hills, green forests and golden summer meadows, rivers and streams, dirt roads, yurts and trailers, grows, unfinished houses made of scrap wood, all rising and closing in toward each other, like a blanket being folded. "I guess I need, like, a map," Celeste said, "or a family tree, so I can keep track of who's related to whom."

"Or not. Just forget about it, Celeste, and try not to be judgmental. Remember that everyone has a story and is worthy of respect. In the city, you pass people on the street and know you won't see that face again, if you bothered to look. The guy begging without a jacket in winter, you pass him by. You don't have to care in the city. But in a small community, we know each other's stories. Educated or uneducated, property owner or destitute." Luna turned off Bear Ridge Road onto bumpy dirt, and they ascended the first hill in the maze of roads and small tracks that eventually would bring them to the heart of Tom and Luna's land. "People here are family," Luna said, "You see them at the store, at the post office, in town. The same faces."

As they rounded a curve, just out of sight of Bear Ridge, there was Jake's truck parked at an alarming angle, blocking the road.

"What's going on?" Celeste asked, believing Luna would know.

Luna didn't say a word. She nosed her car close to Jake's truck, pulled the emergency brake and, without turning off the engine, opened her door and jumped out.

Jake emerged from the cab of his truck. Celeste took a breath. *He's okay.* She turned to Sophie in the back seat. "Stay here. I'll be right back."

"Mommy." Sophie reached out her hand.

"It's okay, sweetie. I'll just be a second. The A/C's on. You stay here."

Sophie grabbed at the front seat.

"Sophie, I'll be right back." Celeste patted Sophie's hand, got out, and closed the car door. Outside was hot and dusty. Celeste walked toward Jake and Luna. As she approached, they fell silent. She felt awkward, distinctly the outsider. "Everything okay?" she asked.

"Give us a sec," Luna said. "It'll be okay. Could you stay in the car? I'll be right there."

"Wait? What's going on?"

Jake ambled over to her and wrapped his arm around her shoulders. "Our neighbor, Jimmy's trim scene was ripped off. A home invasion."

"Their scene? How?" Celeste wanted to sink into Jake, but she pulled away, hoping their brief contact looked like a simple gesture of reassurance between friends.

"They had a big crew working, and two masked guys with guns came in, duct-taped everyone to chairs, and took forty pounds of processed weed."

Celeste looked from Jake to Luna, then back at Jake.

"Why're you here, on the road?" Celeste asked.

"Got people posted on all the roads. There's no way in or out of Bear Ridge. If they're still here, we'll get 'em."

"Oh, shit." Celeste remembered Alexa and Jonah. "The kids went riding!"

"Nah," Jake said, "they're home. Got 'em before they took off."

Celeste turned over another set of emotions, like a slot machine, one set after another. She sighed. "Oh, jeez."

"Celeste," Luna said, "could you wait in the car please? I'll be right there."

"Sure." Celeste tried to mask her humiliation. "Sorry." She felt as if she were a child told to take a time-out. Looking away from Jake, trying to conceal her emotions, she turned to walk to the car. Something on the front seat of Jake's truck caught her eye. Something glinted. It would have to be metal to shine like that. A single object. A gun.

Chills ran through her, top to bottom. When she was almost to Luna's car, another truck pulled up in a plume of dust. Someone got out and joined Jake and Luna in the road.

Celeste slipped into the passenger seat of the car. "Mommy." Sophie looked terrified. Celeste knew Sophie couldn't have heard anything.

"Everything's okay, sweet pea." Celeste tried to smile re-assuringly, then got out of the car, closed the passenger door and opened the back door, sliding into the back seat next to Sophie, who attached herself immediately to Celeste like an octopus. "Everything's fine. Luna's gonna take us home. Alexa is there waiting for us."

"And Jonah?" Sophie asked. "And the horses, and Kiwi, and Trinity?"

"Yep. All the animals." Celeste pointed. "Look, here's Luna." Walking toward the car with Luna was the new arrival.

Luna got into the car, turned around in the driver's seat and smiled at Sophie. "Ready to go home?"

Sophie nodded.

"First, I want you to meet someone special," Luna said. Celeste opened the car door, and Luna continued, "This is Azure; she's going to be your school bus driver. She'll take you to school and bring you home every day."

Azure was tall and large, her bleached blond hair and pink shade of lipstick alien-looking in the dusty roadway. Luna had told Celeste about the transgender school bus driver. Azure reached a giant hand into the car. "Pleased to meet you, Sophie."

Sophie's eyes widened, she grabbed onto her mother, who immediately took the hand extended to her daughter. "She's a little shy," Celeste said.

"No problem. We'll have plenty of time to get to know each other." Azure smiled at Sophie and she and Celeste disengaged hands. "Sophie, see you Monday morning."

After Azure got in her truck, the three vehicles maneuvered around the narrow road until Luna could slip by. Azure drove off in the opposite direction, towards Bear Ridge Road, and Luna accelerated up the hill. As they passed Jake sitting in his truck, Celeste gazed up at him. He raised his palm to her, and then was obliterated by a storm cloud of dust.

Close to the turnoff to Tom and Luna's driveway, an older red truck Celeste had seen on the road before came barreling down the hill. Luna pulled over and stopped. "Our neighbor, Jimmy," she said. The truck parked, and a gruff-looking man wearing a straw hat got out and marched over. He slammed his hand down on the roof of the car.

"Damn. You heard, Luna?" A hot billowing of dust came into the car from Luna's open window. He leaned against the car, took a pack of cigarettes out of his pocket, shook one from the pack, and deftly lit it.

"Yeah, Jimmy. So sorry. But these things always come out in the end. You know that."

Jimmy inhaled deeply on his cigarette. "Not waiting around for that, Luna." He removed a piece of tobacco from his tongue. "Dirtbags got most of our crop." His face reddened and twisted. For a second it seemed he might explode, then he took another puff from his cigarette. "My best Dep ever. Beautiful and gooey. Musta been about forty pounds they got. Oh, they been watching us real close. Knew right when we was ready to go. My guy's coming up next week," He shook his head. "I ain't got nothin'.""

Celeste wished Sophie hadn't heard any of that. The dust was beginning to settle around Luna's car. Celeste looked at the dry brush next to the road and beyond at the surrounding hills, and farther out at the mountains with their dense mottled forests. It looked idyllic. If you didn't know, you'd never suspect what happened on these rutted roads.

"Jimmy," Luna said soothingly, "it could come back to you. It's possible."

"Hey, I'll find 'em sooner than that, Luna. Ain't waitin' around. Pretty sure they was on foot. Found some shoe tracks with a spider imprint going out the backside of our property. Know anyone with spiders on their soles?"

"Don't know. I'll ask Tom, though," Luna said, her voice steady as ever.

"Do that." Jimmy looked toward the back seat and lifted his chin in acknowledgement at Celeste and Sophie, who were clinging to each other. "You in the cabin over there?"

"Yep." Celeste tried to sound calm.

"Okay, Luna. You take care." He banged the top of the car again, this time with two hard, unnerving strikes.

In the big house, Alexa and Jonah were watching *Breakfast at Tiffany's* again. They seemed fine, taking refuge from the late afternoon heat in the cool living room.

Alexa got up from a pile of pillows on the floor. "Mom, we couldn't ride today."

"I heard, honey girl."

"How was the Blessingway?" she asked.

Was that today? It seemed like weeks ago that they'd experienced the warm congeniality of the Blessingway. Celeste fingered the cord on her wrist. "You would've loved the dance performance."

Luna went to Jonah, who was standing now, and engulfed him in her long arms.

"Come on girls, to the cabin." Celeste gathered up Sophie and went toward the screen door.

"Mom!" Alexa protested, "We're in the middle of watching a movie."

"Don't argue." Celeste said, and somehow Alexa understood it wasn't the time to put up a fight. Holding the screen door open for her daughters, Celeste turned back to Luna, who was hugging Jonah tightly. "Thanks for taking us to the Blessingway."

pigs

After the home invasion, Jake slept in his truck on the road. Celeste imagined him, sunk in the ominous darkness with that shiny object next to him on the seat. Tom slept in the outdoor grow. Everyone was on edge, on high alert. The trim shack was closed down for the first time since Celeste had arrived. Bins and black bags full of plants ready to be trimmed were stashed in a cool, dry place that no robber could find.

Celeste had a strange feeling as she lay in bed staring at the rafters. It was as if she was waking up, not from a pleasant dream, but from the nightmare reality in which she found herself. In the shadows of night, only the bones of the cabin were evident. The fresh paint job, new handles on the kitchen cabinets, Tibetan rug on the plywood floor, none of them showed in the dark. Only the pattern of beams and the old-world silhouette of the wood-burning stove were visible. In the nocturnal light the cabin was exposed for what it was: an austere country hut where she'd exiled herself and her daughters.

She couldn't fall asleep. Her hollow, yet seemingly respectable, life in L.A. had been replaced with this perilous existence. How can I raise my children here, she wondered? Everything is unstable and dangerous, jerry-built—the way the houses were put together, the grow rooms, greenhouses, and light deps. Everything improvised, built with spit and glue, without regulation or oversight, without legality. And now she saw the depth of it. When it came to being ripped off, there was no calling the police. No suspects would be read their Miranda rights. In SoHum, it was self-made, self-rule, self-law.

Celeste had been excited about the girls' new school and new life, even feeling settled and acclimated to the ganja culture. Glad to make good money at the trim shack, easily and conveniently. All cash. Yet this recent twist of events brought the lawless nature of the county into focus; she was thrown back into questioning why she had stayed. Next week the kids would start school.

She could have landed in some other small town or suburb with perfect lawn squares attached to the houses, the kind of generic, quaint, innocent town she had envisioned on her drive north from L.A., a place populated by people who were governed by the laws of the larger American society, not by the unwritten laws of a clandestine way of life. She could never have conjured this place: unleashed from corporate and government ties, operating with its own morals. A Wild West culture so arcane it was new again. Not powered by the production of gold, or oil, or minerals, or moonshine liquor, but by unfertilized female flower buds. She'd often pondered whether there was something intrinsically unsatisfying about that—all those female hormones flying around yearning for their male counterparts. In Humboldt, maybe the plant itself had turned biologically lazy, or maybe it had become the secret manipulator of the growers, who planted bigger crops each year. Here, a marijuana plant didn't even have to resort to seed for reproduction, humans did that work too, multiplying its perfect likeness, clone after clone.

The truth, and the problem, was that Celeste felt helplessly drawn to the place, to the vortex of everything SoHum. Like the tide pulled by the moon, she felt compelled by a larger power. She was captivated by the territory and its people; even its nomenclature had become fascinating. But now she'd seen the shadow it cast. The part of the culture she had admired—its autonomy from the rest of the country—had, instantly, become its liability. There would never be a frantic call to 911 saying,

"Our whole crop was stolen." In SoHum everyone was the criminal, and what justice was meted out had nothing to do with American laws. The actions taken against ganja thieves would not be weighed by jury or judge or overseen by a court system.

At the tavern one evening, a man had told her, oddly—boastingly—that he raised pigs. Later, she told Jake what he'd said, amused by this back country bumpkin's pride in his pigs. But Jake had turned solemn. "Some people here keep pigs for a reason."

"Okay . . ." she responded.

"Pigs'll eat anything, even human flesh."

"What are you talking about?"

"Pigs make dead bodies disappear."

At the time it had seemed strange and unreal—an abstraction she'd put out of her head. But now she wondered who kept pigs on Bear Ridge and it made her sick to think of what those pigs might be eating—if the thieves were found.

She knew she'd have to make some changes, quickly. Moving out of the cabin to a place in town, or anywhere not connected to a Grow Scene, as they called it, or a Grow Show. Did that place exist in SoHum? She'd been looking for rentals, so far with no luck. It was time to intensify her effort. For the safety and security of her daughters, she needed to find her own place immediately, then the girls could start school according to plan. Celeste couldn't completely pull the rug out from under them. She wouldn't move out of Humboldt; she needed to find her own place. Her own safe place.

She leaned back into the pillow and concentrated on clearing her mind. The night air vibrated with fear and untamed aggression, like the plumes of glittering dust that flew behind cars on the potholed roads.

※ ※ ※

The sweaty front desk clerk at the motel in Garberville pointed to a side window of the lobby; there Celeste spotted her sister on a lounger next to the pool.

"Thank you," she said, turning and taking Sophie by the hand. "Come on, there's Aunt Greta." Alexa and Jonah followed them outside into the sweltering heat.

Greta was stretched out, eyes closed and head tipped toward the sun. Water droplets glistened on her slim, spray-tanned arms and legs. The girls ran ahead, squealing in excitement. Greta opened her eyes, jumped up, and threw her arms open. "My babies!" She hugged and kissed the girls, then ran her hand through her short blonde hair, pushing wet strands away from her face. Instantly, Greta was laughing and conversing with Sophie and Alexa. "You start on Monday?" Greta exclaimed, "A new school, oh boy."

"Yeah, and it's right by the ocean," Alexa said, "on a cliff. Our teacher said we can see whales migrating."

"Geez, migrating whales while you're doing math."

"And the birds fly by real close," Sophie added.

"Nice," Greta said, and then hugged Sophie so hard that the child yelped.

"Cut it out," said Celeste, slapping her sister on the shoulder. Jonah was behind her, and Celeste stepped aside. "This is Jonah."

"Good to meet you." Greta stood there in her silver bikini, wholly comfortable in her skin. She smiled and shook his hand. Jonah looked like a boy, even with his long dreadlocks and even though he stood taller than Greta. But in the bright sun, Celeste noticed for the first time that a faint fuzz shadowed his upper lip. It wouldn't be long before he crossed that threshold, Celeste mused. His smooth face would soon become stubbled, and his slim child-like body would thicken into manhood.

Alexa stripped off her clothes, down to her swimsuit. Jonah pulled his T-shirt over his head, and he and Alexa loped to the far end of the pool, diving into the deep end. Greta's eyes widened. "Shite, that girl is growing up!"

"I know," Celeste replied. Sophie had her clothes off and was sprinting to the pool. "Sophie, stop running! Shallow end, please."

"Jonah's cute as a button. Kinda looks like Tom. A brown version. With dreadlocks." Greta lifted her chin. "He and Alexa an item?"

"Best friends."

"Says mom."

"No, really. I'm sure. I've talked about it with him. Jonah's great. Super smart. Luna, his mother, is amazing."

"Uh huh." Greta threw one of her I-know-what's-really-going-on smirks at Celeste. "Pretty cute, Tom's son and your daughter . . ."

"Goddammit, Greta. Stop."

"Whatever you say, Sis."

Celeste pulled a chair into the shade. Greta persisted on staying in the hot carcinogenic sun. "I can't believe you made it up here."

"Yeah, well, I get why the drive from the Bay Area keeps people away. It shouldn't take four hours to drive two-hundred miles. And honestly, this place is a shit hole."

"I told you to stay at the River Inn; it's very Julia Morgan, all old stone, beautiful."

"Yeah, I called, no swimming pool."

"Greta, it's got the river at its doorstep."

"Eww, river water, swimming with fish. No thanks. I'll stick with chlorine."

"You make me crazy."

"Nice to see you too. Actually, I didn't mean this rinky-dink motel: the whole fucking town's a shit hole. There's nothing here. What are you thinking?"

"I'm thinking for myself."

Greta stared at her. Greta's hair and features, everything

about her was sharp and defined. In comparison, Celeste had always been unruly and unrefined, and she'd often felt her way forward through life and decisions, unclear about where she was going. Celeste's hair and lips were big and quirky, unladylike. Greta always knew where she was going, and she looked crisp getting there. Greta's version of playing a maternal role—something she'd taken on after their mother's death—was asking Celeste to explain herself. Although it could be a good exercise in self-awareness, it generally made Celeste feel inferior to her older sibling and their encounters usually left her emotionally drained. Greta knew what she wanted. No children. No marriage—although she'd come close once. Yet Greta was exceptional with her nieces, generous with her love and affection.

Celeste had the urge to explain to her sister what drew her to SoHum—the incomparable setting, the spiritual power of the redwoods; but Greta found beauty in a Louis Vuitton bag. Celeste glanced away from her sister's face, past the motel roofline to the surrounding mountains and vast vault of hot blue sky. For Celeste, luxury had become the sweet smell of the country. No rush hour chaos, no concrete underfoot, no hard lines of office buildings. Just unsullied air and earthy smells, rivers and forests—it was solace, satisfying a craving she hadn't known she'd had. As Celeste contemplated reciting her reasons for falling in love with SoHum, she knew Greta would argue its deficits. Certainly, she wouldn't discuss the trauma of the recent home invasion robbery. "So, anyway," Celeste asked, "how's Dad?"

"He hasn't changed into the sweet father figure we always wanted, if that's what you mean."

"What's he saying about, you know . . . my move?"

"The same: you're a fool to have left Victor."

"Goddammit." Celeste looked at the kids, but they were playing Marco Polo, definitely not listening to the conversation; still, she lowered her voice. "Doesn't he care that Victor impregnated his girlfriend?"

"Can't drag me into this one. If you care about what Dad says, why don't you call him?"

"Yeah. Okay."

Greta blinked. "What's the plan with your hair?"

Celeste reached up, spreading her hands protectively over her hair. She could feel the curls and frizz extending outward. "Everyone up here likes it."

"Looks like a red bird's nest dropped on your head."

"Whatever. It's natural."

"Certainly is." Greta exhaled loudly. Then shook off what she was thinking. "So, what the hell do people do with themselves around here? Small town living, ick, like living in miniature."

"There's an event today at the Community House. The Hemp Fest."

Greta looked stunned. "You're kidding?"

☘ ☘ ☘

There was every conceivable ganja-related item at the Hemp Fest, from art posters to roasted hemp seeds for snacking, to finely wrought portraits made of roach papers. As Celeste marveled at the roach-portraits, which were intricate, full of depth and expression from the shadings of burned rolling papers, a man approached the artist to ask if he needed a donation of roaches. Replying in a serious tone, the artist explained that he had to smoke every joint himself down to its nub. "Part of the art."

Greta laughed loudly, and Celeste herded her sister away before things got more embarrassing. They ended up in front of a booth for pot wine. Celeste was offered a taste of an "OG Pinot," which she accepted. She let its compelling green back note develop on her tongue. "It's good, interesting."

The booth belonged to a friend of Jake's, a pony-tailed man in a kilt. He smiled at Celeste and then launched into his spiel, "Between growers and vineyards, California provides most of the highs for our nation; I combine our state's two most prized crops."

He tried to hand Greta a petite white paper cup, but she refused. "My mind hasn't expanded enough to experiment with pot wine."

"Just a taste won't do a thing to you," said Celeste, as she sipped another sample. "Wow, delicious." She was floored by the delicate pot champagne; it tasted the way fresh weed smelled, yet was light and effervescent.

Greta pointed to the arrayed bottles of pot wine. "Aren't you afraid of being arrested for this?" she sternly asked the man in the kilt.

He laughed. "Why? Are you going to tell?"

"It's not secret, is it?" Greta waved her hand grandly around the Community House.

Putting his sample cup down, Mr. Pot-wine came out from behind his booth and approached Greta. She faced him squarely as he came close.

"So," as he spoke he gave Greta the once over, "you probably weren't here earlier when the District Attorney for Humboldt County spoke on our panel. He was just one of the representatives on the Hemp Fest program this morning."

"I missed that," Greta quipped.

"Well, legality is a gray area in SoHum. If I were you, I wouldn't worry about it."

Celeste took her sister's arm, throwing a "Thank you," behind her as she led Greta away.

Jonah, Alexa, and Sophie were already bored. They wanted to go to the rear of the outdoor area where other kids had congregated—a range of ages, teenagers to Sophie's age, and younger—were climbing up and down a dirt hillside. On the adjacent patio, the thick smoke of burning cannabis rose like thought bubbles from multiple clusters of folks socializing.

"Shite!" said Greta, as they stepped onto the patio. "I've never seen so much pot smoke; why do they bother lighting up, can't they just inhale?"

"Not so loud."

"How long do you think I can hold my breath?" Greta squeezed her nostrils shut. "What the hell are you telling the girls, that it's oregano?"

"Would you chill out? Luna had a talk with them. We're good."

In the shade under an overhang, Celeste saw Luna. Her dreads were intertwined with patterned scarves, coiled high on her head. Jonah was striding toward his mom. When Luna looked up and saw him, a wide smile lit up her face.

"I'll introduce you," said Celeste. As they closed in on the buffer of Luna's friends and admirers, Celeste suddenly wanted to turn and run. She remembered that morning when her sister stood practically naked, yet greeted Jonah so comfortably. Greta had nothing to hide. In contrast, Celeste always seemed to be concealing something. With her city-straight sister at her side and the belief that Luna knew, through gossip or intuition, about her and Jake, she felt a tide of embarrassment rise and engulf her. A bolt of fear lodged hot and bitter in her gut. She'd burrowed into SoHum believing she could shed her past. Life with Tom and Luna had seemed rich with warmth and potential, yet the old quandaries she'd left behind in the city had come back to coil around her.

Celeste took a breath, stepped forward and introduced Greta to Luna. She knew her sister's expertly applied eyeliner, bleached, feathered, blow-dried short hair, strong perfume, and pastel-colored outfit took center stage.

Deja, standing nearby, smiled ingratiatingly and passed the

joint that was circling to Greta, who responded, "No thanks. All I need is fresh air."

And a bottle of Pinot Grigio, Celeste thought, but didn't say. Instead, she bumped Greta with her hip and began talking too loudly, hoping to distract. "We're gonna take off to Avenue of the Giants to show Greta the big trees." She forced herself to make eye contact with Luna. "Would it be okay if Jonah came along?"

"Gotta ask him," Luna answered. "Okay with me." Luna turned to see Jonah, Alexa, and Sophie trekking up the dirt hill with some other kids. "If he goes, ask him about the redwoods. He's an expert."

Soon the perimeter of women around Luna swelled. Raine, who occasionally worked in the trim shack, appeared and lit up a joint, just as a woman at the far end of the group lit up a spliff. After the two joints circulated the group a few times, everyone passed them on, except Raine and the other woman. They stepped out of the circle and exchanged the joints they were each holding, both taking long drags reflexively as they carried on a conversation. Celeste saw her sister watching them, and knew she'd hear about it later.

Announcements on the loudspeaker came over the din, and the first notes of live music began, erupting recklessly then morphing into a familiar song. Celeste had taken a couple of puffs off a joint to soften the effects of being with her sister, and she felt the melody soaring through her. The drumbeat was salacious, and she knew the lyrics intimately. "I love this song," Celeste blurted.

"Let's dance." Luna walked toward the band inside. Some of the women in her crowd followed behind, trailing into a disorganized parade.

"I'll get the kids." Celeste went to the far side of the patio and called up the hill, waving them over. "Come on. There's music." They scrambled down the dirt. Celeste gripped both

Alexa and Sophie's hands and pushed toward the band and the crush on the dance floor. Inside was a retreat from the brightness and heat, although people and their humid breath were packed into the space. The area in front of the stage had been cleared, and figures were churning to the music under rotating colored lights. Remembering her sister, she craned her neck to glance back and saw Greta lingering on the patio, talking with someone in the shadows. Celeste couldn't see who. Luna and contingent were already moving joyfully to the music. Jonah joined in with his own distinct bounce. Collectively, they made a clutch of dancers surrounded by the larger crowd, all of whom pulsed and swayed. After a couple of songs Greta materialized, insisting it was time to leave.

On the way to the car, Celeste asked Greta who it was that she had talked to on the patio.

"Jake. He introduced himself."

"Oh! I didn't know he was here."

"Hunka hunka. Too bad he's a dumb hillbilly." Celeste turned to Greta and tried to use her eyes to burn a hole in her sister's head. But Greta continued, casually overriding the vibrational hostility, "Looks exactly like his father. What's Tom look like these days?"

Celeste reminded herself: I only have to endure her one more night. "Same good guy."

The kids were ahead of them, rushing to the car, clearly out of earshot. When diminutive Sophie got to the Subaru half-way across the parking lot, she let out a resounding, "Hurry up!"

"Look," Greta grabbed Celeste's wrist and pulled her to a stop. "This place is interesting. I mean, I get it. But you can't live here. Working as a barmaid, it's not. . . Especially for the girls. Come home. Jesus, lay claim to your house. While you still can."

"I'm not going back to LA." Celeste recovered her wrist from her sister's hand. "I told Victor to put the house on the market. I need him to sell so I can buy a place here." Bile was rising up hot and bitter, Celeste could feel it clotting feverishly in her throat. "Goddammit, Greta, don't tell me what to do."

By the time they reached Avenue of the Giants, doing the tourist thing, driving the curving two-lane road squeezed by the big trees, Celeste had calmed down. Her dearest wish to dump her sister in the Hemp Fest parking lot and wave as she drove away had been resisted. It would be Greta's nastiest nightmare, to find herself stuck there, forced to interact with some random Hemp Fester.

Whatever qualms Celeste had about staying in Humboldt—and after the home invasion robbery there were a boatload—were now put to rest. That incident had been a fluke. She needed to weigh the robbery against the larger picture and then compartmentalize her overblown fears. Having Greta dictate that she was doing the wrong thing was divine reassurance she'd found the right path. Soon, the kids would start school and be enmeshed in SoHum's tight-knit community—the opposite of what she'd left behind in the city, where without realizing it she'd shut out her friends. During her affair at the school where she taught, she'd gone into stealth-mode trying to stay undetected, isolating herself in hopes of keeping her ill-fated relationship with her fellow teacher secret. At the same time, she'd been consumed with yearning for Victor to come home. But when he did return from tour, for brief stints, she'd only be preoccupied with when he would leave, and who he was currently having an affair with. In her beautiful house, sunk in her ostensibly idyllic life, she'd lived in suspended anticipation, caught in a peculiar, endless limbo, everything revolving around her lover, or her husband. Then the bomb of Victor's revelation dropped, allowing her to see her way out.

When she imagined going back to her house, as Greta had suggested, she caught the scent of ammonia. She was always adding drops of ammonia to buckets of water with rag in hand like a deranged Cinderella, trying to scrub her house clean. Unhappiness had irreparably penetrated her house's walls and surfaces. Even the spotless window panes that held precious views to her backyard had been tainted. What kind of a role model would she be if she'd kept her daughters in that ruined realm? This new place had freed her, and her children. Here they wouldn't be asked questions about Victor's new baby, at school, or in random social situations. They wouldn't be forced to process their emotions publicly, humiliatingly.

In Humboldt, Celeste was sentient again. She no longer felt inanimate, as she had for so long. Sometimes, she wondered if moving had been the right thing for her daughters. Maybe it was only essential for her. Yet, she had to believe the right place for her would also be the right place for her kids. Alexa's transformation, from sullen teenager of the city, to beaming girl, happy to interact in her new country life, seemed proof.

Every day Alexa and Jonah rode horses to the river, mucked out stalls, wrote in their journals, and helped in the veggie garden, often inviting Sophie to join their activities. Being in Humboldt had been curative. For Celeste, clipping in the trim shack felt healing—when the venerated, sticky, dark resin coated her fingers, she wondered about her part in the flower bud's journey to transmute a soul.

On Tom and Luna's land, in their orchard, an abundance of fruit-adorned trees bestowed luscious offerings. Devouring a fragrant nectarine, just picked, *still alive*, zinged her taste buds back to life. In the veggie garden, a cornucopia continuously, magically, sprang from the ground. Hot from the sun, a ripe tomato, eaten as juice dripped from her chin to the earth, was pure sensual pleasure.

✳ ✳ ✳

Sophie ran along the winding trail into the columnar redwood forest. Jonah and Alexa had gone ahead. Around a bend, they encountered a loud group of dreadlocked Italian-speaking young people, smiling as they meandered down the path. They smelled strong, like a trim shack, skunky and intense—like fresh dried ganja, and Celeste knew they'd just come from trimming somewhere.

Greta pinched her nose as the last person disappeared around the bend heading in the other direction, and proclaimed, "Italians with dreadlocks who knew?"

"They're 'trimmigrants.' People come from all over the world to work in SoHum, to trim weed—lots of Brazilians, Italians, English—from everywhere."

"Trimmigrants! Crazy. So, why does everyone look like they just rolled out of bed wearing their camo pajamas? Seems no one gets dressed here, or brushes their hair. Pot is a gray area legally, but hairbrushes in Humboldt must be against the law."

Celeste crossed a creek, stepping from rock to rock and reached a hand out to help steady Greta over the coursing water. Mid-stream, standing on a rock in the creek, still holding Celeste's hand, Greta stopped to lecture her, "Celeste, only you could find the land of weed and dreadlocks. I'm worried about your choices here. You can't even get a teaching job. It's so limiting for you."

Celeste had had enough of letting her sister under her skin. She pulled her sister's hand and Greta jumped from the rock onto the thick, quieting forest floor. Throwing her head back, Celeste let her eyes rove above her. "Look around you, Greta. Check out this—this cathedral!" From where they stood, the state park signs and parking area were no longer visible. She envisioned that instead of being a tree zoo, this forest went on forever, in its primeval glory. "You have to be impressed." Celeste watched Greta tip her face upward to take it in. Pin-light shafts of sparkling sunlight pierced the forest canopy. Lush moss and bright ferns stippled the length of a fallen tree lying, melting, into the soft duff. Both sides of the path winding away from them were fringed with enormous fern fronds. They walked on in enveloping silence. The blazing afternoon sun seemed an out-of-place memory as they went farther into the shaded, cool woods. After the trail curved, Celeste spotted Jonah and Alexa, back to back, sitting on a downed tree trunk, scribbling in their individual, but identical, black journals. "Hey," Celeste called, "where's Sophie?" Alexa pointed toward the creek. Sophie was crouched next to the babbling water, absorbed in something.

"What'd you find, sweet pea?" Coming closer, Celeste stared at some felt-like moss growing on a log. Out of the emerald patch a pop of tiny stems dotted with flowers made for a perfect Lilliputian woodland scene. But Sophie was focused elsewhere. Celeste shifted her attention to a mat of yellowed leaves. There, two large slugs, each about the size of a small banana and colored a mottled green yellow, twined together, glistening with slime.

"Oh!" Celeste took Sophie's hand. "That's awesome. Don't tell Aunt Greta; she'll think they're gross." They returned to where Greta stood on the trail, looking out of place, dwarfed by the monolithic tree trunks towering around her. "Hey, Jonah," called Celeste, "are you gonna be our interpretive guide and tell us about redwoods?"

Jonah, chewing his lower lip, looked up from his writing. Surrounded by lush forest, the horizontal log he and Alexa shared was wedged several feet above the ground. He raised his shoulders. "What do you want to know?" A shaft of light pierced the green canopy and streamed over his face, making his honey-colored eyes glow.

"What can you tell us?"

"Well, redwood trees produce twice as much biomass as other trees." For a moment the saturated quiet was restored to the forest. "Um." Jonah followed up. "How 'bout some redwood trivia." He climbed down. Alexa stayed on her perch. Slipping his journal into his back pocket, he said, "They're the tallest trees on earth."

"Mommy told me that." Sophie said assuredly, crossing her arms over her chest.

"Okay, Sophie, did you know that relatives of our redwoods grew in the Jurassic era, when there were dinosaurs?" Jonah went over to a tree and patted its thick, fluffy-looking bark.

"How do you know?" asked Sophie.

"'Cause I was there!" Jonah laughed. He reached down to poke Sophie in the ribs.

"Don't!" Sophie giggled.

"I know from reading about fossils, silly." Jonah spoke in a casual but informed manner, distinctly unlike a sixteen-year-old boy. "Did you know there's a redwood tree in Humboldt that's taller than the Statue of Liberty?"

"Really?" Greta asked.

"Yeah, that's about as tall as a twenty-two story building."

Sophie looked up at Jonah. She shook her head. "My friend has a Liberty Statue. It's this big." She put her hands a few inches apart to demonstrate.

"Sophie!" Alexa jumped down from the log. "The real Statue of Liberty, not a souvenir, wingbat!"

Celeste touched Alexa's shoulder. "Okay. Be nice."

"How about redwood cones?" Jonah raised an eyebrow and tipped his head. "They're only about an inch long, and the seeds are smaller than tomato seeds, but they produce this." He pointed up into the floating, feathery foliage that towered above them.

Leaning into Celeste, Greta whispered, "Shite, where'd he go to school?"

"Homeschooled," she whispered, before shushing her sister.

A month or so before, Jonah had shocked everyone, especially Luna, by announcing he wanted to attend Blue Cove Charter School with Alexa and Sophie. Except there was a hitch, the school wasn't accepting new students. Luna strategized, and asked around to find out what day the principal would be in. On the appointed day they had headed out to

Blue Cove without calling ahead. This was before Victor had come to town, on a beautiful day when Celeste was unencumbered by apprehensions about the way Luna might feel about her. They piled into Luna's Volvo, and drove west. Luna smiled knowingly and told Celeste, "Living back-to-the-land is really all about driving back and forth to the land." As they got closer to the ocean the air cooled and moistened, taking on a salty tang. The countryside was more lush nearer the Pacific, punctuated by stands of redwoods. But the road itself was abysmal—pot-holed—with clusters of orange cones where asphalt had crumbled down the cliff, even in narrow, twisting, hilly spots. Eventually, the paved road gave over entirely to an unapologetic dirt track. After about forty-five minutes of driving, they came to the *major intersection*, where four dirt roads converged—no road signs, or stop signs, just papers fluttering from a plywood bulletin board planted on the hillside.

"The Lost Coast . . ." Luna pointed straight ahead. "The only area of California without a highway along the coastline. You have to hike in, but it's unspoiled."

"When can we do it?" Celeste asked, squinting through the windshield.

"After we finish trimming the outdoor. Before the rains start. Every year we picnic among the elk. Sometimes we camp for a few days. It's so beautiful—sixty thousand acres bordering the sea." Luna turned right, accelerating up a tight winding road cut into the mountainside. Through the silhouette of trees, Celeste saw the glittering ocean below them. They climbed higher, curving up multiple hairpin turns, until the dense forest subsided, the sky opened up, and the school came into view: a cluster of buildings situated on a small campus looking over the Pacific. The light was diffuse, with puffs of clouds casting a delicate lavender tint over the panorama. As they made their way across the empty play yard—it was summer recess—a teacher, obviously a friend of Luna's, approached and engaged her in conversation. Celeste continued to the school office.

The principal, Clara, a short, round woman with silver hair pulled into a bun, was telling Celeste that there were no openings for new students, when Luna bounced in with Jonah, Alexa, and Sophie.

Clara went mute mid-sentence. "Luna!" she finally exclaimed, seemingly stunned.

Smiling graciously and giving Clara a quick hug, Luna explained that Jonah would very much like to attend school in September with his good friends, Alexa and Sophie. "You know that Jonah's never gone to school before—except for those few science classes at the junior college in Eureka, which we talked about last year."

"Yes, yes, I remember." Clara nodded enthusiastically.

About a half-hour later, they were back on the school playground, having secured placement in the best teacher-to-student ratio, K-12 charter school in Northern California.

❋ ❋ ❋

In the redwood forest, Jonah leaned against the tree trunk. Celeste smiled at him, grateful for his intelligence, and his biracial status, or whatever it was that had motivated the principal to treat him like a rock star and allow his friends, Alexa and Sophie, to attend school with him.

"Redwoods can live to be more than 2000 years old." Jonah was saying. "Only a few of those are left. There's no law against cutting down an old-growth redwood, if they're not in a state park. Anyway, when a tree is cut down baby trees grow around the cut stump." He pointed to the depths of the forest where a stump the width of Celeste's car had a circle of trees towering around it. "The tree sprouts use the roots of mama as their own. The new circle of trees is called a Fairy Ring. The baby trees are clones of the cut tree. Most of the remaining forests are made up of clones."

"A fairy ring . . ." Alexa repeated dreamily.

"So, even though a tree was cut, the genetic material of the tree, which coulda stood when the Romans ruled, is still regenerating itself. A living thing that old!" He threw his head back to scan the forest understory. "It's really cool the way redwoods move water around. They pull it from the air and circulate it through their entire mass, creating the environment they need, creating a rain forest."

Celeste put her hand on the nearest tree trunk and pressed her cheek against its pithy, reddish bark—listening for the heartbeat.

school

As always they took the footpath to the big house for break-fast. But the moment the screen door slammed behind them, Celeste wanted to herd her daughters back outside. This morning, Tom, Luna, and Jake sat at the large wood table. Luna's eyes were red and swollen. Celeste had never seen Luna look vulnerable, not even after they'd heard about the home invasion robbery. Alexa and Sophie went quietly down the hall, presumably looking for Jonah. Luna and Tom didn't move; they seemed stupefied.

Jake said, "One of the twins died last night."

"One of the Skunk Twins?" Celeste asked. Luna looked up sharply. Celeste's gaffe fell heavily, she'd used the ugly tag for identification purposes only, but there was no explaining it away. "I'm so sorry."

"Yeah," Jake replied, "still don't know which one."

"What happened?" she asked. The memory of the two boys flying through the air in front of Jake's truck, out of the black-ness, into the beam of headlights, came back to her.

"Crashed their motorcycle into a tree. One died on the road. Other one's in the hospital."

"Oh, my God, I'm so sorry." Celeste wasn't sure whom she was addressing. She was desperate to make amends and won-dered how much Luna hated her. She wanted to help, somehow. Glancing toward the kitchen, Celeste almost asked if anyone would like her to make coffee or breakfast, but it seemed taste-lessly mundane and inappropriate under the circumstances.

Jake tipped his head sideways, toward the door. He got up

from the table. Celeste followed him outside. In the sunlight, he took hold of her, and spun her around, as if they'd been dancing all night. She stepped back, slightly dizzy.

"Talked to your sister."

"I heard. How'd you know she was my sister?"

"Baby, she looks like you!"

"Shhh," she whispered, anxious about Luna and Tom hearing them. He grabbed her hand, yanking her down the path toward the cabin, like an impatient, impish boy. "Jake," she tried to keep her voice down. He swept her along the hilltop in his slipstream. "Jake." She prayed that Luna and Tom wouldn't hear her as she hissed, "Stop!"

He let go of her hand and turned. They were near the steps to the cabin's porch. Breathless from running behind him, she went up the steps and opened the door, ushering him inside. Jake smiled wickedly as he passed her, his hand running over her breasts. "Not here," she said, exasperated. They faced one another inside the cabin. Suddenly, he seemed extra big, outsized, a giant. Usually it was just her and the girls in the cramped space. Then it struck her again, like the first time she'd set eyes on him—he was so familiar, so appealing. "You gotta stop, Jake. Seriously. My kids are here."

"You're always so fucken stressed," he said. Outside Celeste heard birds screeching in the trees. Jake continued, "Why don't you get over it and smoke some weed."

She had no idea what she was doing in a relationship with him—she wasn't sure it was a relationship. He was her worst liability, yet he was also her conduit to some lost bloom. She shook her head. "You don't get it."

"No." Jake looked smug. "You don't get it. Why not have some fucken fun, Celeste."

"That's right. I'm no fun." They stared at each other. "Not where my kids are. Not in front of your dad and Luna."

Jake opened his arms. "Come here, baby."

It was private in the cabin. Her body yearned to let go. But she shook her head "No" and tried to shake off her mixed-up emotions. "God damn it!" Celeste shouted. "Somebody just died." Now she felt like crying.

Jake stepped towards her. "I know, I know." He wrapped her in his arms, and she let herself fall against him. Then he pressed his pelvis into her and nuzzled her neck.

"Oh, shit, Jake. Really? This doesn't work." Celeste pulled away. "It just doesn't work." She said again, this time for herself.

He shrugged, then murmured, "It's all good."

"I can't do this anymore." She took in a breath, and let it out. For him, she knew, everything was about the fuck he wasn't getting. That big directional penis led him around. "It's the age difference," she said. Jake sat down on the spindly wooden chair that was perpetually on the verge of breaking. The cabin got quiet; outside the birds screeched. "Want some coffee?" she asked.

"Yeah."

"Just know, it's over."

"Yeah."

Celeste put the kettle on the camp stove and got out a jar of ground coffee, spooning some into a paper filter. "How'd it happen, with the twins?"

"Guess Jimmy was behind 'em when they crashed. Last night, late, like one or two."

"Jimmy?" she asked, confused. "Jimmy, the neighbor over here?"

"He was trying to talk to 'em."

"At two a.m.?" Celeste was incredulous. "He was driving behind them because he wanted to talk to them in the middle of the night?"

"They always ride at night. Yesterday Jimmy found a foot-path at the back of his property that hooked up to a motorcycle trail. He followed it to their grandfather's land. Jimmy talked to the grandfather, but the boys weren't there. So he went looking for 'em at night. . ."

"Jimmy thinks it was the twins who did the home invasion?"

"It was."

Outside the slapping sounds of the girls' flip-flops were coming up the porch steps. The door banged open, and they barreled in. Alexa stopped short when she saw Jake. Sophie bumped into her from behind and fell down.

"Take it easy." Celeste pulled Sophie up and brushed her off.

Alexa was frozen, blatantly staring at Jake, wide-eyed and slack-mouthed, as if she'd never seen him before, like he was some sort of alien being.

"Alexa!" Celeste blared.

Alexa's head slowly turned toward her mother, yet her eyes stayed glued to Jake, trance-like. Finally, she snapped out of it and brightly, loudly, announced, "I'm starving."

Celeste shook her head. "I'll make something." She bent over to view the paltry selection of food below the counter. "What do we have?" she asked, thinking out loud.

"No, Mom." Alexa protested. "There's nothing good here."

"How 'bout oatmeal?"

"Hey." Jake stood up. "Let's go to town for Sunday breakfast. Waffles, at the Woodrose. My treat."

"No thanks. We're gonna picnic at the river. We have the whole day planned. Tomorrow's their first day of school."

"Mom," pleaded Alexa, "Waffles. Please. Jonah too."

Sophie pulled at Celeste's T-shirt and echoed her sister, "Mommy, pleeease."

There was nothing that would make the girls happy now—except breakfast in town, and going to town meant that the best portion of the day would be squandered. "Damn it, Jake."

"What?" he asked innocently.

※ ※ ※

They ran into Eddie in town; he'd already heard the news about the twins. Celeste knew what the patrons would be bantering about at the tavern tomorrow night.

"Those boys," Eddy said, "never got a chance. Not with their mom OD'ing when they was so young." Jake nodded and spoke in low murmurs that Celeste couldn't decipher, probably telling Eddy details about the rip-off. It was a good thing Luna and Tom had stayed home; Luna couldn't have stomached the gossip.

Eddy blurted out, "No shit." His back straightening, before he went back into a huddle with Jake. In the bright sun, the bald spot at the top of Eddy's head glinted out Morse code, his dreads fell in straggly, snarled pads around his shoulders. Jake continued talking in a low conspiratorial tone, and Eddy listened, rapt and attentive.

It seemed so cruel.

Standing in front of a real estate office, the girls and Jonah milled aimlessly, joking and poking at each other, their bellies full of waffles, content and satiated. Celeste's attention wandered as Jake and Eddy talked. She strolled to the front window of the office; photos of houses for sale were attached to the glass with yellowed tape. Leaning in, she looked closely at a picture of a property for sale near Holper Creek. The small farmhouse nestled next to a large oak on a gently rolling hill. Celeste took off her sunglasses; she'd noticed that house on the way to Blue Cove School; it captivated her when she saw it that first time. The farmhouse was old but looked well built. She remembered that the surrounding land was as romantic as a plein-air painting. Celeste checked the price scrawled below the photo a second time, wondering if she'd missed a zero. Compared to real estate prices in the city, the little house—and its five acres—was laughably cheap. Numbers rotated in Celeste's head. Victor hadn't agreed to sell their house in L.A., but even on what she made bartending and trimming, she might be able to eke out a monthly mortgage on property priced that low. *Owner will Carry.* The numbers rolled some more. If she put down twenty-percent—or less—she wasn't that far from being able to buy. Except, if she used the money she had toward a down payment, it would leave her flat broke. Without the stability of a teaching job, she'd be unable to get a mortgage through a bank. But if the owner carried, she wouldn't have to submit to corporate rules.

Luna had implored Celeste to embrace the Ganja Goddess. "Stop griping," Luna had commanded a month or more ago. They'd been canning tomato chutney in the kitchen, and as Luna stood over a giant canning pot billowing steam, she'd told Celeste, "You want to buy your own property, but you won't embrace the Ganja Goddess. If you were willing to grow, there'd be no worry about selling your city house." Luna slapped the lid back on the pot. "We're privileged in SoHum, blessed by the Goddess. Embrace her, Celeste. Options will open up for you."

Yet, Celeste maintained her resolve not to grow. However ambiguous legalization was locally, growing pot was against federal law. She wouldn't put her children at risk. But there were no available rentals to tide her though. Garberville wasn't like the city, with its endless beehives of apartments. Every other week, when a fresh stack of local papers appeared, Celeste checked hopefully. Occasionally there would be a lonely listing for some inadequate rental, but when she called it would already be gone. Luna had told her that because most local houses had some kind of grow connected to them, homeowners wouldn't advertise. A friend, or someone with a trusted connection, would be chosen to live in the place, run the grow—get a cut of the profit.

Inside the real estate office a woman sat behind a desk. "Hey," Celeste called to the kids, pointing to the door of the real estate office, "I'm going in."

※ ※ ※

When they returned to the ridge, it was late afternoon. Still enough time to help the girls organize their school backpacks, but that last lazy day of swimming and picnicking at the river had been lost.

In the heavy afternoon heat, Celeste cleared a place on the counter to put down the bags of groceries she'd bought in town. Recently, she decided to cook and eat in the cabin and avoid the big house as much as possible. It would be tricky, but if everything went well with the farmhouse, in a month or two they'd have their own home.

After using a small ice chest as a refrigerator the entire summer, she wanted to buy a little propane fridge and leave it as a thank you gift for the rent-free cabin Luna and Tom had provided. Celeste wanted to talk with Luna about it, but every time they were together she felt overcome by something— something unstated, but as real as an elephant with thick, ash-gray skin, sitting in every room they inhabited together. Celeste assumed it was because Luna knew about Jake, and the fiasco of leaving her children with Victor.

Oddly, Celeste didn't feel the same distance from Tom. Perhaps he didn't know about her involvement with Jake, or maybe he was more accepting and philosophical about it. Whatever the reason, she was thankful. The trim shack was back in working order after being shut down during the rip-off scare. Celeste had come to think of the trim shack as a place of refuge. She could make good money and blend in, just one of many workers. Tom was always around, going in and out, checking up, weighing and bagging pounds, taking away the stripped stems, bagging up the shake, always making jokes.

Someone knocked at the cabin door. Celeste froze. No one knocked. Either the kids burst in, or someone yelled for her. She opened the door, surprised to find Luna, her dreads un- tamed, her eyes bloodshot, puffy and glazed-looking. Celeste had a vision of embracing her, pulling her inside, holding her, tenderly winding and calming each dread back into place.

"Come in."

"Tom urged me to talk to you. I need help."

"Anything, Luna. Anything."

"I'm putting together a memorial for Damien."

"Oh, for the twin?" Celeste asked.

"Yeah. Damien died. We're hoping Danny will be out of the hospital by next week so he can be there, but that's uncertain."

"Whatever you need, Luna."

"I have Anya's birth coming up."

Celeste felt for the cord around her wrist without looking down. Still there.

Luna continued, "I need someone to work with me in case she goes into labor and I can't be at the memorial." Luna's shoulders drooped.

"Here." Celeste pulled out the rickety chair, the only one in the cabin. "Or." She pointed to the futon on the floor, the cozy spot where she slept every night. "How about the futon? You can relax, Luna. Much more comfy." Celeste wanted to take care of Luna, heal her, bring her hot, sweet tea.

Luna lowered herself onto the chair. "This is fine." She was quiet for a moment, then began, "It's important for the date of the memorial to get out there. So kids stop leaving things at the crash site."

"Kids?"

"Teenagers. The twins' friends. They've got this shrine going at the crash site, with bottles of Crown Royal, vodka, joints, other stuff . . . stuffed animals. They need something organized." She brought her hands up to her hair, patting it as if to check that it was still there, then gathered strands away from her face.

Grabbing at her ponytail, Celeste pulled her hair tie out and handed it to Luna. A whisper of acknowledgment crossed Luna's lips, but she shook her head. "I just got off the phone; I rented the Community House for next Sunday. So we have a date."

"Tell me what to do."

"Well, the kids know how to put memorials together. Lots of practice, unfortunately." The cabin went quiet, before she continued, "Our community's lost so many young ones."

"Drug-related deaths?"

"And accidents—on back roads, ATV's, crazy stuff. So, so many tragedies . . ." Luna's voice lost steam. "Anyway," she sat up straight, as if she were trying to rise above the depths of those casualties, "can't leave it up to the young people. They won't do an organized pot luck. They bring candy and ganja and then no one is well nourished. Those events spin out of control. They need structure. Some kind of schedule of events would help. Someone to lead, and . . ." Luna paused, then began again, "Laminates with Damien's picture need to be made up. We'll have to find a good picture of him. We need flyers, and someone to post them in town. We need someone to lead at the microphone . . . I already said that . . . anyway, there's more."

"I'm so glad you asked me to help because . . ." Celeste's temples pounded as she forced herself to speak, "I feel like you're not . . . happy with me anymore. I mean, you must be upset because of my relationship . . ."

"No." Luna interrupted, raising her palm. There was a moment of quiet; Luna focused on something behind Celeste, toward the back of the cabin, it was as if a glass panel was lowered between them. Luna continued to stare blindly beyond Celeste, through her, unseeing. Then, her demeanor changed. Slowly, almost robotically, Luna said, "I'm disappointed in myself. I promised to make sure the twins stayed safe, and I let them down."

"Oh, Luna!" Celeste jumped up and threw her arms around Luna. "Those boys were in another world. You had no control over them."

"I didn't do what I should've done, what I promised myself I'd do." She made a deep guttural sound. Not a sound that seemed to go with crying, not a weeping noise, but more of a long hiccup or gurgle, an escaped interior sound, which accompanied a single teardrop rolling down her ebony cheek, falling on her chest. It left a stain on her faded T-shirt.

Later, in the middle of the night, Celeste sat up, woozy and scared. The repeated echo of that sound woke her, as if the strange noise that Luna made got stuck in the walls of the cabin, as a dying creature would get stuck behind wallboards and scratch desperately over and over to get out.

☀ ☀ ☀

Celeste sent Alexa to fetch Jonah. From her car, looking up the hill, Celeste saw the screen door open, and was surprised to see Luna appear on the porch with him. The big house had wooden stairs from the porch to the driveway —as opposed to the cabin's wonky dirt steps. Celeste watched as they made their way down the steep stairs.

Luna got in the passenger seat. "Thought I'd join the festivities."

"The first day of waiting-for-the-school-bus festivities?" Celeste asked.

"Right," Luna laughed. Her eyes weren't as red or puffy as when she'd visited the cabin the day before.

On the ridge road, parked on the dirt shoulder, they all clambered out of the car. Next to the landmark of stacked rocks they waited together, milling around, watching for Azure to come around the bend in the small yellow bus.

Celeste remembered the first time she'd seen those rocks: in shock over meeting Tom for the first time in so many years, she'd felt lost and dismayed. Now that old, cherished image of Tom had been overlaid with Jake's face. Celeste turned toward Luna, guilty over her thoughts, and just then, Luna looked up, drifting onyx-colored eyes her way. Celeste glanced away, unable to breathe. She'd tried to talk with Luna about

Jake—but had been quickly and completely shut down. Luna had her own troubles.

In the thick dust on the side window of the Subaru, Alexa drew a peace sign, and then wrote "wash me." Jonah wrote "don't" above that, adding "conserve H_2O," and then "$\pi \times pie = yummy\ ^2$." Sophie drew a heart and wrote "Amy" inside it.

"Who's Amy?" Celeste asked.

"Amy's the baby's name."

"The baby?"

"Daddy's baby."

"Oh. Did Daddy tell you that when you talked on the phone yesterday?"

"No," Sophie shrugged. "But I like Amy. It's pretty."

Celeste understood now, it was as if Sophie were playing with dolls. "Does Daddy know it's a girl?"

Sophie shrugged again and looked up at Celeste. "Amy's a good name." Sophie was excited about having a half-sibling. She'd been bubbly about it lately, especially after the girls' weekly phone conversation with Victor. The Blessingway triggered many of Sophie's recent questions about births and babies; she didn't seem to differentiate that it wasn't her mother who was bearing her new sibling. Celeste had recently suppressed a laugh when Sophie said something sweet and funny about the baby. She caught herself wishing Victor was there so they could share a discreet smile about the cuteness of their daughter. But how twisted was that? Celeste shook her head. "Mommy, when will the baby come?"

Alexa spun around, turning on her sister. "Shut up!"

"Hey," Celeste said.

"Shut your trap about stupid 'Amy'," Alexa hissed, inches away from Sophie's face.

Celeste put both hands on Alexa's shoulders. "Stop it. You're angry Alexa, but not at your sister."

In the distance a large raven called from a tree top, then swooped across the sky. Alexa tossed a cold stare back at her mother and turned away, stalking back toward Jonah, who watched her closely, looking stricken and shocked. Celeste squatted next to Sophie, wrapping her arms around her. "Sweet pea, you can talk all you want about the baby with me." Celeste brushed Sophie's hair out of her face. "Okay?"

Sophie gave a weak smile. "Okay." Sometimes Sophie chatted endlessly about the subject of the baby, asking a litany of questions. When she did, Alexa did a certain thing with her mouth: a strange tightness extended over her lips. It could almost be read as a smile, except Celeste knew it wasn't. It was too closed, too clamped, like an expression made when trying to get an uncooperative jar to open. It reminded Celeste, uncomfortably, of a look she'd seen Greta make. After Victor left, Celeste took Alexa aside to explain the break up to her, but she couldn't find the right thing to say, there was so much that Alexa didn't need to know.

At last, the school bus rounded the bend, with Azure smiling her pink-lipstick smile behind the wheel. After kisses, the kids loaded onto the bus and Luna and Celeste waved good-bye. Sophie pressed her face against the window. "Love you," Celeste mouthed, then threw a kiss. "That hurts," Celeste said, as the bus pulled away in a dust cloud.

Luna's warm hand landed on her shoulder. "At least with Azure, we don't have to worry about their safety." Celeste knew that must be true, with Azure's female soul and linebacker shoulders, the kids would be safe, despite traveling the treacherous road to Blue Cove School.

"How are *you*, Luna? First time you've seen your boy off to school."

Luna looked toward the tree tops on a distant slope and sighed. "Just glad Jonah knows what he wants."

Driving back up the hill, Celeste thought out loud, "So I guess this is my new morning commute." Quite different than the 405 freeway that she and the girls used to traverse everyday in L.A., from the Westside to their school in the Valley. On the 405 each car was an opponent ready to pounce into the smallest opening, however unsafe. Before Celeste set foot in her classroom in the city, she'd already run an emotionally harrowing gauntlet. "Lots of potholes, no traffic." Celeste remembered when she and Luna had come upon trucks patrolling this same road, renegade fashion. As long as she didn't happen upon that scene again, she could continue to believe that the rip-off, and the fallout from it, was an aberration.

"Tom talked to Jake yesterday."

Celeste gulped and glanced at Luna. "About what?"

"Helping with the memorial setup, in case Anya goes into labor. I asked Tom to do the setup, but he won't. He refuses to leave the property during the harvest moon. Jake was adamant he wouldn't go either, but Tom talked to him," Luna sighed, "so Jake agreed to help."

memorial

Harvest season meant that all of SoHum was ripe and fragrant. Tom and Jake's monster plants were so tall Celeste couldn't reach the tops: she could only gaze up at the heavy buds that spilled outward, glittering with lusty, stinky resin, as if they'd been frosted with sparkling sugar. Everywhere, whether driving or walking in town, she passed through invisible clouds of the pungent odor, skunky-sweet and unmistakable, except possibly when the smell could be confused with a flattened skunk on the roadway. Celeste heard tales of people leaving dead skunks near their property to throw off suspicion. In the heat of that third week of September, the smell of ripe ganja was ubiquitous. Summer stretched on. People murmured and smiled at one another about the good weather as the buds got bigger and more resinous. It seemed the heat would go on forever.

When the day of the memorial came around, Luna was attending to Anya, who'd gone into labor during the night. Somehow, Luna had known it would happen that way. Celeste wondered about that, and also about the irony that she and Jake were thrown together again. They shared no small talk in the cab of Jake's truck as they cruised Bear Ridge Road on the way to the Community House. He sat behind the wheel with the forest gliding past, the wind from the open window making shallow cotton waves on his T-shirt. His profile had the chiseled look of a classical statue. Desire welled up in her. But she'd made her decision, *absolutely no more Jake*. It was too ruinous, too enmeshed with the remnants of her failed relationship with Tom, wholly impossible to sort out. Yet, in an odd way she was closer to Jake than to anyone in SoHum. From the beginning, they'd had a visceral relationship that was honest and raw. Too bad he lacked the maturity to distinguish among her many selves: the passionate woman, the girl tripping on mushrooms, the responsible mother, the animal woman. But, oh, that first time in the liquor room was so good; she couldn't afford to think about that.

A truck pulled in front of them from a side road. "What the hell?" Celeste exclaimed.

The truck was completely covered in fully-grown pot plants. Ropes and bungee cords secured plants to the top of the truck; on the front and back, more bulging plants flapped over the bumpers. Jake raised an eyebrow. "Look." Peeking through the leaves and buds was a sheriff's emblem. It was a sheriff's truck dressed in just-cut cannabis plants, like a float from a country parade. Saw-toothed leaves whipped in the wind, beautiful colas flopped, big and perfect, ready for harvest.

"How heartbreaking."

"Oh, dude," said Jake ruefully. "Might be from the Edwards' property. They live on that road. Holy shit!" He lifted his chin toward the rear-view mirror. Behind them Celeste saw there were other trucks following them also piled with plants. "Sheriffs musta called in the whole fucken crew."

"Will the Edwards go to jail?"

"Probably. Sheriffs can be bad. A CAMP helicopter used to just load up and fly off. Then you just wave goodbye. And cry. I watched Dad cry once." Jake kept his distance from the sheriff's truck in front of them. "They're gonna drive that truck up and down Main Street so everyone gets a good look. Gotta tell Dad. I'd like to turn around . . . but that would look suspicious."

"Is Bear Ridge safe? Should we be afraid?"

"Looks like a targeted bust to me. The cops have been sniffing around the ridge ever since the twins crashed. I'll call Dad when we get to the Community House. And Jimmy. He'll know what's up. See if we can get KBUD on the radio. Maybe they're reporting. Someone knows what's going on."

Celeste turned the radio on—nothing but static on every station.

"Bad stretch for reception," said Jake.

Celeste sank into the seat. "I look forward to one nice, boring day." Fear lodged in her gut, in the same spot where it had previously carved out a home. The truck in front of them took another curve. She watched the windblown plants shift pitifully.

"Once I fucken CAMP'ed my mom."

"What?"

"Ya know about CAMP?" Jake glanced at Celeste.

"Campaign Against Marijuana Planting? Yeah, Luna filled me in. Federal and state funded."

"Exactly. So, I was little, maybe eight. Me and Ziggy—my best friend, dead now—anyway, we're like in the veggie garden playing, and my mom had some plants in there."

"Pot plants?"

"Yeah."

"This was Luna?"

"No, my mom, when my parents were still together. So, we're playing CAMP. Ziggy's the helicopter, I'm the cop. We pull up her plants." Jake shook his head. "She was fucken pissed."

Celeste looked over at Jake. "You know," she said, "kids act out what goes on around them." The children of this particular world, living in the realm of growing, in the land of marijuana farming—in Growland—were witness to the culture's devastating secrets. There were no antidotes for something impossible to explain to an outsider. Celeste wanted her kids settled in the safety of their own home, quickly. She was pushing hard to get the paperwork for ownership of the farmhouse done, but the process was taking its own time.

Sandwiched behind and in front of sheriff trucks swathed in pot plants, Jake drove—carefully—over Bear Ridge Road. The river had to be close by. If they pulled off the road they could probably hike down to the river bar. Celeste wished she could be there now, lounging in the sunshine with her daughters and Jonah, watching water drip off Sophie's eyelashes, soaking up heat that had been absorbed by river rocks. She longed to feel carefree—without the buzz of fear about the newest grow-related catastrophe.

Yet, the truth was that without the pot economy she wouldn't have the opportunity to buy the farmhouse. The daughter of the old couple that had lived in the farmhouse was going to personally hold the mortgage, which was an exceptional bridge to carry Celeste over the waters of financial disclosure. In SoHum people didn't have to be legit on the books. There *were* no books. It was perfectly normal to look pathetic on paper. Victor's refusal to sell their house in the city was not an obstacle: a single woman supporting two daughters on a bartender's salary could buy a house, without disclosing other income. Growland would give Celeste, and her daughters, freedom and autonomy.

☙ ☙ ☙

A few people were already busy setting up folding tables when Celeste and Jake arrived at the Community House. Celeste took Luna's Indian bedspreads from the cloth bag and began to spread fabric over the tables.

Jake reappeared about a half-hour after they'd arrived. "Word is the bust is over," he said, standing close to her. He spoke in a low voice, "Doesn't seem they're going after anyone else, but Dad says we're gonna take everything down tomorrow. Not taking any chances."

"What'd Jimmy say?"

"Didn't know about the bust, but he talked to the twins'

grandfather yesterday. Jimmy says the grandfather won't let Danny back on his property. Not 'til he tells where they hid it."

"Their own grandfather thinks they did it?"

"They're fucken thieves, Celeste. The grandfather says he's gonna see it gets returned to Jimmy, every last fucken ounce. Says he holds Danny responsible for Damien's death."

"What if they didn't do it, Jake? Then that boy will be accused at the worst possible time in his life." Celeste stopped arranging a tablecloth and looked into Jake's green eyes. "Where will he go if his grandfather won't let him back home after the hospital?"

"Just hope Luna doesn't bring him back to Dad's."

"What?" Celeste froze, stunned. "She wouldn't do that." In theory, Celeste could extend the benefit of innocence to the boy, but on a practical level she didn't want him anywhere near her children. Regardless of what he'd actually done, or not done, he was trouble. She'd known it the first time she'd seen those twins.

"Hope not. Gets out Tuesday." Jake stared at Celeste, then shrugged before he turned and wandered off.

The tables filled with offerings as people began to arrive. Candles were lit. Garden flowers in Mason jars appeared. A gray-haired woman in a paisley gown arranged Native American medicine bundles of sage and tobacco on a red cloth. A wooden bowl was piled with joints. A paper bag filled with candy was plunked down. Swarms of teary-eyed teenagers and twenty-somethings streamed into the building, holding onto one another, whispering. Outside on the hillside leading up to the Community House, oversized pickup trucks parked nose to tail.

Celeste stationed the laminates in a basket at the entrance. She'd been up until two in the morning tying a ribbon to each laminate. Just looking at a ribbon, she could feel its slippery texture in her fingers. Double knots. Two hundred laminates. The photo of the light-haired boy with pale and strangely vacant eyes had become permanently imprinted on Celeste's brain. The feature that stood out most to her, however, was the arm of the boy's twin brother. She hoped it wasn't as obvious to everyone else. There had been no way to cut it out gracefully. Those twin arms thrown over each other's shoulders were interwoven, impossible to excise one from the other. Below the photo, printed in ornate script, was "RIP, Damien Broudy, October 9, 1986 September 15, 2002." As the mourners came in, each of them picked up a picture of the dead twin in its plastic sleeve and draped it around their necks.

The bulletin board leaning against the table nearest the podium was covered with pictures of the twins—a few as toddlers and the rest as adolescents. The centerpiece was a blown-up photograph of the brothers with other young boys, all around ten or eleven years old, posed in front of an emerald lake. One boy held a small fish by its tail; another boy playfully flexed his arm muscles like a strongman. They were shirtless, skinny, smiling. At one point, Cloud joined her in front of the board. He pointed to each boy, reciting the circumstances of his demise: overdose, gunshot wound, passenger in a car wreck, and now, fatal motorcycle accident. The only boy in the picture who was still alive was Danny.

People began to sit down as the band set up on the stage, clunking the heavy sound equipment. When the memorial got underway at last, with Cloud leading from the podium, it was almost two hours later than the time Luna had told Celeste to list on the flyer. A few young men came up to speak about Damien, telling emotional stories about their childhood. Then a man with cursive tattoos on his neck waved his arm from the audience.

"Come on up, Justin." Cloud gestured. Justin made his way to the podium through a cluster of mourners. The crowd was hushed and watchful. The previous speaker handed a glass pipe to Justin, who whipped a red plastic lighter out of his pocket and fired it up. Smoke spiraled upward and there was a long interlude as he inhaled, held it, and then blew smoke out into the audience, as each of the other speakers had done. Homage to the Ganja God.

"Yo. Hey." He bent to the microphone. "Uncle John Broudy." He nodded his head toward the twins' grandfather sitting in the front row and then looked around the room in a daze, speaking in a faltering voice. "Me, Damien, and Danny—cousins, man. Grew up tight, man. This's fucked." He shouted, "Fucked!" He pressed his thumbs into his scrunched-up eyes, as if pressure would stop the bleeding out of tears. "Wish Danny was here, man, not in the hospital. Yo." He waved to a woman who was filming the ceremony. "Dude, love ya," he said, making an elaborate hand signal for the camera.

Celeste was standing in back of the audience. She leaned against a door and tested the doorknob, slowly and delicately. It was unlocked. As quietly as possible, she pushed it open. Turning sideways, she slipped outside, finding herself in blinding sunlight in the parking area behind the building.

The Community House sat on a knoll, with a steep hill rising behind it. Celeste crunched across the gravel lot, past rows of parked trucks glinting in the sun. The town spread out below, Busy Bee Grocery, the post office, the laundromat, and, set back from the sidewalk, one of the many churches, its center porch entrance planted with yellow and red flowers.

Celeste turned and looked up at the forested hillside; mossy steps curved up from the parking area and disappeared into the woods. The steps looked lush and romantic, as if from a fairy tale. They beckoned her. Each stair had a cap of rocks and tread covered in velvety moss. Her feet sank into the soft green mat, leaving imprints that quivered slightly as they sprang back into place. Celeste took off her sandals and climbed the stairs barefoot. Each step a revelation of plush, dewy delight. The forest was dense, stippled with shadow and light, a clear bell-like sound of water resounding through it. At the top of the stairs, she found the source: water fell over a rock ledge in shining droplets, forming a delicate trickle of tears. Against the surface of the mottled stone outcropping, verdant ferns clung and glistened. Looking back down the curving steps, she was surprised to see how far she'd come. The Community House and town were no longer visible through the trees. She had an enveloping sense that she'd been trans-ported. Water pooled at the bottom of the rock wall, flowing off in a narrow gully that diverted it from the Community House below. Celeste stretched out on the furry moss carpet, breathing in the forest air and the mineral, metallic scent of water on rock. She stared at a tender, fractal-patterned fern, then felt her body become heavy.

Rumbling vibrations of diesel truck engines woke her. Frag-ments of light in the forest had changed hue, from bright white to a diffuse golden glow. Water dropped from the rock outcrop like strands of multi-faceted diamonds. She rubbed her eyes; her dream came to her whole, like a round, full bubble, not in disjointed segments as usual: she and Luna had been talking and laughing, while they floated—flew—inside an old Volkswagen Beetle that Luna had described owning long ago. Suddenly careening to earth, they hurtled down a mountainside. Celeste reached out, grabbing a tree branch as they went; she pulled herself out of the car window into a large oak tree growing sideways out of the mountain. Celeste looked down at her body, it was covered in fur. When she cast her eyes away, to search for Luna, everything had changed, the mountain was gone, and Luna was hurtling through a dark, deep abyss.

Celeste shook off the dream. She rolled her neck, stretched, put on her sandals, and went down the hill, stepping carefully as she descended the soft, slippery steps.

Some of the trucks lining the road had departed. The band played loudly inside the Community House. Disparate groups mingled in the gravel area out back. Celeste spotted Jake's blue T-shirt through the crowd. She wanted to get back to her daugh-ters, but she and Jake had to clean up before they could leave.

Eddy and a few others were talking to Cloud. Celeste smiled and said hello, raising her hand in greeting as she passed them, moving quickly toward where Jake was standing. His back was to her, his right palm flat against the side of the building, his arm supporting his body, tilted at a strange angle.

"Jake?"

He whipped his head around with an odd, astonished look. It struck her as funny, and she laughed. Then she saw Harmony, and Jake so close to her, his arm against the building encircling the niche in which she stood.

Celeste turned away. She wanted to run, but controlled the urge, walking as quickly as possible over the gravel, with as much grace as she could muster. Halfway down the hill, she heard Jake's voice behind her, but she kept going.

☘ ☘ ☘

On Tuesday, Celeste was called to substitute teach at Garberville Elementary. Standing in front of the classroom, curious third-grade children staring at her, the squeaking sound on the white board as she wrote her name—the sights and sounds of the classroom reassured and comforted her, like pulling on pleasantly worn clothes with just the right yielding fit.

The principal droned on, sounding scratchy and distant through an old P.A. speaker. According to the lesson plan Celeste found in a folder marked "Substitute," his "Thought of the Day" was meant to be an inspirational message. It bore little resemblance to the sweet morning ritual of singing with her students at her Waldorf School in LA. Finally there was a click and the disembodied voice was gone. The first assignment was to have the students write about what the principal's words of wisdom meant to them. Celeste strolled the aisles between the desks. "After you write your two sentences on the Thought of the Day, we'll get to know one another."

"Good work," she said to a boy well into his first sentence. A girl on the other side of the room raised her hand. Celeste went to her. "Please, tell me your name."

The girl had big, bright eyes. "Tamara," she said shyly.

"Hi, Tamara. Do you need help?"

She nodded in response, and Celeste knelt next to her desk. Suddenly Celeste was engulfed in a cloud of fresh-cut marijuana scent, intense and unmistakable. Mortified, she resisted pulling the neckline of her cotton dress to her nose and sniffing it. She'd made certain her clothing was pristine; it wasn't her exuding that smell.

Although she tried to concentrate on helping the girl, Celeste had trouble getting over her shock at a third grader smelling like a trim shack.

"Did you have a question?" Celeste asked, robbed of that sweet nostalgic sense she'd had about teaching just seconds before. The cannabis stink had knocked it right out of her.

Tamara nodded, pointing to a word she'd written, "Is that right?" She looked up at Celeste with pure, innocent eyes.

As the morning wore on, Celeste realized it wasn't just Tamara emitting the familiar odor. At least a couple of the other children smelled like they'd just come from a harvest as well. After the lunch bell rang, Celeste walked the kids to the cafeteria, watched them file in, and then went back to the empty classroom.

"Hello?" A slim brunette peered around the open door, and then swept into the room. "I'm next door," she said, pointing to the wall. They introduced themselves. She had luminescent skin and an interesting scar across her forehead.

"What grade do you teach?" Celeste asked, taking her sandwich out of a paper bag and smoothing the noisy bag flat.

"Fourth grade. This is my second year . . ."

There was a commotion outside. A girl came running into the classroom. "Miss Farrar, Zack threw his apple again!"

"Where, Raven?"

"The cafeteria."

"Is Mr. Gordon there?"

"Yeah."

"Well then, Mr. Gordon will deal with it." The girl deflated like an emptied balloon. She looked at Celeste and back at Miss Farrar, as if to plead, one last time, for action. Then she gave up abruptly and ran back outside—but not before the smell, that same strong whiff of fresh pot blossomed into the air where she'd stood. Celeste flared her nostrils and pulled away, an inadvertent, visceral reaction. Miss Farrar, or Jasmine, as she had introduced herself, laughed. "You haven't lived here long," she snorted.

Celeste wanted to explain that she'd been trimming all summer, she wasn't a prude. But she'd been sworn to secrecy by Luna. Besides, it wasn't the presence of marijuana or pot farming itself that disturbed her: it was the shock of the smell of it on schoolchildren. But, of course, why wouldn't they smell of it? They lived in the midst of it. The harvest was probably hanging to dry inside their house—or trailer, or cabin, or yurt—in which case, Celeste knew, it would be impossible not to smell like it. Do peanut farmers' children smell of peanuts? Or orange farmers' children smell of oranges? Even if they did, those smells wouldn't lead cops to arrest someone. But, peanut farmers wouldn't be bringing the harvest inside their homes to watch over it. And anyway, she thought, most American farmers don't harvest their own crops; underpaid migrant workers do the work.

"It's just that time of year." Jasmine smiled warmly. "You must be new to SoHum, how long have you been here?"

"We came up in July."

Jasmine put her hand on her hip and cocked her head. "Are you staying at Luna and Tom's?"

Celeste laughed. "That's us."

"My parents used to be land partners with Tom and his first wife, back in the day." Jasmine leaned against the desk. "Harvest season goes on for quite a while. You can get a whiff just walking down the halls. Guess you have to get used to it. Doesn't bother me, but I grew up here." She slapped her hand on the desk. "Last year, I was teaching fifth grade, going over equivalents with my students—ounces and pounds—I asked the kids if anyone knew how many grams were in a pound." Jasmine laughed, "They all started looking at each other, and then I realized, of course they know how many grams are in a pound. One girl said, 'There's 464 grams in a pound.' And then this kid in the back yelled, 'No, dummy, that's *with* the turkey bag.' I almost laughed out loud."

"Well." Jasmine looked up at the clock. "Nice to meet you. Better get back." She turned to leave. "See you around town."

At the end of the school day most of the children streamed out of the classrooms to the school buses, but a few stayed behind waiting for their parents to pick them up. Celeste recognized one of the fathers as a regular from the tavern. When she saw him from across the room, her spine stiffened. She didn't want to be outed as a bartender. But he looked right at her, waved, and called, "Hello," in a casual, friendly way. Celeste sighed, relieved. Surely there could be no regulations against bartending while teaching at an elementary school, but it still didn't bode well, especially in a small town. It wouldn't help her land the teaching position she wanted. Would the administrators even have called if they'd known? Maybe, she mused, I should consider trimming full time.

✹ ✹ ✹

Garberville scrambled with pedestrians, trucks, and cars; the small town was overrun with people looking for work. The predominant group consisted of American trimmigrants; Jake called them the "walking dead." They roamed in bands, lured by rumors of quick and easy cash, on a quest for the golden trimming job. Because they lived outside, or in vehicles, the longer they stayed, the dirtier, and grayer, they became, dawdling around town, walking single file with their dogs by the roadsides. At twilight, columns of transients rambled down narrow paths to camp on the river bar below Garberville.

Other distinct waves of people arrived and then receded. Almost every weekend some festival would draw crowds; the largest, Reggae on the River, brought diverse skin tones to town. But as summer faded, there were fewer and fewer faces of color. Celeste came to realize that her initial impression of the area as racially diverse was incorrect. Turned out SoHum's multi-ethnic state was festival-related. Once, when Celeste had complained to Luna about standing out like a sore thumb in a crowd because she was a redhead, Luna had responded, "Oh, baby, I'm Black! I spent years personally integrating SoHum." Yet perplexingly people spoke about the area's diversity. Slowly, Celeste came to realize they were referring to a diverse spread of class and strata: the environmentally conscious intellectual embracing the old-school clear-cutting redneck, the old white poor mingling with the young white ganja rich. There seemed to be a large population of lesbians, gay men, and transgender people. But when she stood in the elementary school classroom that morning, it hit her just how white SoHum's population really was. Every child in the classroom was Caucasian, except one girl, who could have been Latina—or, more likely, Native American. There was more ethnic diversity at the expensive private school she'd taught at in the city.

In the Busy Bee Grocery parking lot, transients and trim-migrants roamed around cars. Celeste found a spot, as far away from the action as she could manage. Rummaging in her purse for her shopping list, she entered Busy Bee. Beside the refrigerated drink case was a chainsaw-carved redwood sculpture of a growling bear, a variety of tourist souvenirs, posters of state park forests. She stopped at a life-size poster of Bigfoot—covered in fur. The animal man. Celeste laughed.

"Hey. What's so funny?" Jake asked, appearing out of nowhere.

Celeste shook her head. "Where'd you come from?"

"Across the street. Saw you park." Jake gazed expectantly at her. "What're you laughing at?"

"Just the absurdity of things." She coughed, checked her list, and took off down the cereal aisle. The day before, Jake had called and they'd talked for the first time since the memorial. He said he'd only talked to Harmony for a few minutes and that she'd been on her way back to the Bay Area. Celeste insisted it didn't matter; he should forget the whole incident. She apologized for her reaction. "I had no reason to be upset."

Jake followed her to the produce section. "You look all, like, school-teacherish."

"I subbed at Garberville Elementary today."

Jake had hungry eyes. "I like you in a dress."

Celeste reached for some bananas. "What're you doing in town?"

"Gregor's store is opening this weekend."

"Oh. Nice."

Celeste paid for her groceries and Jake picked up her bag. When they emerged in the heat, Jake pointed across the street to a new store. "Been helping all day."

"There's Cloud," Celeste said, "with Gregor." It was easy to recognize Gregor; he always wore a kilt. He and Cloud were talking near the new storefront and its bright new sign. "Trim It Up" specialized in machines that trimmed pot. The new business had agitated the community; many didn't want a sign saying "Trim It Up" on Main Street. Apparently, the same outcry was heard years before over the Hemp Connection sign.

Local trimmers feared that trimming machines would destroy the economy and culture of SoHum, obliterating an important source of income. But Tom said it would take years to get to the point where machines were used widely and even then, a bud processed by machine still had to be shaped, if only briefly, by human hands.

Celeste took her groceries from Jake and put them in her car. "Thanks," she said, "I gotta go. Luna's picking up the kids from the bus."

Jake put his hand on her shoulder. "Do you know?"

She turned, "What?"

"About Danny."

Celeste shook her head.

"Luna picked him up from the hospital this morning."

"Where is he?" Jake didn't respond, he just shook his head, and Celeste knew. "At Tom and Luna's? Are you sure?"

"Dad's fucken pissed." From across the street there was some commotion. Jake turned to look, then refocused his gaze on her, direct and serious. "But Dad's letting her do it. I guess Jimmy came over this morning and started screaming shit."

Celeste felt like the weight of a millstone had fallen on her. "Jake, I gotta move out of the cabin now. I can't wait for escrow to close on the farmhouse."

"Where will you go?"

"Jesus, I don't know!" Celeste was frantic. And scared. She had to get her daughters out immediately. It could be mere days before the deal for the farmhouse closed, but that was too long. Why would Luna expose Jonah and her girls to a damaged, reckless boy like Danny? She scrambled into her car, anxious to get to her children.

"You working at the tavern tonight?" Jake asked through the open window.

"I'm supposed to." Her mind reeled. She had to call Delores and beg for the night off. The last thing she wanted was to leave her kids at the big house with Danny there. As she turned onto Main Street, she glanced in her rear-view mirror; Jake was still standing in the Busy Bee parking lot, watching her drive away.

Celeste drove fast, too fast, on Bear Ridge Road. She tried to distract herself from the horrific thoughts zooming in her head by remembering how happy she was to be teaching again—before her emotions had been tempered by the way the kids smelled.

So many of the people who crossed her path smelled like they'd just come from dancing with a ripe crop. Celeste went out of her way to make sure that she and her daughters never carried that reek. In public, she didn't want to be identified as being involved in the trade.

After a full day at the trim shack, she'd be immune to the smell on herself, but she was fastidious about stripping her designated clipping clothes off—always outside—leaving them in a basket on the porch. She never brought them into the cabin, where the odor would infiltrate other clothing, bedding, and . . . her children. The resinous stink on her hands was difficult to dissolve; she'd scrub with salt and olive oil, follow with a good soaping, and finish with a rubbing-alcohol rinse.

In the trim shack, she was now able to distinguish the notes of different strains: the tangy smell of Sour Diesel versus the floral scent of Granddaddy Purple. But she couldn't come close to matching Jake's uncanny ability. From a bag of buds he could tell—by smell and sight—not just the strain, but whether it was indoor, outdoor, dep, or hydroponically grown, even discerning the enclave where the crop had been grown.

Celeste worked hard to be discreet, while in Garberville a business called Trim It Up was opening. This contradiction was a measure of the power of Humboldt County's economy, and the whole of the Emerald Triangle, with its culture of flagrant secrets. Growers benefited from pot being illegal, but so did law officers. The local sheriff stations were flush with unreported confiscated grower cash. SoHum, the Ground Zero of growing, reflected the disparity of a culture spun from lies, yet hiding in the light of day. The townspeople leading the fight to have the "Trim It Up" sign barred from Main Street were attempting to cling to the pretense that Garberville was a regular town, not a town all about ganja. But it was all about ganja. A company town—without a company.

Once, despite her careful efforts, Celeste had given herself away. She and the girls were at Busy Bee, in a line of people waiting to pay. She'd been marveling at the display of trimming supplies grouped together on the shelves of the check-out lane, last-minute grab items next to the candy and gum—Fiskar clippers and rubbing alcohol—when a blonde surfer-type dude in line behind her smiled and delicately pulled a fresh pot leaf from the back of her T-shirt, letting it drift to the floor. Celeste mumbled thanks and looked away, embarrassed.

Behind her he spoke softly, "We're all on the same team, sweetie."

goodbye

In the big house, Alexa, Sophie, and Jonah were at the table doing homework. Celeste looked down the hall, casting her eyes about, searching the recesses for Danny, but she didn't see him or anything out of place.

"Mommy." Sophie ran to her.

Celeste kissed Sophie on the top of her fragrant head. "How was school?"

"We heard seals," Sophie said excitedly.

"Sea lions," Alexa corrected.

"They bark. Like dogs," Sophie explained.

"How cool." Celeste was relieved, everything seemed as it should. There was no evidence of the twin; Jake had to be wrong. She went toward the kitchen. "Luna, thank you so much for picking the kids up from the bus stop."

"How was substituting?"

"It was good, actually." Celeste took in the gleaming darkness of Luna's skin, and thought of the sea of white children's faces in the classroom that morning. She was so used to looking at her daughters' golden glow and Jonah's mocha skin color that Caucasian children seemed to lack vigor or health. Of course her own skin tone was the palest of pale; only her freckles and red hair gave her color.

"I saw Jake in town, on my way home." Celeste said to Luna.

"Yeah, he's helping Gregor open that new store."

Celeste stepped closer. "He told me you picked up Danny from the hospital."

Luna looked up from wiping the counter with a sponge. "I did."

A chill went through Celeste. They exchanged looks. Placing the sponge on the counter, Luna swiped at her hair, pushing a dreadlock off her face. "Sometimes it's necessary to step up and help out. No one else is offering Danny a place to stay. I'm not turning a child away."

"But Luna . . ." A sound behind her made her turn.

Danny stood, almost hidden, in the shadowed hall. Celeste met his light blue eyes across the distance. His features were not unattractive, but Celeste could only think of the night when two sets of light eyes had appeared coldly reptilian.

"Danny," she tipped her head, acknowledging his presence. "I'm sorry for your loss." Celeste didn't know what else to say. It was obvious that she didn't want him there. She couldn't pretend otherwise; she *wouldn't* pretend otherwise. Danny faded back into the hall, without responding to her.

Jonah looked up from his studies. The whole house felt suddenly tense, artificially quiet as if they were staying perfectly still until the music started again.

"Come on, girls, let's go to the cabin." Celeste waved her hand. She moved toward the screen door. "Thanks again for picking them up, Luna."

In the cabin, she called Delores, pleading for the night off as her cell reception wobbled in and out with every sentence, Delores' response was absolute. "Sorry, doll, ya gotta work; ain't got no replacement." Celeste considered not showing up, but she had to keep the job; it was already a part of her financial profile for the acquisition of the farmhouse. She didn't have a teaching position yet, but she did have a regular job at the tavern.

Everything will be fine. Believe it, make it so. My children will be safe. Everything will be fine. She repeated the mantra over and over.

☘ ☘ ☘

That night, Jake came into the bar with a woman. Celeste saw them enter in her peripheral vision. Immediately, jealous girlfriend symptoms returned. The bar was busy, loud, crowded. Jake stopped near the entrance to talk to Gregor. Celeste couldn't see the woman's face.

"Here you are," Celeste announced as cheerily as possible, placing drinks in front of a couple seated together at a table. She went back behind the bar and when she looked up Jake was inches away from her, on the other side of the bar.

"Hi, Celeste."

She shook her head and looked away, flooded with rage and adrenaline. "Jake, please."

"I want you to meet someone." The woman was next to him. Celeste turned slowly to face her. "Mom, this is Celeste." He gestured. "This is my mom, Pandora."

Celeste stared.

He went on. "She's got, like, a studio where you can live."

Celeste felt she'd been hurtling down a superhighway not knowing where to exit as the feelings came up and then whizzed by again. Exits with names like: "Jealousy," "Anger," "Hope." She was dumbfounded.

Jake's mom smiled. "Nice to meet you." Pandora had deep lines etched in her face and thin, long jet-black hair. "Heard so much about you." She wore a low cut top that made it obvious she'd had a boob job. Her clothes showed off a still youthful figure, but her breasts were the first things you noticed, flags flying high and kooky, uneven and unnatural. Way too close to her collar bone, they looked as if they had migrated upward. Celeste couldn't help but stare.

"So, you're an old friend of Luna's?" asked Pandora. "Are you from Chicago too?"

"Oh," Celeste's mind reeled. *No, actually I'm the old lover of your ex and the new lover of your son.*

Jake was throwing dagger eyes.

Celeste stumbled along. "Um, actually I'm from . . ."

"It's in town," interrupted Jake.

"What?" Celeste asked.

"Mom's place is in town."

"Oh." Celeste turned toward Pandora. "So, you have a studio to rent?"

"Well, it's unfinished." Pandora smiled demurely. Celeste decided it was a practiced smile. "Some of the drywall's up," Pandora added. "The studio's in my house; I'm an artist." She threw her hair back and caressed her neck in a slow affected movement with her pinky extended. "An artist needs a dedicated studio. So I decided to have my back porch enclosed. Eventually, I'll paint and teach art classes there, but it's not finished yet." She sighed loudly. "My carpenter chased his bimbo to Hawaii." Her voice lowered. "Asshole."

"Oh," Celeste said, passing another exit on the superhighway, this one called "Disappointment." She didn't want to move to an unfinished room inside Pandora's—or anyone's—house. "How much is the rent?" Celeste asked. "You know I have two daughters, right?"

"No problem with your kids, and rent's no problem. I don't want money. I need help, in my grow room, and I have a mother room for propagating clones that I need help with too. So, I'll do a work trade. My carpenter got the mom room set up and then ran off. I just can't do it by myself." Her tone changed again. "And the A-hole still wants a cut!"

"But . . ." Celeste looked at Jake. "But . . . I don't know anything about propagating clones. I'm not the right person."

Jake turned to his mother and said, "Just a minute." Then he bent over the bar, blocking his mother's view, whispering in Celeste's ear. "I got this for you. Fucken say 'yes'. It's a gift."

※ ※ ※

After work, late that night, Celeste went to see Pandora's small clapboard house on a Garberville side street. Pandora led the way through a cluttered living room, past the kitchen to a long back room with a bank of windows and a glass door on the back wall. No drywall on half the walls, and the floor was dirty plywood, but, Celeste thought, I'm used to that.

"There's the bathroom," Pandora said proudly, pointing to an adjacent door.

"What's out here?" Celeste cupped her hands to the window.

"Here." Pandora flipped the switch, and a bare yellow bulb illuminated a row of tall marijuana plants in an unkempt, but private, fenced-in backyard.

"I'll show you my mom room, where I need the most help. I just can't keep up with it."

Celeste followed Pandora out of the studio, down a few steps and across the yard to the back of the garage. At a padlocked door, Pandora took out keys and struggled a moment with the lock. When the door opened, a blinding white light radiated from the room. Celeste looked away to avoid the intensity of light, as Pandora disappeared into the room.

Celeste hesitated. "Uh, isn't it bad for your eyes?"

Over a loud buzzing, Pandora shouted from inside, "Don't look at the bulbs."

Tentatively, Celeste stepped into the room, high-intensity electric noises crackled and bright lights blazed. "Whew."

"Haven't you seen an indoor before?"

Celeste shook her head; she was overwhelmed. When her eyes adjusted enough to look around, she thought the place looked like a combination potting shed and lab. Under white metal hoods, which cast the most intense brightness, large plants clustered. Light sources were everywhere. Shelves lined with rows of trays had smaller lights over them. Each tray with divided foam squares held a single, diminutive cannabis plant. Pandora pumped a plastic sprayer and held the nozzle to the trays, letting a soft mist fall over little stems.

"What's that? Is it something poisonous?"

"Water." Pandora gazed at Celeste. "Are you always, like, worried about everything?"

"If I'm going to be working in an environment like this, yes, I want to know if I'm exposing myself to anything toxic." Celeste shrugged. "Anyway, what would you want me to do? I don't know anything about this."

"First, you water and fertilize the Moms, do some leafing, maybe some potting up. That kinda stuff. Then I'll teach you to cut clones. See if you have the magic."

✻ ✻ ✻

The next morning, Celeste took the kids to the bus and then went back to Tom and Luna's, opening the screen door to the big house, she saw Luna at the kitchen sink.

Luna turned to her and smiled. "Good morning. Would you like some tea?"

"Good morning. I'm okay, thanks. How's Anya doing?"

"Great. That baby is beautiful. Such a calm birth."

"Awesome." Celeste watched as Luna put the kettle on and fussed with some loose tea. She felt a tremendous swell of love and gratitude. "Thank you so much for everything you've done for us."

Luna placed her penetrating eyes on Celeste. "Everyone's having trouble with Danny being here. You're not alone."

"I know," said Celeste. Nothing would change Luna's mind about protecting the boy. Though the grapevine named the twins as the robbers—and Celeste now believed they'd done it too—Luna was steadfast. If Danny were proven guilty, Luna would still be capable of forgiveness. Celeste admired that, even as she prepared to haul her stuff off the ridge to another uncertain living situation. She respected Luna and her determination to harbor a troubled young man.

"Luna," Celeste almost cringed as she spoke. She hated what she was doing. But it was better than exposing her daughters to the potential storm of the remaining twin. "We're moving out of the cabin today." Celeste didn't want to tell her that they were moving to Pandora's, and she held her breath hoping Luna wouldn't ask where they were going.

Luna stirred honey into her tea without any register of surprise. Had she expected it?

"It's been a pleasure, Celeste."

"You and Tom have been so good to us. So generous. You changed our lives." Celeste wondered where Danny was, probably somewhere close by, listening.

"We'll miss you, Celeste. We'll miss the girls. Jonah especially will miss them. Will they stay in the school?"

"Oh, yes,"

"Good."

A stillness floated between them. Luna didn't ask questions. She was like that. Her way was complete acceptance. Everyone should make their own determination. But nothing could sway her. Not Jimmy, not Jake, not Tom.

And certainly not me, thought Celeste.

mother room

Pandora chatted as Celeste sorted the kids' clothes and tried to figure out where to put them. Rows of stacked canvases leaned against the walls, taking up valuable space; there was no closet, and furniture was scarce in the studio. In the almost three months Celeste and her daughters had lived in SoHum, they'd somehow acquired a remarkable amount of stuff.

Pandora talked incessantly about living the artist's life, though her paintings looked lifeless to Celeste. After a while her voice became noise, irritating static Celeste was forced to listen to. Pandora's monologue lurched from her artistic abilities to her love affairs, to why she'd gotten breast implants and what a spiritual experience that had been, and finally to her higher connection with children. "It's just natural for me. The artist's consciousness is all about getting back to the child's mind, the innocence of creativity without the critical grown-up voice that interferes with the impulse." Pandora perused her canvases and enthused. "I teach a children's painting class on Saturday. Your daughters would love it. I can see they have the artist in them."

"Sounds good," said Celeste.

"It's only forty dollars a class. I provide the supplies and environment. My new series starts Saturday."

"Well, actually, I'm saving for our farmhouse right now."

"They'd gain important knowledge of art and life. There's a waiting list, but I'll let your daughters in." Pandora smiled ingratiatingly. "The first class is free."

"Oh. Okay." Celeste resisted rolling her eyes. "This Saturday. A free art class for the girls. Sounds like a plan, Pandora. Thanks."

A class led by Pandora would be a pallid stab at replacing the outdoor activities her daughters had become accustomed to, but a plan for Saturday would help Alexa give up her dogged insistence that she was going horseback riding with Jonah over the weekend. It didn't seem to matter how many times Celeste explained that as long as Danny was at Tom and Luna's, Alexa couldn't go back.

Broken-hearted and angry, Alexa was furious at Celeste for taking her away from Jonah. Celeste explained that she would still see Jonah on the school bus and at school. The only real change would be not living next to each other. Yet Celeste heard the same subtext that Alexa heard: *You and Jonah won't be riding horses to the river everyday or doing random art projects together. You won't be sitting next to each other in the coolness of the great room in the hot afternoons, or writing in your journals side by side, as you have done almost every day since you met.*

For Celeste, being in town, meant having consistent cell reception and wireless internet. While the girls were at school, she walked to the health food store, and revisited the enchanted steps at the Community House. In the studio, she scrubbed the floors and wiped up mounds of desiccated fly carcasses from the aluminum window sills. She made clean and comfortable areas for herself and the girls to sleep on their futons. Although, looking out to the enclosed backyard at Pandora's, she couldn't help remembering the sweeping views from the cabin porch, those distant mountain ridges that layered themselves in shades of green against the sky.

Sophie's biggest upset about leaving Tom and Luna's involved Kiwi, the pony, and Trinity, the dog. Sophie cried in the mornings, worried that Trinity was waiting for her on the cabin porch, a big puff of black fur sitting dutifully, waiting for her to open the door, kiss him, and rub the soft backs of his ears—a ritual enacted every morning since they'd arrived. Celeste considered calling Luna to check on Trinity, but decided that would be ridiculous—he was Tom and Luna's dog.

When Saturday morning came, Alexa was still not talking to her mother. It had been four days since they'd moved and Celeste began to wonder if she'd done the right thing. Alexa was sticking to her plan to ride horses and spend time with Jonah at the Big House over the weekend. Celeste had said "no" repeatedly and was losing patience with her bull-headed daughter. Yet the move felt so sudden, she could understand Alexa's anger. It was disorienting not to be in their cozy cabin near Luna, Tom, and Jonah.

Celeste hated working in the grow room and the mom room. Pandora was haphazard in her communications about what to do and how to do it. She'd yap a few confusing instructions, then leave Celeste to some mind-numbing task. Celeste had crouched on the floor, and pulled yellow leaves from the bottoms of the mother plants for hours the day before. Working for Pandora was worlds away from the advantages of trimming for Luna and Tom. At the trim shack she'd earned cash, time passed quickly in the lively social circle. Working in Pandora's grow rooms was solitary, time seemed to lengthen excruciatingly.

She was doing exactly what she didn't want to do, living in a place with a grow scene, in town. Everyday, she had to remind herself it was only temporary, just a stepping-stone, a small inconvenience, a temporary fill-in until they slid into an important new phase of life. Soon they'd have a stable, safe home of their own. A little discomfort now would be worth it. It was possible they'd move to the farmhouse in one week, or a matter of weeks.

Saturday afternoon Pandora took the girls to her children's art class, which she taught at a rented studio near Chinook Creek. Alexa was so unhappy she wouldn't even look at Celeste waving good-bye from the sidewalk as Pandora drove them away.

At four o'clock, the timer in the grow room would make a small clicking noise and the banks of hooded thousand-watt lights would switch on. Celeste watched the clock until a few minutes after four, waiting for the lights to steady and the electrical buzz to die down to a unified drone. She struggled for a moment with the lock, and then the door swung open. The room was a dazzlingly bright, humming womb. Lines of plants in black plastic pots sat under the light hoods. Pandora explained that the plants were in the vegetative cycle, eighteen hours of light. Pandora's electric bill, thought Celeste, must be outrageous.

She was scheduled to water and fertilize. When her eyes adapted enough to the retina-killing brightness, she took the list of fertilizers she'd been given out of her pocket. She went to the shelves of grow supplies and stared at the large collection of brightly labeled plastic bottles and jugs crowded together. One label had an air-brushed image of a forties-style pin-up; in heels and a red swimsuit, the girl bent over, her ass high in the air, head turned back jauntily to wink at the viewer. "Wet Cherie. Plant Penetrator." Well, sex sells, mused Celeste. And the target audience is male. The quart bottle had a peeling price sticker. Celeste took it down. *One hundred and sixty-eight dollars.* Celeste read the label aloud, "Biologically active formula dramatically intensifies flavor, fragrance and taste. Only the best organic nutrients microbrewed for your indoor and outdoor growing needs." She laughed, and mused over the industry's real bonanza. Like Levi jeans in the Gold Rush, supplies for the growers were where the big, long-term money was.

Grow stores in Humboldt were like dandelions, sprouting everywhere. There were half a dozen in town and more dotting even the most remote outlying areas. In Blue Cove, Celeste had seen a crude sign for "Nursery Supplies," and another, smaller sign below read, "Visualize Your Soil." Obsessing over soil was the regional pastime. Mountains of plastic bags filled with specialty soils were hauled into SoHum on semi-trailer trucks everyday. Arriving from the north, an army of trucks importing bagged dirt to the countryside rumbled in, while other semis hauled more bagged dirt from the south. The fat, heavy plastic bags were patterned, colorful, whimsical, serene with nature scenes, or designed in abstracted camouflage, all holding the newest, best, most unique soil blends. Grow supplies were ubiquitous, displayed in the windows of the grow stores or being driven by purchasers, in their truck beds or trailer rigs. The detritus of grow supplies were everywhere, too. In front yards in town or further out of town at every property Celeste had seen, emptied bags of soil neatly stacked or in chaotic piles, used plastic fertilizer containers with peeling labels.

Just that morning, getting coffee in town, she'd walked by a parked pickup with its bed packed with black and white plastic trays and cases of Oasis foam, which she now recognized as supplies for a mom room.

There was a sound. Celeste had been lost in thought. Someone was at the door of the grow room. She froze and looked around; there was no other way out. Her heart pounded. "Who's there?"

The door opened and Celeste yelped. Jake stepped into the room.

"Oh." Adrenaline prickled over her skin. "My God." She grabbed Jake's arm in relief. "You scared me!"

Celeste looked up at him. His face was weirdly ashen. She stepped back. "What's wrong?"

He lifted his hands and rubbed the top of his head with his palms.

"What happened Jake?"

"Jonah was shot." He mumbled.

"What?" She tried to make sense of his words.

"At the river." His voice wavered as he spoke. "They rode the horse down. Jonah and Danny. A deal went bad. They got shot." His body quaked. "Jonah died on the river bar."

"No!"

"Danny was trying to sell that fucken pot to some gangsters from the city. He musta told 'em to meet him at the river." Jake stopped rubbing his head. "At The Crossing." He brought his eyes to hers. "The cops caught the guys in town. They had the gun and the pot." His bloodshot eyes flashed. "Two pounds! Killed over two fucken pounds." Jake's hands flew back to his head.

"But Jonah wouldn't do that!" Celeste cried.

"He didn't know. I'm sure he didn't know. Danny probably asked him for a ride to the river." Jake's head tipped forward. It was quiet except for the whirring of fans, the buzzing of ballasts, and some garbled sound Jake was making. Celeste moved, her arm flailed, hitting one of the bottles she'd been looking at. It fell to the floor, landing on a plant which wobbled and tipped, spreading soil over the floor. Jake immediately righted the plant, grabbed her hand, and pulled her outside. He slammed the grow room door and locked it up.

Daylight seemed less bright than the room they'd emerged from, adding to Celeste's sense of unreality.

"Where're the girls?" Jake asked.

"Your mom's art class . . . Oh. The girls . . ." Celeste said numbly. She looked at Jake, her thoughts seeping slowly, individually, each one adding another drop to the sick brew. Jake looked pallid, almost yellow. Tears fell from his eyes. His whole body shuddered. Celeste reached her arms around him, and they held on, racked with inharmonious weeping.

Jake spoke between sobs. "Danny's alive. Shot in the back. Probably never walk again."

Celeste sucked a breath in. "It was Jimmy's pot he tried to sell?"

"Of course."

They staggered inside, crossing through the studio, still hanging onto one another.

Celeste cried out, "Luna and Tom?"

Jake's head fell forward, lolling side to side. "Bad."

Together they hobbled into the bathroom. Jake let go of her and went to the toilet to piss. She leaned over the sink and threw handfuls of water at her face, then lifted her head, water dripping. "It can't be."

Jake flushed the toilet and turned back to her. A volcanic sob shook her. He bent to hug her, nuzzling her neck. Then he lifted her T-shirt, rolling his wet, slimed face against her skin. Celeste caught a glimpse of them in the mirror: a man at a woman's breast. The hollow shock that rang through her was not reflected, just a man rooting for closeness and proof that he was alive. She reached behind her back, unhooked her bra, pulling it with her T-shirt over her head. With a low groan, Jake buckled his mouth over her nipple and bit down. She cried out in pain. He brought his face up, close to hers, and they peered at one another through the briny distortion of tears. Tenderly, he slid his tongue over her lips, and then his tongue probed her opened mouth, in search of answers.

On the floor of the studio, they made hard, elemental love, filling the emptiness and finding her center. After climax, as her breathing steadied, Celeste closed her eyes. Behind her lids, she saw other eyes, twin sets, and Jonah's blameless eyes. She saw Luna at Jonah's bedside, tucking him into bed between the pillow and sheet, his angelic face like an iris through which light passes, bearing witness to his own unexpected death. Celeste saw Luna's last kiss on his forehead and heard her incantation to him, bedtime words to help him fall softly.

❋ ❋ ❋

Alexa flung the screen door open and ran outside. Celeste grabbed Sophie and went after her, in a wild dash across the small backyard. When Alexa reached the bay tree, she clung to it, pressing her face against the scabbed bark. There had been no gentle way to deliver the news.

Alexa stuck to the tree and wouldn't respond when Celeste tried to rub her back and soothe her. But she didn't cry. Sophie sobbed and stretched up her arms. Finally, Celeste sat on the lawn, took Sophie into her lap and rocked her. In time, Alexa burst into sobs and asked despairingly, "Where's Jonah's journal?"

Celeste was taken aback. "Honey girl, I don't know." Celeste had no idea if his journal had been found and didn't like the idea of asking.

Alexa stared at her mother. Her brown eyes overflowed with fat, shining tears that rolled steadily down her cheeks.

"Oh, sweetheart," murmured Celeste. Alexa teetered a moment before she collapsed, falling next to her sister, allowing herself to be folded inside her mother's embrace.

Later, Celeste tried to call Tom and Luna's house a number of times, but the phone just rang. She considered driving to Bear Ridge, but Jake had gone there. She knew he'd watch over them; at least Tom and Luna would be safe. She planned to go the following day.

Before bed, Celeste repositioned the three futons so they touched each other. Sophie abandoned her futon altogether to curl in the crook of her mother's arm. Alexa lay with her back to them. Celeste put her hand on her arm, eventually falling asleep to the soft repetitive sound of Alexa's sobbing.

The next morning, Celeste's senses went haywire. The girls were still asleep. She got up as quietly as possible to go to the bathroom, overwhelmed by the strange sensation that her eyes were not really open, as if she were seeing things from nerve cells on her skin. Feeling her way around, she bumped into things, touching walls to determine if they were there. Her insides were upside down; her stomach was in her throat, bloated and aching. Everything was askew, profoundly changed and hurt, though the outside world masqueraded as normal.

It was unimaginable that Jonah was really gone. When she stumbled back into the studio, the girls were awake, nestled in the white crumpled sheets on the futons, staring up at her. They looked as lost as orphans. She tried to smile reassuringly. "Come on. Let's get dressed and walk to Main Street for breakfast." Her plan was to bolster them by staying in command and appearing calm. But everything felt hollow in the face of death.

The day was cloudy and close, the humidity suffocating. Celeste held Sophie's hand, and Alexa followed listlessly. Rows of houses flanking the hot sidewalk gave way to a less residential area of town. They passed a church. One more block and they were on Main.

Celeste opened the door of the café. The girls went inside, and Celeste followed them in. The glass door closed with a hiss, like a vacuum seal behind them. It was cooler inside, but dense with the smell of fried food and Celeste almost gagged. Everyone in the café looked toward them. A waitress writing someone's order looked up. Another waitress clutching the handle of a steaming pot of coffee gazed their way. All the faces, old and young, swiveled in the direction of Celeste and her daughters, who stood grief-stricken and defenseless.

Celeste wanted to shriek: "What are you people doing? Jonah's dead."

It was life-as-usual, Sunday breakfast, enjoying the day. Did they even know they were living under the shadow of death?

The waitress motioned. "Go ahead, hon. Have a seat in the booth."

They settled; Celeste wondered if they should have come out. Alexa and Sophie hid behind menus. Eventually, the waitress came over and took their order. Celeste asked for tea and dry toast, though she didn't think she could eat it. After the food was in front of her daughters, they just poked at it.

"Eat. Please," Celeste pleaded. Her cell rang, and the girls looked up expectantly. She had a sense that they thought it would be news that some mistake had been made and Jonah wasn't dead after all. Or it would be Jonah himself, calling from the other side, reporting—as he would—on what he'd learned about his new realm.

It was Jake. "Hey, we're going to the river." His voice sounded so normal.

"To the river?"

Alexa scooted over on the seat, pushing into Celeste. "Mom." She waved her arms in front of Celeste's face.

Celeste raised her elbow defensively while bending away to hear Jake, who was saying ". . . a gathering."

Alexa spoke loudly, "ask about the journal."

"Word of mouth," Jake continued

"Hold on a sec." Celeste turned to her daughter. "Alexa, I'm trying to hear."

"Please, Mom!" Alexa's eyes skittered and flashed. She lowered her voice, "Please." Alexa was fervent, vibrating, almost shaking.

"Okay, I'll ask," Celeste said, "Give me a minute."

Alexa stared blankly, nodded, and then shrank back into the leatherette booth. Celeste turned back to her conversation. "Sorry."

"Hey," Jake sounded breathless, as if he were running, "Dad and Luna are leaving now."

"To the river?" Celeste asked.

"The Crossing."

"Okay, we'll go after breakfast. Listen, Jake, do you know if they found Jonah's journal?" There was no response. "Hello?"

"Yeah, I can hear you. Actually, Luna said his journal wasn't with him. It's odd; he always had it."

✼ ✼ ✼

On the strip of dirt above the river, cars and trucks lined the road, parked haphazardly for at least a quarter-mile. The asphalt blazed heat as Celeste and her daughters pressed through the thick air to the path. At the trailhead, Celeste paused briefly to stare: *DO NOT CROSS CRIME SCENE*. A sickening feeling turned in her gut. Yards of the crime-scene yellow-and-black plastic tape wound around a metal fencepost then flared down to the ground, where it split into tails trodden into the dirt.

"Come on." Celeste grabbed Sophie's hand. She and her daughters descended the first crumbly bend to the river, choking on the powdery dirt they kicked up on the steep trail. Dazed flies buzzed through the air; Celeste swatted at them ineffectually. Wild anise plants gave off a heavy, sweet scent. At the bottom of the path, the Scotch broom hedge closed up the end of the trail before the river came into view. Celeste grabbed the stems and pushed them aside; Alexa jumped the embankment to the river bar, then Celeste made the leap herself, turning back to sweep Sophie down.

People were everywhere; many were naked. Children ran and played on the riverbank. The pebbled beach was studded with bright colors of piled clothes and towels. It didn't look like the place she knew so well: the serene river spot Celeste had come to consider her own. She scanned the river bar without letting her sight fall on any one person, then went in the direction of the large flattish boulder that lived half-in and half-out of the water—the familiar spot where she and the girls always situated their things. It wasn't until she got right up to the boulder that she realized the rock held a scattering of people and their belongings.

"Oh." Celeste swallowed her surprise. "Hello."

Anya looked up, her tiny baby strapped to her chest, breathing faint, cooing breaths. "Celeste." Anya and Celeste embraced, and both began to cry. Anya squeezed words out, "It's so terrible."

"Mommy, Mommy." Sophie pulled the bottom of Celeste's shorts.

"What, sweet pea?" Sophie gazed imploringly at her mother; she didn't speak, but raised her arms. "Sweetie," Celeste said. "Let's sit together."

Anya lifted a diaper bag out of their way and let it drop in the pebbled sand. Celeste settled herself on the rock, and Sophie climbed into her lap, curling into a ball.

"Your boy is beautiful," Celeste said to Anya, thinking of Luna's boy, inconceivably gone forever. Celeste suddenly remembered how adamant Alexa had been about seeing Jonah over the weekend; she shuddered at the thought of what might have happened to her daughter if she'd allowed her to go.

Anya was stroking her baby's back. "I can't imagine what Luna's going through."

All the breath went out of Celeste. She dropped her head, letting it rest on Sophie.

"Luna and Tom are over there."

"Where?" asked Celeste, jerking up to look.

"I don't wanna point." Anya lifted her chin toward the river, and Celeste saw Luna and Tom across the water on the opposite shore. They sat, naked, their backs against a rock outcropping on a small half-circle of beach. Celeste crumpled down around Sophie, crying all over again. Soon, the pressure of a hand was on her shoulder and Anya whispered, "Look."

Gazing up, she saw Tom and Luna standing. They walked to the river holding hands, entering the water together. The movements and voices of the crowd on the beach died out to silence. Everyone froze. Even people in the river suspended their motions as the multitude watched Tom and Luna wade deeper into the river and then plunge under the surface. Everyone seemed to be holding their breath in concert with them underwater. Time passed. Sunlight flashed and gleamed over the undulating river. Then rising forms appeared; Tom and Luna emerged side by side, with their heads thrown back and mouths open, gasping air.

No one moved until, finally, a man at the far end of the beach broke the spell. He pulled his shorts off and dove into the deep pool at the base of the rapids, close to Tom and Luna. A woman with a child on her hip waded into the shallows, and then, simultaneously, people began moving toward the water, shedding clothes like empty husks on the sand.

Celeste held Sophie's hand at the waterside. Soon people bobbed everywhere in the river. Celeste turned, searching for Alexa, finally catching sight of her purple bathing suit at the far end of the river bar, obscured by a tall cluster of willow shoots. Celeste pulled Sophie's hand, and they left the crowd and crossed over hot pebbles, arriving at the silted ground from which the willow stems grew. Alexa was bent toward the ground, holding a stick like a blind person, tapping it slowly from side to side, her thick plume of dark hair thrown forward, covering her face. Celeste picked Sophie up, and they moved through the stems until they were next to Alexa, who didn't stop to look at them. Heat radiated off the ground with the intensity of a desert, but the air was as sodden as a lung. Celeste put Sophie down, wiped sweat off her forehead, and spoke to Alexa as gently as she could. "What're you doing, honey girl?"

Alexa kept moving the stick from side to side. "I had a dream it was here."

"What?" Celeste asked.

Alexa stopped tapping the stick. She looked up with empty miserable eyes. "Jonah's journal." Her voice was thin and sounded both exhausted and exasperated. "Mom, don't you see?" she said, as if trying to explain something to a child for the hundredth time—something that should be obvious. "If they didn't find it, then it's here. Somewhere. It's gotta be."

Celeste felt frozen inside, unable to formulate the right actions necessary to help her daughter.

Tears streamed down Alexa's cheeks, and she exclaimed, "He always had it!"

Celeste grabbed Alexa and squeezed her. She whispered in her ear, "I promise I will help you look for the journal, but will you come swim with us now?" Alexa's body went limp in her mother's arms. "Please, sweetheart." Celeste gripped Alexa's forearms and drew her away, gazing into her eyes imploringly. In grim agreement, Alexa nodded.

They stayed at the river for hours, going in and out of the water, keeping their bathing suits on as few others did, until the day turned dark. Later, it got darker still, and the water turned black and melted into the sky. A bonfire roared up, throwing sparks on the river bar. Folks kept arriving. Food materialized and was shared among the people, along with joints and some hash smoked in a small glass pipe. Even though there was a big crowd, the night stayed quiet. For a while, Celeste sat on a rock with Luna and Tom and they held hands. Except for the crackling fire and the sound of rushing water, everything was hushed under the bright twinkling of stars. When people spoke, they talked quietly to one another and said just what was necessary. A bag of grapes was passed around the fire, another joint, a torn baguette. It wasn't a party scene. It was something else entirely.

grid search

Celeste thought it had to be morning, but it was still dark outside. Sleep evaded her. In the evening, she had dropped off, exhausted, at the same time as the girls, falling into tangled dreams. She woke after a few hours, the long room floating in shadows. Still, she was warm and comfortable, snuggled with Sophie, who slept safely curled into her, Alexa's form was just visible on the nearby futon. Celeste felt lucky and thankful. She now measured everything by Luna's loss.

The rain made layers of plummeting sounds; she listened to the variations of the rhythms: splashes falling into puddles, irregular gushes coming off the roof where the gutter was filled with debris, sounds of rustling leaves as they swished against each other. The sky began to lighten. At last the shadowed forms gave way to a colorful and glistening wet day. Looking up from her futon, she could see a tree bough swaying over the stair railing. Green, ovate leaves fluttered and dripped, hanging tentatively by invisible connections. She wondered how long they would hold. She felt like those leaves—just hanging on.

On KBUD, the weather report predicted that the rain would turn to sun the following day. Celeste had promised Alexa that when the rain stopped they would go to the river to hunt for Jonah's journal though she held out little hope of actually finding it. If the journal were there, she assumed the police would've found it. But the act of searching would be important for Alexa. Cathartic. Cathartic enough that she'd give up her fixation, Celeste hoped. Instead of mourning Jonah, Alexa obsessed about finding his journal. Every day after school, she'd gone on Celeste's laptop, learning everything she could about grid searches. Celeste felt that in Alexa's mind the journal had come to represent Jonah himself.

Alexa turned over on her futon and opened her eyes. Celeste smiled and whispered, "It's early. Go back to sleep. There's no school." It was Friday, almost a week after Jonah's body had been found. There was no school on Fridays; Blue Cove School was in session only four days each week. Luna had explained it was originally set up that way so that parents had one less day to make the trip to school during pot harvests.

Alexa's eyes stayed open. "Can we go to the river today?"

"It's raining."

"So what?" She sat up in bed.

"Shhhh." Celeste pointed at Sophie asleep next to her.

Alexa continued in a loud whisper, "Mom, you promised you'd help me."

"I will. But it's been raining. I said when the rain stops."

Alexa began to say something, then hesitated and fell silent. Finally, in a shaky, low voice she said, "I have to tell you something."

A jolt of fear bolted down Celeste's spine. She sat up to lean against the cold wall. "Okay," Celeste whispered. Sophie shifted around on the blankets, but stayed asleep.

Alexa fixed her tawny-colored eyes on her mother in an intent gaze. "You know Jonah's journal was secret?"

"Yes." Celeste's mind raced. Examining Alexa closely, she couldn't fathom what her daughter was going to say. *Alexa and Jonah were lovers? Alexa's pregnant? Jonah was dealing drugs?*

The words exploded out of Alexa. "Jonah was gay." She reached her hand out to her mother, her voice plaintive and trembling. "He was ready to tell Luna. He was going to tell them. Don't you see, Mom? He wouldn't want a stranger reading his journal." Tears streamed down her face. "I had a dream it was in the sand. We have to find it for him."

☀ ☀ ☀

Four days of rain wasn't going to make it easy to search for a small black journal. Left unsaid was that if it were there, it would certainly be water-logged and ruined. But Celeste had a promise to fulfill. After breakfast, they went to the hardware store. Alexa picked out a pocketknife, measuring tape, and string. While they waited to pay, Alexa turned to Celeste and implored her, "Mom, I really need a lot of people to do a good grid search."

"Sweetheart, that's why we'll have better luck tomorrow, when the sun's out. We'll get a large group then, for sure."

Alexa shook her head and stared at the floor. "No." She looked up. "I'm not waiting anymore. Call Jake."

☀ ☀ ☀

The mud was impossibly slick. They skidded down the trail, bumping into one another. Celeste brought umbrellas, but there was no way to hold them and negotiate the path, so she left them under a shrub. Sophie slipped and fell twice. Muck plastered her hair and backside. Celeste had a fleeting thought that they should turn back, that it wasn't even safe, but when they got to the thicket at the rise, just before the river bar, the rain dwindled to a drizzle. Celeste pushed the Scotch broom aside, and they jumped down onto the pebbled sand.

The river was mud-colored and swift, higher and wider than Celeste had seen it, the beach narrower and reconfigured. The rock they always used as their landing spot was almost submerged; only one point jutted from the water. Trees, shrubs, leaves, and grasses looked fat and fleshy; tree trunks on the far shore, up the wooded mountainside, like chameleons, had dramatically changed color. Trunks and branches glowed green; what used to look like shaggy bark revealed itself to be brilliant, glowing moss.

Their shoes sank into muck as they walked; when they lifted their feet shoe-shaped impressions filled quickly with water. Alexa clumped off toward the swale of willow brush at the far end of the river bar. It looked like the rain had turned that area into a marsh. "There's so much land to cover; why don't we start somewhere else?" Celeste suggested.

Alexa swung around angrily. "Mom! Are you going to help or not?"

"Sorry." Celeste sighed and trudged forward, holding Sophie's hand. She scanned the chocolate-colored river, trying to visualize it as it had looked during the many hot summer days they'd spent there. It was almost bank-to-bank now, farther down the narrows. Just the week before, it had tapered into calm, clear greenish-blue pools—the way it must have been the last day Jonah was there on his horse. The river saw everything and knows everything, Celeste thought. She envisioned Jonah on his last ride, Tatanka trotting up the river bank. Sharing his saddle with the other boy. Jonah always generous and helpful, even as his time wound down.

Celeste lifted her head at a sudden slanting brightness. At the intersection of sky and mountain was a long scrap of intense blue. "Look, Sophie." Celeste pointed up.

"Will it stop raining?" Sophie asked.

"Maybe." A steady mist floated in the air, yet the drips off the elbows of trees and from leaf to leaf in the surrounding forest made it sound as though heavy rain was still sizzling around them.

"Hey!" Jake and Cloud leaped down to the river bar.

Celeste waved, relieved to see them. They wore T-shirts and jeans, no umbrellas or jackets. Cloud had a hat on. Now Celeste felt silly having insisted on layers of clothing for her children. Her sweatshirt felt soggy, as if she were sheathed in a damp sponge. The natives knew how to dress. Celeste looked at Sophie, mud covered and probably wet through. She had brought the girls a change of clothes, but the car was a slippery hike back up the hill.

Jake and Cloud tramped over to them. Cloud looked different with a hat on. His face seemed younger, more ordinary, without his crown of blue-inked curls. His lips, an unusually tender shade of pink, widened into a smile. "Hey there, Celeste."

"Thank you for coming," Celeste said. "Sorry we're doing this in the rain."

Cloud tipped his head back to the sky. "It's hardly coming down."

Jake gave Celeste a hug. "Dad always says, 'If you don't like the weather in Humboldt, wait five minutes.'"

"So." Cloud clapped his hands, then rubbed them together. "At your service." He looked around as if expecting to find a starting gate.

Jake's arm hung around Celeste's shoulder. She felt ashamed and confused by their sweaty, teary, manic love-making the day Jonah died. They'd crossed borders of decorum, once again. Yet, strangely, she also felt the episode had helped them, elevated them. Some part of her believed they'd honored Jonah in the most primitive way, channeling him into a breathing entity, or a spark of life-force. Celeste kissed Jake briefly on the cheek and stepped away.

"Where do we start?" Cloud asked.

"Alexa has a plan." Celeste yelled towards her daughter, "Are you giving orders, boss?"

"Yeah," Alexa called back, raising her new, fluorescent orange tape measure. "Over here."

They assembled in the slick, muddy swale among the scrubby willow stems. Alexa lined them up, side by side. She'd tied string across the area and gathered a pile of sticks. "Sophie," Alexa said, "you stay with Mom. Right with her.

Understand?" Sophie nodded. "This is our start point." Alexa gestured to a line of string. "Jake," said Alexa, "right here is where Jonah was found, right?"

Celeste flung her head to face where Alexa had pointed, shocked that her daughter knew where Jonah's body was found. Celeste hadn't allowed herself to consider exactly where the shooting had taken place, but Alexa had gleaned the gruesome details of the violence that had taken her friend's life. "Who told you about that?"

"Jake."

Celeste swung back to look at Jake, but he'd turned toward the river. He must have told her on the day everyone had gathered at the river with Tom and Luna. Celeste was dazed. It was hard enough that this horrific act had occurred, but to want details about exactly where and how it had happened seemed too grisly to endure. But of course Alexa would have to know, in order to do a search. She'd devoted every available moment since Jonah's death to researching how to find an item in a crime scene, with a tenacity and fearlessness that Celeste had never seen before.

"Spread out." Alexa handed the tip of the measuring tape to Cloud and began to unreel it carefully. "Six feet between you." She pushed another stick deep in the mud. "Totally examine everything in your six feet. Don't move forward until you see every little thing." She reeled the tape measure in, handed the case to Jake, and stepped back again, measuring out another six feet. "Okay." She plunged another stick in the mud. "Start here, Mom." She handed the metal tip of the tape to Celeste. "The thing is," Alexa said, "you have to be sure you see everything. So go super slow."

Once they started walking their lines, Celeste knew it was an impossible task. The powder-fine, whitish crust mixed with rain had made a slick, extra slippery mud. The willow stems were difficult to negotiate; though flexible, they poked painfully. To do a proper job, she'd have to get on her hands and knees and crawl. She looked over at Alexa, who was doing just that. Celeste crouched down, examining bits of sticks, dried-up leaves, and rocks, everything coated in mud, sorting through things with a stick and her hands.

At one point, Celeste saw something translucent and picked it up, rubbing it against her pant leg. "Look what I found." She held up a smooth piece of blue glass between her fingers; the light shot through it as if it were a beautiful gemstone.

"River glass," Cloud yelled from across the marsh.

"Can I have it?" Sophie asked. "Please?"

"For you, sweetie." Celeste deposited the prize in Sophie's palm and was rewarded with a kiss. She refocused, gazing again at the whitish mud, at the sand, at a beetle coursing intently around a root. She leaned over and then gave in, crawling around and through the willow stems on her hands and knees, getting to know their spiraled leaves, silvery-blue on the undersides, with a tendency to flutter. Sophie stayed near, walking by her side, sprinkling complaints about being hungry, wet, tired.

Finally, it stopped drizzling, and the sun, although hidden by spent clouds, washed everything in bright, diffuse light. The trees, the river bar seemed scrubbed clean. Everything sparkled. Time passed slowly as Celeste deliberately picked through her assigned area.

"Mommy, I'm hungry." Sophie pleaded. It had to be the third or fourth time she'd heard that. Celeste sighed, surrendered, and stood up. Celeste's jeans were wet and heavy with mud. "Alexa," she yelled, "I'm taking a short break." She tried rubbing her hands together to get off the half-dry caked-up mud.

Alexa popped up out of the scrub. "Come on. At least finish your pass."

"Sorry. Sophie needs a break." Celeste pushed her stick in the wet ground to mark the spot where she'd stopped, and she and Sophie picked their way carefully up an embankment. She boosted Sophie onto a ledge, covered with flattened yellowed weeds that, while wet, was not muddy. Celeste pulled an apple from her sweatshirt pocket and handed it to Sophie.

"I don't want an apple."

"It's all I have. We have some other food in the car." Sophie took an unhappy bite.

Flocks of birds flew over the river, having appeared en masse after the rain stopped. Celeste raked her gaze over the river bar. The different types of birds seemed to stay with their own kind. At waterside, brownish, tiny birds bounced, pecking at invisible things, while larger birds swooped and squawked over the water and through the forest. Jonah would probably have been able to name them.

It was turning into a dazzling day but Alexa was oblivious to it. She'd been swallowed up by a great tide of grief. They all were. It was as though everything was perceived through a thick pall of unbending fact: Jonah was dead. Sitting there, soaking wet, muddy and grieving, Celeste knew there was no other place she'd rather be than at The Crossing with people she loved doing something for Jonah—and for Alexa, whose determination made her proud.

Celeste started to pick at the mud that had hardened in Sophie's hair, but Sophie batted her hand away. From her vantage point, she could see Jake, Cloud, and Alexa as they worked parallel to each other moving slowly, crouching or crawling.

Locating her cell phone in her front pocket, Celeste pulled it out with her mud-encrusted hand. It had been almost two hours since they'd parked on the road above the path. The yellow crime-scene tape that had been wound around the metal post at the trailhead the last time they'd come to the river had been repurposed. Woven in and out of the chain-link fence, the yellow and black plastic strips spelled out "Jonah, RIP" and further down the fence "Danny." Below the names, flowers were strewn, beaten into the ground by the rain. It was a scraggly shrine: a short run of chain-link along the dirt boundary of Bear Ridge Road. Celeste thought it ironic and unfortunate that Jonah and Danny's names were elegized together, as if one had not been responsible for the other's death. Linked together for all time.

Jake stood up from the scrub. He rolled his neck from side to side and arched his shoulders. "Shit. My back's killing me."

"Jake," Celeste called down to him, "why don't you take a break?"

"Yeah." He stretched his arms over his head, and then swung himself out of the swale and walked toward the embankment. His T-shirt was wet through; he must have been cold, but of course he'd never say so. Celeste watched his easy, deliberate movements as he turned to half-sit, half-lean against a protruding rock. His hair had grown out from the short cut he'd gotten in the summer; longer hair softened the lines of his angular face.

Jake bent down. "Oh, hey," he called out. Celeste watched from above as he fell to his knees. "Hey!" He made a whooping noise, and then yelled, "I found it!"

He reached his arm under a large boulder in the embankment, and then Celeste couldn't see him anymore. But when he jumped back, he was waving the small black book in the air. Alexa screamed and ran, reaching Jake first. She and Jake jumped up and down ecstatically. Celeste helped Sophie, and they slid off their perch.

Jake opened the book and leafed through it. Suddenly his stance changed; his exhilaration melted away. He froze as he read the journal. They crowded around him, pushing in. Jake's hands began to shake uncontrollably. He turned the book around, opened to the last page of writing. The left side was densely scrawled, but on the opposite page the script was loopy and erratic. The pages were damp, but the ink had not run. Celeste could see the word "love" written many times.

"He wrote it" Jake struggled to get the words out as he choked on tears, "here." The bottom of the page held the last written words, "Is love infinite? Will my love go on forever? I love you all."

❋ ❋ ❋

Celeste knew the road by heart: every pothole, every hairpin turn, every steep grade with its loose spray of gravel. Ahead of her, Cloud drove Jake's truck. She followed, watching as the truck dodged some potholes and lurched through others, each sway causing the two men's heads to bob. From a distance, the back of Jake's head looked small and vulnerable.

Her car lagged farther and farther behind the truck, not to avoid dust—the rain had put a temporary end to that—but because this was a solemn procession.

The road to Tom and Luna's held so many memories. Each time she drove it felt like a test. Besides its curves and clefts, it always held a new influence. This time it was the recognition that Jonah wouldn't be at the other end.

The girls had changed out of their wet clothes and the interior of the car was warm. The comfort seemed indulgent, at odds with the bumpy road and the loud crunch of gravel, and the ache of it all.

Celeste glanced at Alexa. She was holding together, the journal resting in her lap. Jake suggested that Alexa hand the journal to Luna and Tom personally. Celeste suspected that after Alexa completed her task she might come unglued, but for now only quiet tears rolled down her face.

When Celeste pulled next to Jake's truck, Cloud and Jake were already on the porch. The screen door opened and she watched them disappeared inside. Celeste turned off her engine and looked in the back seat. Sophie had fallen asleep slumped over her seatbelt.

Gently, Celeste took Alexa's hand in her own. "Are you ready? Should we go up?"

Alexa stared at the journal. She was quiet. Then she raised her eyes. "Can I do it myself?"

"Oh." Celeste brought her hand to Alexa's hair and then to her soft, wet cheek. "Honey girl, are you sure?"

"Yes." Alexa grabbed the door handle, hesitated, and looked back at her mother. For a second, Celeste thought she changed her mind, but she wiped her face. "I'm sure." She took a deep shuddering breath and opened the car door, letting it slam after her.

Sophie startled awake and straightened up. "Mommy. Mommy."

"Right here." Celeste climbed into the back seat, unbuckled Sophie's seatbelt, and let her sprawl in her arms. In a groggy haze, Sophie drifted back to sleep, her muddy head resting on Celeste's shoulder.

She watched Alexa cross the driveway and climb the wooden stairs to the big house. Holding the journal as if it was a fragile, new-born, breakable thing, she lifted each foot and set it down carefully on the step above. At one point during the summer, Jonah, Alexa, and Sophie had scrambled up those narrow wooden steps, the object being who could count them the fastest. Twenty-nine steep steps. Celeste wondered if she had fully appreciated those lovely summer days with her children—and Jonah.

The low sun slanted through the car's dirty windows. Alexa arrived on the porch and stood at the screen door. A long moment passed before she went inside.

Celeste closed her eyes and let her head fall back against the seat.

She woke when the car's interior lights blinked on. It was dusk, and Alexa was getting into the passenger seat. Sophie was fast asleep across Celeste's lap.

Alexa's face was hidden by the headrest.

"Are you okay?"

"Yeah."

Celeste leaned over to the window and gazed up at the house. She saw Luna's silhouette framed in the open doorway, a still-life in shadow, and then Tom's tall, familiar form moved behind her, their back-lit figures merged into one unrecognizable shape.

Luna stepped forward, out of the doorway. Underneath the porch light, her dreadlocks glowed with a new halo of white. She raised her hand, brought it to her mouth for a kiss, and threw it out into the darkness.

Acknowledgments

In a full classroom, Kathy Wollenberg and I sat attentively. Carolyn See, standing at the helm, asked the question: if you wrote a novel what would it be about? I knew immediately.

Kathy and I first met in David Holper's classroom, and it was from that class that our initial writers group formed. Since then there have been many iterations of our group, yet Kathy and I have held steady, her truth and caring guiding me forward. For her loyal presence I am forever grateful. Kathy's award-winning novel, *Far Less*, is important and wonderful.

Thank you to Kyle Morgan and Humboldt State University Press for saying yes to *Growland*, after years of rejection from far and wide, turns out there really is no place like home.

Many hours, days, and years elapsed working to bring this book to fruition; many people read, critiqued, and supported me in the process. Thank you all: Janine Volkmar, Darlene Marlow, Julie Sylvia, Kristin Kirby, Amy Barnes, Roger & Kristi Clark, Gail Wread & Tommy Rosin, Lena Hittelman, Lupine & Nina Wread, Joanie Otay Wread, Nina Cochrane, Pamela Palmer, Holly Poslusny, Patty Davis, Katie McGuire, Dee Nelson, Elena O'Shea, Becca Barkin & Ron Sharrin, Jan Flynn, Ray Oaks, David Holper, Midge Raymond, James Hall. Thank you to Janine Woolfson for her insightful overview. Peter Brown Hoffmeister, your kind words of encouragement meant everything to me.

I thank my children, each one a beacon of light; Tia, your design talents astound; Myla, you are our driving force; Sachi, your art glimpses other dimensions; Louie, your photographs expand the world. To my grandchildren, Kayvan and Layla, for making life sweet again.

Finally, I thank my beloved husband Stewart Moskowitz. Nothing would be possible without you.

Made in the USA
Middletown, DE
17 November 2022